A NOVEL # SALT &
SACRIFICE

by John Carlyle O'Neill

Paperback ISBN: 978-1-940014-60-9
E-book ISBN: 978-1-940014-59-3
Library of Congress Control Number: 2015942003

Cover design and interior layout by Emily Shaffer Rodvold at Lift Creative
Typeset in Alegreya Regular.

Printed in the United States of America
First printing: 2015
17 16 15 14 13   5 4 3 2 1

Wise Ink Creative Publishing
837 Glenwood Ave
Minneapolis, MN, 55405
612-200-0983 • www.wiseinkpub.com

For orders other than by individual consumers, the author grants a discount on
the purchase of 10 or more copies for special markets or premium use (such as
nonprofit donor gifts). For further details or to order, visit www.itascabooks.com.

Dedicated to
William & Kimmie

PROLOGUE

THE YOUNG FUGITIVE'S PACE SLOWED AS HE stumbled across a frozen mountain stream. Sweat was already beginning to freeze in his thick hair. The hounds were well trained—even with their prey in sight they traversed the treacherous snow-covered forest floor undetected. Powerful leaps and bounds landed silently in the deep powder. Jet black, they hugged the shadows of the tall pines, moving like smoke across the freshly fallen snow.

The stumbling figure's strength was failing; the broken arrow lodged in his upper back reduced his pace to a crawl. His cloak was frozen at his knees, where the blood had pooled and frosted over. The cold had seized him. The young man was shaking, becoming less surefooted with every labored breath. In spite of the pain, he greedily inhaled the hard, cold air. He found comfort only in the aroma of the tall pines. The fugitive's partially clad feet were beyond numb; he imagined the feeling of warm sawdust between his toes.

Bracing against the sharp wind, he stumbled toward the edge of a gorge. He forced his way through a jagged narrow opening in the rocks. The arrow snagged and his cloak became tangled. Every movement he made wrenched at the splintered arrow protruding from beneath his shoulder blade. Tasting blood on the icy air, the hounds at his heels were clawing through the gap toward his ensnared limbs. Shedding his cloak, the emboldened fugitive lunged forward blindly into the wind-torn darkness. He plummeted lifelessly, hammering into a dense snowdrift below. His body narrowly avoided the rocks as his momentum forced him through the snow pile. He surged aimlessly through the deep powder until he could once again feel and hear the harsh wind around him.

Clinging to consciousness, the disoriented runaway's weary eyes struggled to focus on the cliff above. Then he saw them. Dark wolf-like shapes were swimming through the deep snow, wading down the ledge toward him. He wrapped a tattered garment snugly around his neck. This was the only barrier between the hounds' fangs and his arteries. He concealed his dagger beneath the white blanket of snow, then went limp. Only one thought remained for the delirious contender: *their blood is warm.*

To the beasts, the smell of fresh blood was intoxicating. In their hunger, the hounds' patience wavered. They pounced at the young man's lifeless form with eager claws and gnashing teeth.

— I —

Entombed in the depths of Saltz Mountain, a man sat alone. Outside of his cavern, hundreds of exiles labored to death unearthing the endless fortune of rock salt from the great mountain. Hammers and booms echoed throughout the sprawling maze of winding shafts, and yet the brooding man sat motionless. He could hear a group of familiar voices drawing closer; it was apparent that this loner did not enjoy company. The voices were gruff but jovial.

The banter began to taper off. As they drew nearer the men went silent; they entered the ring of torchlight cautiously. In their own way, each man avoided making eye contact with the figure before them.

One finally spoke. "Archer, we found another handful holding court in the shafts."

"And this message required three couriers." His dead eyes fixed on his subjects.

No response followed; the men stared at the gravel floor. Their deference pleased the lord. Without a word, two of them shuffled off into the darkness. Once the others were out of earshot, the disfigured man rose to face his remaining follower. The empty-eyed leader's back was torn and scarred from decades of lashings. His rugged face had been marred over a lifetime of struggle. What stood out most, though, were the cross-shaped scars seared into his sunken cheeks.

The master's cold eyes met his follower's. He spoke unenthusiastically, straight to the point. "Are any of them workers?"

"Two are known producers; the rest rarely pull their weight."

"Are they newcomers?"

"No sir, only one."

"It only takes one."

A silence fell between them. The courier was unnerved; he was desperate to leave but knew better. The scar-faced man took his time in deciding how to proceed. He was slow-moving but calculated. Archer had not been blessed with any exceptional physical gifts. He was not exceedingly tall nor intimidatingly strong. He did not seem impressed with his own intelligence, nor was he overtly charismatic. Yet, at a glance, only one conclusion could be drawn of the man: he was in charge.

"Dock the two useful men water for a day. Don't allow them food for three," Archer said, after what he considered a moment's thought.

"What of the others?"

The master continued, with no change in tone, "Flog them in front of the rest at serving time—then throw them into the pit. The men need a show. As for the newcomer, let him watch the pain he's caused, then send him to me."

"Do you think they'll fight, sir?"

"Don't they always?" Archer was emotionless and distant—bored with it all. "Do as I say."

"At once, sir."

The pit was a crater carved into the mine's floor filled with jagged protrusions, bones, and broken weaponry. Custom dictated that any disputes between workers would be settled in this arena. This practice had been in place long before Archer's reign. The rest of the salt miners watched the spectacle from above, and liquor was rationed out to all. Archer often used the pit to punish stubborn slaves; the crater's walls had a knack for exposing the limitations of their humanity.

"Wait," Archer snapped. The underling stopped dead and turned to face his master. "Take the women."

A grotesque grin fanned out across the subject's mangled black teeth. "Thank you, my lord," the rodent snickered.

Archer did not attend the festivities that followed. He had seen enough. From his quarters he could hear the whips crack, which told him the disobedient were being beaten. Then came the whistling, hooting, and hollering, clearly his women were putting on a good show. Soon after, bloodthirsty roars filled the shafts. The chaos that erupted from the depths told him that the transgressors were battling to the death, for only one man was ever allowed to leave alive. All told, it took a little over an hour from start to finish; then the newcomer was brought forth.

Two guards dragged the man by the chains around his ankles into Archer's cavern. The links clinked in the gravel as they hauled the mangled heap to a halt at their master's feet. The smaller of the two gave the man a hard kick to his stomach. The slave groaned.

"He's still with us, sir," the smirking brute announced.

"Leave him," Archer commanded. Darkness hid the master's face. The men left without another word.

Searching for his captor in the shadows, the prisoner pulled himself to his knees. He was white-haired and gaunt; his blue eyes flickered pathetically in the faint torchlight. Undetected, Archer stared at the pitiful soul before him. The slave had been badly beaten; tears drifted down his filthy, swollen face. The lord remained calm and silent like the darkness around him. The exhausted captive collapsed into the gravel. The disheveled heap lay in a ball of chains and wept before the disfigured lord. The way he groaned spoke volumes; hardship was not new to the starving miner.

Choking down his sorrow, the man began uttering the Lord's Prayer. Archer listened, mouthing the forgotten words as the slave prayed them aloud. When the believer had finished, Archer emerged from the shadows so his captive could bear witness to the grotesque scars that adorned his sunken cheeks.

"Tell me, Christian—does mercy triumph over judgment?" Archer demanded.

When the horrified man saw the crooked crosses burned into the wild-eyed monster's face, he immediately hid behind his hands and returned to prayer.

"Stop talking to yourself, you fool. Your childish dreams can't save you now."

Crippled by fear, the faithful soul lacked the boldness necessary to stand his ground. Fear of death left him defenseless. The lord could feel him crumbling; he drew his spear and went for blood.

"Coward, you fear that your God can sense your victims' blood in the sand. You were warned—God has no place in this mine. Your flesh will rot; that is the heaven that awaits you. Enough of this pathetic nonsense. Renounce your Messiah, and I will spare you."

The slave sobbed into the salted gravel, "I can't—I won't."

"Of course you can. You have told the truth before, I'm sure of it." Archer paused; his patience was drawing wire thin. *"Am I a fool?"* he asked.

"No, sir."

"Do you think I do not know that your persecutors would not have sent you here, had you not renounced your Father?"

"They were going to kill my children."

"Renounce him—*renounce him now.*"

"Never again; there is nothing left for you to take from me."

A twisted grin contorted Archer's long disfigured face. He mocked the pitiful man before him, "Ah, I see. Now that there is nothing worth living for, you can finally pronounce your undying faith—*to a God too weak to reject you.* I am sure this pleases your

Father in heaven—that you would risk nothing for him."

Before his prisoner could answer, Archer backhanded the feeble man into the coarse gravel floor. He lifted the broken slave's face from the debris with an outstretched foot. The lord glared disgustedly at the frailty before him. He pressed his heel into the man's throat. His flailing victim began to lose consciousness, so he let up. Coughing violently, the man grabbed at his neck.

The defeated slave was choking for air, but suddenly found the courage to speak. He fought back to his knees as his eyes went white. He addressed his persecutor in a fierce broken voice, *"When the dark water rises, the Lord will come for you."* The prophet's words fell on deaf ears; Archer's rage had taken hold. All he saw was weakness; all he heard were lies.

"You were lost—and now you are found," Archer spat.

With that, he plunged his spear into his prey. In one powerful motion, the wild-eyed lord wrenched the emaciated man's body up into the air. His ensuing roar reverberated throughout the shafts. His heart pumped molten fire as an influx of adrenaline coursed through his veins.

Just as suddenly, he let his victim fall to the floor. Desperate to escape the taste of burning metal, he stumbled toward his jug of spirits. When his vision began to blur, he fell to his knees. The disfigured master battled his memory; a familiar dizziness was taking hold. He lunged for his jug and drank deeply, but the images only intensified. The lord collapsed with his head in his hands nursing his pounding skull. Images flashed through his over-stimulated mind as the terror set in and nightmare became reality.

"Don't touch them," he squealed.

Several henchmen rushed into the cavern to investigate the misplaced pain in their master's voice. They found him kneeling before the murdered believer with his face in his hands.

"Is everything alright, sir?"

"His stench is giving me a headache. Get him out," he stammered.

"Should I send the women?" another guard asked. The despot hurled his empty jug at his men. The vessel shattered against a far wall.

"No, leave me be." The lord's speech was broken. The disfigured master could hear the crows all around him now; he could feel them racing between the shadows.

"Aye, sir," the servant answered uneasily. The henchmen grabbed hold of the dead man's chains and dragged him off into the darkness.

Archer collapsed to the ground. The crosses seared into his face were throbbing as though his flesh had just been branded. The man dared not open his eyes; the resounding crows only intensified. The maddening screeches took hold. He could smell the blood and taste the fire.

"No—do not touch them," he begged.

The lord was on all fours, refusing to open his eyes. He could hear the whips crack and the women scream—the memory was strong. When he saw his father's eyes, his cursed memory became reality. Writing on the cavern floor, *he was a small child again....*

Archer's mother tore through the cupboards until she found the shears. Her mind raced as she scrambled toward her youngest daughter. She ran her hands down the young one's frame. Her breasts were still small. She would pass. Her daughter was shaking as the sound of pounding hoofs drew down on the estate. The mother swiftly directed her attention to her elder daughters. She paused. Locking eyes, they all knew this girl's womanhood was undeniable. Undeterred, she handed the shears off to her eldest who hurriedly began cropping her sister's hair. Soon after, a servant woman came rushing down the steps and threw baggy men's garments over the young girl's head. Archer's other sister grabbed a handful of ash from the fire and desperately smudged the young one's face to mask her beauty. They prayed she would pass. The women were moving frantically; the young boy was speechless. His panic-stricken mother ushered him toward the pantry. The child began to cry when he saw tears filling his mother's determined eyes.

"Son, shut your ears and close your eyes. Don't make a sound," she instructed. There was shouting and yelling coming through the shuttered windows from the courtyard. Sounds of battle burst forth as his mother closed the cabinet doors.

With the cries of dying men subsiding, the horses calmed.

The victorious commoners could be heard heckling their victims. The boy curled up toward the back of the pantry with his eyes shut tightly and his hands held firmly over his ears. The raiders had bound the wealthy landowner and slain his loyal servants.

Several brutes had already begun stealing jugs of wine from the storehouse. Trudging through the courtyard, the largest among them turned his sights toward the estate. He kicked open the doors and his men tore into the house. Hurling anything they could find, the women did their best to fight them off. They bit and clawed at their attackers. Archer hid helplessly as the violence raged. The servant was a large, powerful woman; armed with a spear, she stood guard over her master's youngest daughter. She plunged her weapon into an attacker before she was cut down. Archer heard his older sister cry out as she was dragged toward the courtyard. Her girlish tone gave her away immediately. His arrow-ridden father strained against the ropes that bound him as his family was dragged off toward the storehouse. The boy could hear him raging, shouting at the attackers until his voice was raw. Amidst the chaos, soldiers took to looting the household of all its precious goods. The worst of them filled jugs with wine and headed toward the storehouse with something else in mind.

Archer could hear the rummaging thieves ripping through the house; he remained huddled toward the back of the cupboard as the sounds drew nearer. The door was yanked open and light spilled into his hiding place. A bloodied hand snatched the boy's ankle. The raider dragged the squirming child out into the courtyard, where he was forced to watch his father's torture. Humiliation reigned, as far worse was being done to his mother and sisters. The persecutors kicked him and mocked him at his father's feet.

The man guarding the young one was missing a couple of teeth from the fight to subdue the landowner. The overweight mercenary held a sword to the boy's neck and demanded half-heartedly, "For the last time, just tell me what I want to hear."

Archer's incapacitated father was secured to a post, slowly dying in the hot sun. Servants lay dead all around him; they had fought bravely to protect his family. He looked into his son's terrified eyes and said, "I am sending you as lambs among wolves."

The landowner was pummeled for not obeying his captor's order. The boy looked on in horror, tears streaming down his face. The women's screams sliced through the fragmented air. Crows screeched and circled overhead. The child watched powerlessly as the raider ripped his father's metal cross from his neck.

Holding the crucifix before the man's eyes, he demanded again, "Get on with it, you sorry bastard." The words were not his own; he had studied someone else's act. This man was not at all invested in his captive's renunciation, but the glimmering chain might be worth something. With some luck, the others would never know he had snatched it.

Clinging to consciousness, Archer's father would not even acknowledge the hired thug's presence. Instead, he shouted out into the broken air, so that his son would never forget, "The Lord is the way, the truth, and the life. There is no way to heaven, but through him!"

"Alright, alright. I get it. Keep your God, my friend. He's all you have left now anyway." The hefty man sighed. He was using his tongue to inspect the space where his lost teeth had been. Others were bringing everything of value out of the estate and loading the goods onto carts pulled by mules. Looking over his shoulder, the persecutor checked that the coast was clear. He took the opportunity to pour some of his wine into the beaten man's mouth. The Christian spat the red liquid into the sand.

The persecutor shook his head and lumbered toward the shade, shoving the child out of his way. It was hot and he had grown thirsty; he reached for his goatskin to drink the warm wine within. The hired hand was content to let the landowner cook in the hot sun a little longer. After all, he really did not care whether or not the man renounced his God—the pay was the same regardless. Besides, he had beaten the man enough not to warrant any suspicion from the rest. He was mostly concerned with making sure he got his cut of the livestock. The groggy mercenary closed his eyes and blocked out the women's muffled cries.

The heap was snoring in the shade when the rest of the raiders returned from violating the women. They laughed at the lazy oaf. The largest among them gave the lump a kick and growled, "Get up. You're lucky the boy didn't cut your throat as you slept."

A few of the others taunted the believer slowly dying before them. They mocked and paraded around him, making vulgar gestures. The carts were full to the brim with loot. Most of the men were ready to move on—all except for one.

The leader snatched the medallion from the sluggish hired hand and snapped, "Holding out on me, are you, boy?"

Wiping the sleep from his eyes, the man pleaded, "No, Castor, I—"

The brute waved his subordinate off as he inspected the object carefully. The others began preparing to ride onward. Two drunken henchmen were ushering the women back up the hill toward the estate.

"Is it silver?" the lazy man inquired.

"Awake now, are you?" Castor sneered. "No, just iron—some God." Moving the metal between his fingertips, he locked eyes with his stubborn prisoner. Tired of how things were progressing, he placed the chain on his sword to dangle it over the fire until the crucifix burned red in the tumbling flames. With a leather-gloved hand, he grabbed the glowing red-hot medallion. He threw the child into the sand and let the blazing crucifix swing in front of the boy's gray eyes.

"God is merciful. Be strong, son," the father sighed, focusing only on his child's gaze, and refusing to look at his attacker. The slowly dying man was nodding in and out of consciousness. Without warning, the persecutor pressed the red-hot metal into the boy's cheek. The nearly molten iron instantly seared the child's face.

"Damn you to hell, you coward," the father cried out.

The wild man bore his mangled teeth at his prisoner and taunted him, "Pray for your persecutors, remember?"

Castor violently wrenched the boy up by the hair and pressed the still-smoldering cross into the child's other cheek. When his victim clawed at him, he flung him into the sand. Archer's mother screamed.

None were prepared for what followed—she yanked the shears from her disheveled dress and plunged them into the nearest raider's neck. The battered woman charged at her child's attacker with the bloody shank in hand. The devilish man snatched the woman by her throat as he pushed his sword into her. The makeshift dagger slipped from her fingers into the hot sand. The towering beast groped as he pulled her close to nibble at her neck. He slowly withdrew the weapon from her womb; she fell to the ground beside her son. All the men looked on in disbelief. A few hands had moved toward their swords, but it had all happened so fast. Drunkenness, regret, and fear all clouded their judgment. They exhaled their shame as the broken woman bled out in her son's small arms.

"That's why you always keep the bitches bound," the murderer barked at his inexperienced henchmen. He trudged toward his associate. The man was choking on his breath as he clung to the mortal wound in his neck. Castor heaved his bloodied sword to finish off the woman's victim.

"Renounce him, father—please, father—renounce him!" the child begged.

The butcher allowed a twisted grin to unfold, for this had never been about God. Castor smiled at the young one and asked, "Child—do you renounce your father's lies?"

"I do. There is no God. God can't save me!" Upon meeting his father's tortured eyes, the child wept at the anguish he found. The dying man looked to those who had stood by; not one among them dared to meet his glowering eyes.

The madman came close to his prisoner's ear. "Listen to your boy, Christian, and it will all end. No more pain, no more shame. Renounce the false idol that has abandoned you. Do this, and your son will live—*renounce him*," the devil hissed.

"You are weak—your soul will burn," the God-fearing man snarled boldly at the evil before him. A couple of the younger soldiers were taken aback by the intensity of this shattered man's beliefs. Most of the others were too ashamed or too jaded to take notice. Patchily bearded guards escorted Archer's sobbing sisters back into the estate to get them cleaned up.

The faithful landowner looked at his child with love. "There is still hope for you, my son—you are far too young to be tested."

With empty eyes, Castor pushed his sword into his captive's chest. The child watched his father die. Nightmarish crows pervaded the sky of memory; their screeching filled the air. Thunder boomed from the westward horizon. With the winds increasing, the men hurried to cover the carts. The wild-eyed soldier cut the ropes that had bound his prey. The believer collapsed into the sand. The unaffected brute slid the necklace back onto his sword again to dangle it over the fire, playing with the heat. His stare enjoyed the tumbling flames that bit and licked at the smoldering metal; the blood began to burn on the blade.

They were almost prepared to ride on when pounding hooves came to an abrupt halt nearby. A man that all the raiders knew braced against the wind as he pushed toward the violent scene. The new arrival was hefty, with kind eyes that could flip in an instant. His glare dashed from the dead woman—to the child's mangled face—to the brutalized father—then back at his men. Finally, his fire fixed on the monster he knew was responsible for most all of the mayhem.

"Castor, what is this?" the newcomer's deep voice demanded.

Fumbling for words, the startled intimidator dropped the blazing crucifix into the fire. It began to spit and melt in the hot coals.

"What is this?" the new arrival roared at the rest.

Lightning flashed and thunder shook the valley. The men shied away from their boss. The irate man lifted Archer's mother's face out of the sand by her windswept hair, taking in her beauty with complete disgust.

"And look at the body—hell, that's ten coins lost, right there. Damn it, Castor, I expected you idiots back hours ago."

"Sir, I—"

"Not another word. If I can't trust you with this, what can I trust you with? You're pathetic."

"Patricio, the Christian would not renounce his God," Castor protested.

The fiery-eyed man put his hands to his face in frustration. Pulling them down slowly for emphasis, he shouted, "I don't care. You have seen how I do business. If he doesn't renounce him, you kill him quickly and then you say he did—you sniveling shit. Gods help me—please, gods help me." Patricio groaned. "And you're the one that wants a larger cut? Hell, you aren't worth half of what I pay you—not half."

"Sir, I—"

"There aren't that many rich ones to go around. You just don't get it. You won't lead another raid for me—not one."

The leader glanced at the child and his rant intensified. "By gods, look at this one's face—" The scrawny boy's mangled cheeks made him worthless; nobody would want a servant they had to feel sorry for. At wit's end, Patricio snatched a jug of wine from a hired hand. He lifted the vessel into the air to polish it off.

The ringleader continued with rekindled resolve, "I could have gotten five pieces for that boy before you mucked him up."

"I'm trying to break in the new blood." Castor wished he had not spoken the words as soon as they left his mouth. A cold rain began to fall on the hot sand; the cooked earth steamed around the fallen. The horses were uneasy with the storm at hand.

Shouting over the steady winds, Patricio roared, "You are hell-bent on making martyrs out of these poor fools." The leader began pacing furiously around the courtyard. He made it a point to stand over his fallen henchman's corpse. "And this one—is he broken in yet?" The humiliated subject dared to glare at his master.

Castor looked to his accomplices. He found no support.

"By gods, you are worthless," Patricio scorned.

Pushing past Castor, he addressed the rest of his brood, "I want everybody to look around! Know this: I can read a man's face as easily as a dog's. I know fear and I know pain. I know hate and I know pride. But shame—leave shame on a mutt's face, because it doesn't belong on a man's. Avoiding my eyes won't save you either because I don't need to see it; I can smell it on all of you. A man doesn't stand by. A man doesn't know shame."

"Sir, I—," Castor pleaded.

"Shut your mouth, boy. I should have left you where I found you," his master raged. The enforcer had become a snail. While watching the gruff one squirm, a newer henchman chuckled somewhere behind Patricio. The furious leader spun around to locate the watery-eyed young man, desperate to hide his grin.

"Am I amusing you?"

"No—no, sir—," the nameless mercenary stuttered. Castor gave the young man a smug snarl. Without hesitation, Patricio backhanded his towering associate.

"Wipe that stupid look off your face. I hope you had fun today, Castor, because after this you won't be able to afford a woman for a long time. Hell, I should sell you to the mines to make up for this day's losses."

"Patricio—"

"Give me your sword."

The animal reluctantly handed the blood-soaked weapon to his master. The rain was falling steadily now.

"What of the boy?" a younger soldier asked his commander.

The child was refusing to let go of his fallen mother. The leader could tell by the looks on some of the mercenaries' faces that they did not approve of what Castor had done to the child. Patricio looked away from the dead and caught a glimpse of a man attempting to sneak three women out of the far end of the estate.

"Now, what the hell is this one doing?" Patricio grumbled. Up the hill, the intoxicated fool was pushing the women toward a covered cart.

The flabbergasted leader gave a loud commanding whistle and shouted, "Ay! Where the hell do you think you're going? Not a damn thing here belongs to you. Bring me my bounty." Turning on his heels, the disoriented young man sheepishly led the women down the hill toward his master. Rain-soaked dresses clung to their curves; even through the storm the girls looked profitable. Patricio's mood eased a touch.

"Well now, what's left of the women will be sold in the next province," the commander said, giving the child a nudging kick. "Look at this kid's face, Castor. What's wrong with you?" he demanded. Glaring at the animal, Patricio wiped the cold rain from his brow. He handed the lowly dog's sword off to his associates.

The towering brute said nothing. He had reason to fear this man.

"As for the boy—he will live. Sell him to the salt mines. He could turn out to be like his father. I know it's good for business, but I can't risk him wandering around spreading his old man's lies. After all, our orders were to kill the poor fools. It wouldn't look good if this one returned to lay claim to these lands, now would it?" Patricio feigned a grin to his men. Even still, disappointment remained fixed on his full face. He had little tolerance for casualties, and even less for losses. By now, what remained of Archer's sisters came into full view. Patricio was more than content with his harvest until his eyes fell on the smallest among them, the one with closely cropped amber hair. All the men sensed a change in their leader. Castor began to shy away.

"Who broke the young one?" Patricio did not shout. Silence followed; several eyes turned toward the unarmed brute cowering at their leader's side.

"This isn't supposed to be about money," Castor grumbled.

The commander's eyes flashed; he had heard and seen enough.

"Cut this fool's tongue out, and put him in chains. Sell him to the mines with what remains of the child," Patricio ordered. His tone left no doubt about his command's sincerity.

The monster panicked and ran for the nearest steed. A stocky guard was ready; he swung his club forcibly into Castor's knee. The joint shattered and the beast toppled into the wet sand.

Wielding clubs, the band of men beat the giant into the ground. The child lay beside his mother. He had no tears left to shed; the evil man's sentencing did nothing to mitigate his grief. The pounding rain soothed his torn face, but he felt no relief. In the midst of the violence, the Roman took a knee beside the fallen woman and her son.

"Nature does nothing in vain," Patricio consoled the trembling child.

The others were busy beating a terrified Castor into submission; all were eager to show their disapproval of the man's actions. More than anything else, though, they regretted their own indecision. Rising to his feet, Patricio knew it would be a nasty business getting the child to let go of his mother. Out of pity, the dark angel drove his heel into Archer's unsuspecting face. Following the powerful blow, the child collapsed into the bloody sand at his mother's side.

Those who were not handling the situation pulled the bodies into the house and began torching the estate. The flames worked their way from room to room, destroying everything that could not be taken. Every structure in the compound was razed; the smoke rose defiantly into the storm. As the raiders left, a soldier hammered a sign into the mud at the entrance to the villa:

DANGER PLAGUE

— II —

DEEP IN THE MOUNTAINS, A FORGOTTEN OLD
man stood guard atop his sentry tower. From his position, it was a two-week journey south through deathly cold, wood-
lands, and cliffs to the outskirts of barbarian territory. After that,
it was still a twenty-mile trek to the nearest trade post. A decent
map would show that the northern border jutted out and to the
west to include this land in the realm of occupied domain, forming a landlocked peninsula that existed only in the minds of men.
This was wind-torn wild country—impassable, infertile, unforgiving—yet there he stood, alert and ready.

The soldier exhaled steam into the frozen air as he watched
the sun rise over the snow-covered mountains. He uncorked his
jug and took a brisk swig of its fiery contents. On cue with the
rising sun, a relentless morning gust ripped across the mountainside.

"Damn this salt," he growled.

A massive salt deposit lay nearly a quarter mile below this
tired old soul's feet. Otherwise he would have never set foot on
this great peak buried away in a no-man's-land called Saltz
Mountain. Ton after ton of salt had been mined out of this tow-

ering rock for untold centuries. The Northerners had worked the deposits long before the Romans seized control of the operation. Salt—*white gold*—sustained the armies, preserved the food, and was even a form of currency. This highly useful, coarse, edible substance spurred extensive trade routes; men went to all lengths to secure it. An army of slaves worked themselves to death in the darkness of the mines so that the gray rock could be manipulated into precious sand.

The bowman atop the tower was Thadius. He had come to the mountain for work five years earlier, just after his wife's death. The former soldier had served his post well, and it had made him rich. The guards of Roman descent were paid handsomely in salt. The cunning old dog had been shipping his salary along with the other bundles, destined for the most established traders in the Roman Empire. Once these parcels reached his sons back home, they were able to sell the contents for a hefty profit. On Thadius's instruction, the proceeds were used to buy several farms.

Grimacing against the wind, the watchdog groaned. "You're the one that wanted this, you old fool," he scolded himself under his breath.

The Roman was well aware that he could have walked away from this dreaded mine the year before. That summer the warden had bribed the humble marksman to get him to stay. After a great internal debate, he decided to take the money. The guard agreed to serve for two more years; he would be sixty by the time he made it home to see his grandchildren. At least the earnings would ensure that he would never work another day in his life—this was the plan. Of course, it had been much warmer on the mountain when he counted the silver; the seasons had played a cruel trick on the old man.

As commander of his post, Thadius had two duties. First and foremost, he was to sound the horn and fire three flaming arrows high into the sky if an army was approaching. Secondly, if anyone ever walked out of the abandoned mineshaft behind his tower, he was to shoot them dead. The man's corpse was then to be sent around the mountain to the main mining operation on the southern face. This way, the branded number on the slave could be taken note of, after which the body would be fed to the hounds.

The idea of an army approaching from the north was laughable. An attempt to navigate anything larger than a well-supplied expeditionary force through the maze of gorges and wild pines would result in a very healthy serving of casualties and suffering. If and when an approaching army finally arrived, what was left of their number would probably throw down their weapons to beg only for a seat by the fire. As for his second duty, in the event that some lowly, flea-bitten wretch walked out of the Northern Shaft alive and well, Thadius had promised himself he would open his prized jug early. Of course, he would first fire a well-aimed arrow through the man's heart. But that night, he would give a toast to the miraculous stranger that had emerged from the shadows. For surely he would have been witnessing the work of the gods.

In truth, the guard's position was obsolete, but he knew his post was safe. His job security could be attributed only to Nero. The warden delighted in threatening lollygagging guards with a winter at the outpost on the northern face at half-pay. Not surprisingly, a few of this year's outcasts were already beginning to get on the elder's last nerve. Thadius looked to the abandoned shaft's opening curiously. A flash of anger shot across his weathered face as he took note of the bushes that obscured his view. The old dog had told his men on several occasions to clear this thicket. That fall, his much younger associates had only half-heartedly cleared a few sections of the overgrowth. Their commander was not impressed or satisfied.

"Worthless bastards," Thadius grumbled. The old man had grown accustomed to muttering to himself. It was a welcomed consequence of the countless solitary hours he spent atop his tower.

Drawing his bow, the sentry fired at the post near the abandoned mine's exit. The missile was absorbed by the overgrowth and never found its target. Frustrated, Thadius reloaded twice more. Neither shot made it to the post. The thicket's many swaying branches batted the arrows down; the commander shook his head. No matter, this outpost was more of a tradition than a necessity. Besides, he was being paid handsomely to watch this doorstep to nowhere, overseeing whatever numskulls Nero banished his way.

"To hell with it," he mumbled, more annoyed than concerned.

Over a century had passed since the Northern Shaft had been operational; even then, there was no evidence of a link between the mountain's two mines. Hundreds of slaves had run off into the maze-work over the years in an attempt to escape through the long-lost passage to freedom. Half returned a day or two later, begging to be whipped and given back their pickaxes. Most were never seen again. Anyone worth talking to believed that tunnel collapses and floods had made escape impossible.

As for sending the body around to the southern face so that the slave's number could be recorded, Nero could dream. Thadius's crew only made the trip to the mountain's main camp during the warmer months. The slight risk that the slaves could tunnel into the abandoned shaft and escape kept them put. There was no chance they would be lugging some slave's body through the snow so that the warden could update his numbers. The poor bastard would be killed then thrown off the nearest cliff—that would be that. As far as he was concerned, it would go down as just another number lost to the salt. The weathered watchdog chuckled at the idea that Nero thought they would actually lug a body around the mountain, only to be fed to the hounds.

"That conniving spider," Thadius cracked, before taking a long draw from his jug.

The idea that Nero, of all people, was concerned with accurate record keeping was an exercise in hypocrisy. The man spent his every waking hour rigging the scales so that he could siphon a fortune's worth of salt out of the operation each year. The entire charade was hilarious to Thadius. He took another long swig, then emitted a deep plume of steamy breath into the frosty air.

The elder could not help thinking about what he had seen the last time his crew made the trek around the mountain to the main camp. The stone fort was jam-packed with building materials. He recalled the massive beams that had been dragged up from the valley by oxen and slaves. The soldier had never seen such massive lengths of timber. The other guards had been very withholding; none could give him an answer as to what the great planks were for. Dozens of beams had been strewn about the encampment, and more continued to arrive. That was not all—Thadius's brood was disappointed to discover that there were no women. None of the usual merchants had been around either. Not a single outsider could be found at the mining operation—this was unprecedented.

Even more perplexing was the firewood. Nero had men working around the clock, chopping down the trees that speckled the southern face. The fuel was heaped into mounds all around the storehouse. Not only that, there were massive spools of heavy-duty rope, surrounded by hundreds of drums of tar, scattered around the mine's entrance. The ground was torn and grooved all the way down the barren mountainside from the great wave of industry. Armed guards were in place at the entrance to the storehouse—this too was unprecedented. Several new sentry towers had been constructed, situated at consistent intervals down the mountainside. The mountain had become a fortress.

Dozens of new guards had been hired, consisting mostly of foreign mercenaries, none of whom spoke Latin. Thadius had looked for the warden's trusted henchman, Dimitri, but Nero's sidekick was nowhere to be found. Those he could communicate with informed him that Dimitri had been disappearing for several weeks at a time. The veteran guard had been stunned when Nero offered him a raise in pay to keep him on Saltz Mountain. After witnessing all of the improvements and the increase in manpower, his confusion gave way to anxiety. Thadius did not know exactly what Nero was up to; all he knew was that it was a well-guarded secret.

The archer's stomach growled as a grueling gust of wind tore across his bearded face. Bracing against the cold, his thoughts returned to his post. Thadius and the five men on guard with him ate even better than the hounds on the southern face. If not for the cold, they would have had no discomfort at all. The younger men missed the women; being older, the commander only felt these pangs occasionally. Wine was well stocked, as was firewood. He and his men dined on wild rabbits and deer that he picked off from his tower. The Roman's eyes were beginning to fail him, but his accuracy with his bow was still unrivaled on the mountain. Thadius had a natural intuition; he would shoot where his target was going to be. He took into consideration the wind, the speed of the object, and the inaccuracy of his own eyesight. Then, with perfect form, he would send an arrow whistling through the air.

"Excellent," he said under his breath.

Barring his slightly yellowed teeth, the hunter stood slowly so that the old timbers making up the sentry tower's floor would not creak. A plump rabbit, with a thick winter coat, emerged from the thicket around the mine's opening. Rabbit stew was his favorite. He pulled his bowstring taut and fired. *It's a shame*, he thought, *such beautiful little critters. Too bad the gods made them taste so good.*

The elder loathed having to climb up and down the tower's rickety ladder. Not to mention trudging through the deep snow to carry his fresh kills back to the barracks. His knees were not what they used to be. The young soldiers who kept watch with him were a bunch of—

"Talentless, lazy ingrates," he muttered as he slung his bow over his shoulder and reached for his spear. The soldier took another long pull from his jug, pausing briefly to take in the majestic scenery before making his way down the hillside. His gazing eyes squinted abruptly, focusing on a disturbance in the brush.

"By gods, you rotten little son of a—"

The hunter fumbled for his bow and scrambled to take aim. It was too late. A snow fox had darted out of the thicket to snatch his fresh kill. The hungry man watched the well-camouflaged bandit disappear into the dense brush with his breakfast in tow.

"That pest has been pilfering my kills for three years now." Even still, the makings of a smile crept across his wrinkled face.

"Little rat," the hunter grumbled under his breath. He went silent. His eyes locked on the tree line. Thadius was fortunate to have had his bow at the ready—two doe had emerged from the pines to his right.

"Wait for him," he mumbled. There was an old buck that traveled with these females. The marksman had seen them all together down the hillside, out of range, several times over the past few weeks. The buck was very cautious—always the last to come out into the open.

"There's my boy," Thadius whispered, pulling the bowstring back.

The target was almost out of range, partially concealed behind a felled pine. The hunter did not have a kill shot. The cold would make it unbearable to track the deer more than a mile, so he held position. His prey began to trot casually toward the females, busy snacking on a patch of grass buried beneath the snow. The beast's impressive antlers bobbed as the powerful animal made its way out of the edge of the forest. The buck turned broadside in the clearing. The bowman's nostrils flared, already smelling the fresh meat cooking over the fire. His callused fingers released. The bowstring snapped and the arrow sailed through the icy air. With surprising speed, he reloaded and took aim.

The first arrow landed perfectly just behind the buck's powerful front shoulder, just below the midway point of his torso. The beast reared up as the second shot caught him just in front of his back leg. He darted off haphazardly; fifty yards later he took his last breath. The wise buck died mid-stride, skidding to a halt on the steep mountainside. The patch of snow around the animal went red; Thadius wiped a lone tear from his coarse cheek. The uphill draft that had concealed his scent bit at his face.

"Damn wind is making me tear up. No chance I'm lugging that big boy up to the barracks alone. I'd better wake those lazy fools."

The commander began making his way down the ladder. He was not sure if it was the timbers or his old bones creaking as he descended from his tower. Their camp was just outside the opening of the long-abandoned mineshaft. Thadius trudged up the mountain through a foot of fresh snow to a stone fort with a thatched roof and chimneys on each side. He opened the heavy wooden door of the outpost. Five young guards were slumbering inside, still drunk from the night before.

"Wake up, you lazy logs," he bellowed.

The men groaned.

"Thadius, would you shut that door before all the heat gets out?"

"Quit your crying, *Pecius*. When I was your age I served on the front, in the thick of things. I saw men lose limbs to the frost. It wasn't all drinks by the fire and plenty of fresh rabbit for me. Far from it." He finished with a contemptuous laugh, his eyes staring blankly at the fire for a moment as he remembered the hell.

"Thadius," Pecius rebuked, "we've all heard it *all* before.

Now, will you shut that infernal door?"

The other guards had gotten their bearings. Brushing the sleep from their eyes, they now stood at attention. Pecius remained bundled in furs by the fire. The outspoken noble had been banished from Rome by his father, sentenced to ten years of military exile to be served under Nero at the mines. This punishment came after his father had uncovered his plot. The young man had attempted to kill his older brother so that he would inherit his family's fortune in its entirety. Pecius regretted being caught, but not much else. He did not have the discipline nor the demeanor of a soldier, although he was quite deadly with a sword in his hands. Thadius was sure the scrapper had never seen more than a skirmish. To make matters worse, the arrogant snob was Nero's second cousin on his mother's side. Nero ran the entire mining operation and was accountable only to Alexander, one of the wealthiest men in the empire.

Pecius was connected.

Every now and then, a poorly armed barbarian force would try to plunder the salt carts. The ore mined at the mountain was transported bi-weekly to a weighing station a few days to the south, which later shipped the product to the refinery. During transport, several guards protected the unrefined rock salt. Before being assigned to Thadius's post, Pecius had guarded the supply convoys. During his tenure the self-satisfied noble had cut down dozens of these ragtag bandits, mostly starving old men armed with clubs. Of course, Pecius had been pulled off escorting the carts once Nero discovered he was stealing salt to pay for indulgences at the trade post. That is how the deviant aristocrat wound up under Thadius's command—banished by a family member once again. It was an arrangement both loathed and barely tolerated.

"Ah, the fearsome, Pecius," Thadius growled. "I hear your sweet cousin never sent you out on the last salt delivery before winter."

"What's that supposed to mean, old man?" Pecius sneered. The Roman had lost his status, but his air of superiority remained intact.

"It means you have never seen a *real* barbarian. Do I have to spell it out for you?" A few of the others chuckled. Pecius glared; the smiles vanished from their patchily bearded faces. The spiteful noble shrugged off his furs as he pulled himself to his feet.

It was well known amongst the veterans that every year before winter, the barbarian lord himself stole the final shipment. It was tolerated that one load a year would be taken. The arrangement worked out well for all parties. One load was not much; it would never become so costly that the army would be called upon to attack the village to the northeast. In exchange, the lord agreed he would not attack the mining operation. Nero always sent any new guards he wanted to get rid of to escort this doomed shipment. Pecius had always been spared.

"I have cut down droves of barbarians, and you better—"

"I better what?" Thadius roared. He would not tolerate insubordination. "Watch your tone with me, boy," the commander warned as his eyes filled with fire. The arrogant soldier knew he had crossed a line. Thadius trudged around the fireplace; large clumps of wet snow fell from his furs as he collected himself. Aside from Pecius, his men watched him respectfully.

The elder spoke, "One day—and I hope that day never comes—you men may find yourselves face to face with a true barbarian raider," he said, pausing by the fire to warm the bones in his wrinkled hands. His eyes were entrenched in the rolling flames before him. "The raider is a merciless killer. He wields Roman steel taken from the lifeless hands of your fallen brothers." The veteran walked across the room, addressing each man until he stood toe-to-toe with Pecius. The privileged guard stood tall, obnoxiously indifferent to his superior's babblings.

Thadius spoke gravely, "I pray that your confidence does not fail you, Pecius, when you hear the fearlessness in his battle cry and see the *hate* in his eyes."

— III —

A MAN ON THE BRINK OF OLD AGE WOKE IN A cold sweat, gasping for air. His white head was pounding. This was Lord Pallas, the Master Engineer of Rome. His dreams varied depending on his mood—he would either lay brick, hoist timbers, lay out columns, or, his least favorite, look for missing documents. These sorts of quirks are the trappings of a fiercely disciplined mind. Pallas rose out of bed and the dizziness took hold. He found himself clinging to a chair as a sharp pain shot up his left arm. Quite suddenly, he leaned over to vomit on the marble floor at his feet. A large dog brushed past him toward the turbulence.

"Ay! No, you filthy mutt. Get your fat head out of there," he snapped as another horse of a dog barged in.

Pallas commanded them to sit. The two hounds quickly sat and were still.

"That's better, girls, give a man a minute to figure out where the gods left him this time," he grumbled. Pallas felt the cool marble floor under his toes; he sniffed what he deduced was his mistress's perfume in the air.

"Right," he continued aloud to his hounds, as he jostled the smaller one's neck, "I made it home last night after all."

The engineer's compound was an imposing structure; it provided an unobstructed view of the beautifully crafted city. Not a bad dwelling for a Greek immigrant—the bastard son of a dairy farmer. Of course, you would never know Pallas was Greek or even foreign, for that matter. He had buried his accent, along with his lowly upbringing. The master approached the veranda; he pulled back the curtains allowing the moonlight to fall in. Thousands of torches speckled the ocean of humanity before him. Rome's hills were slowly being uncovered by the early morning shadows, cast by a sun that was still an hour from rising. Even surrounded by all this beauty, he felt nothing.

In his fifty years on earth, Pallas had never admitted to being bored; he had always associated the concept with laziness. To him, boredom was indicative, in all but the occasional rare case, of an acute lack of creativity. To be fair, he believed most people were never actually bored, but rather lacked a better word to describe their feelings. These individuals hid behind the veil of disinterest like children who were actually lonely, frustrated, or disappointed. The engineer was not sure, but he feared that maybe he too had finally succumbed to the flawed mentality.

Only an hour had passed since Pallas vomited onto his bedroom floor. This did not stop him from bouncing around the dimly lit courtyard, rattling off orders to half-asleep servants. He knew them all by name, so no one could avoid his pursuit. The aging wolf was an experienced orchestrator and expeditor. At a glance, he would accurately assess an individual's abilities, then delegate tasks accordingly. His clear, firm delivery was the mark of a battle-tested leader.

The man's head was still throbbing. On impulse, he shoved a horse aside and dunked his aching skull into the murky trough. He shook his head from side to side in the refreshingly cool water, exhaling violently through his nostrils. With a powerful jerk, he flipped his full head of white hair back out of the water, sending a jet across the faces of two young maids as they attempted to hurry past. Pallas spun around in the direction of the girlish screams.

"Ah, excuse me ladies," he joked to the well-formed girls with disgusted looks on their faces. "You know how Lucinda is always trying to get me to take more baths." It was very early and the maids were in no mood to laugh; they forced polite smiles.

"No apology is necessary, Master Pallas," one of them replied dutifully.

"What are your chores today, young ladies?" their master asked in a stern tone, which caught them both off guard.

The sisters exchanged nervous glances. The older of the two responded this time. "Icarus has assigned us to mop the kitchens, and then—"

"Nonsense, mopping is enough for today. I have something more important that needs to be done." His stone-gray eyes darted all around the courtyard, then he roared for his loyal house warden, "Icarus!"

"Yes, sir," Icarus responded, seemingly from nowhere.

Soon after, his bald head appeared out of one of the third-floor windows.

"Ah, Icarus," Pallas said with a smile. "See to it that Ariel and Bella go to the market today to pick out garments for Lucinda. Make sure they have a little extra for lunch."

"Of course, sir," Icarus replied hurriedly. He was coming unraveled; his wife was nagging him in one ear, while his boss was tugging on the other.

"This is a top priority," his master barked.

"Of course, sir. I will be down in a minute," the humble servant added, with more than a hint of agitation.

"Lazy old bird," Pallas jabbed. He rolled his eyes theatrically for the girls. They felt very important when their employer referred to them each by name in front of the others. Bright white smiles stretched out across their gorgeous, sun-kissed faces. The two of them rushed off to get their mopping done as quickly as possible.

As the sisters disappeared into the estate, their master froze. Triggered by a sound, or possibly even a primal sixth sense, Pallas cocked his head. Over his shoulder, out of the corner of his eye, he caught a glimpse of a scrawny young man stumbling across his courtyard. It was his nephew, Antonius. The old dog's hard eyes flashed.

"Antonius!"

His roar filled the entire courtyard, reverberating off the roof's clay shingles as it climbed. All the servants stopped dead in their tracks. Antonius's heart skipped a beat. Pallas almost never yelled; when he did, he made effective use of the tool. The wolf stomped across the courtyard, stopping an inch from his nephew's lifelessly pale face.

"Hear me, Antonius. If I catch you stumbling out of my storehouse again, I will beat you senseless. Thank the gods your mother isn't alive to see the worthless, drunken bag of bones you've become. Here you stand, nearly twenty, *and still* I can barely trust you to sweep the damn corridors."

A few servants struggled to muffle their chuckles. Antonius was a wisecracking shrimp who had grown up within the walls of his uncle's compound. The privileged freeloader could sense the laughter, and it was maddening. In a moment of weakness, he had the misfortune of entertaining a burst of drunken confidence. His fiery eyes ignited as he found the courage to speak.

"I don't need this shit-hole."

Pallas let out a brief chuckle before returning fire, "You're right. The world is just waiting for a talented stable boy such as yourself. You dodged me yesterday. I hear Icarus had you shovel shit from sunup to sundown. I guess it was for the best—even you can't muck that up."

Several more servants chuckled aloud at the furious look that flashed across Antonius's twisted face. He was humiliated and unwinding fast. Then an unfortunate idea became reality: in an ill-conceived conniption, the drunk swung his bony fist at his uncle. Pallas used his powerful left forearm to block the pathetic right hook with ease. If he had even an ounce of respect for his nephew as a man, he would have countered with a blow of his own. Instead, in the blink of an eye, the gray wolf lunged forward to grab his assailant's ear. He crushed it between the calloused fingers of his powerful left hand.

"Mercy, Pallas. By gods—let go, old man," the squirming fool demanded.

"Does that wine make you feel strong, boy?"

In a flash of anger, he yanked his nephew by the collar and drove him hard into the courtyard wall. The bumbling bag of bones stumbled backward before collapsing; no servants were laughing anymore. Pallas stormed into the storehouse, emerging moments later with a barrel of cheap wine. He slammed it down next to Antonius's throbbing head then looked at his house warden, Icarus, who had just come down to the awkwardly silent courtyard. The servant did not seem the least bit surprised by how his morning was unfolding.

"If this worm doesn't finish this jug by sundown, I never want to see him on these grounds again." His victim groaned in protest. A toothy grin fanned out across Pallas's heavily whiskered face. If he were going to get rid of the drunkard, he would have done so years ago. Icarus knew this.

The loyal servant lifted the jug to gauge its weight and responded, "Of course, sir." Pallas took a knee to face the brazen freeloader.

"I swear—if you weren't my late wife's dead sister's youngest son." This also happened to be how his uncle introduced him to visitors and company of all kinds.

"I was my mother's only son; I'm your only nephew," whimpered Antonius.

"Curse the word. Only by association, you fool. We share no blood. Shun the gods that dealt me such a useless little rat. If those scheming politicians in Rome only knew half the muck I have to deal with." A handful of servants chuckled. Pleased to have won back his audience, the old wolf grinned.

The engineer had devoted his life to construction. Somewhere along the way, the buildings and his love for teaching his craft had become a mind-numbing chore. Here he was, an aging man with nothing left to do but build, and every day was becoming worse than the one before. He wanted to relinquish his position but feared to disappoint the emperor. The man had killed for less.

The Greek started his career building bridges and outposts for the infantry in the North. He met General Alexander on the front, a man who eventually proved to be a true friend. Without him, Pallas never would have been allowed to become the man he was. Decades before, Alexander had personally recommended the builder to the Imperial Engineer's staff. Pallas proved himself worthy of his friend's recommendation and swiftly moved through the ranks. Always eager to shed accountability, it was not long before Rome's lawmakers had the talented foreigner overseeing all construction funded by the emperor.

Over the years, Pallas kept in touch with the former general. It was no surprise that Alexander—a business titan—and Pallas became so closely entwined. After all, a builder is only as good as his suppliers and equipment allow. Fortunately, the lord ensured that his friend had the best of both; as a result, the Greek thrived. Alexander was a stabilizing force in the North that brought vast wealth to the empire; to cross him could mean war. As the lord's well-known associate, Pallas enjoyed a sense of job security that few of his predecessors had ever been privy to.

— IV —

T HE ENGINEER LEFT HIS COMPOUND A LITTLE
after dawn. He instructed a servant guarding the gate to
keep the hounds back. Despite leaving his beasts behind, he was
not worried about muggers. Pallas wore no gold or jewels and
dressed in cheap garments. For protection, he carried only a thin
iron bar just over sixteen inches long, roughly three pounds in
weight. He had refused to carry a sharpened edge since his early
years in the Roman Infantry. As a young man, he had marched
many good men to their deaths and cut down even more with his
sword. All the bloodshed had never hardened him. To this day, he
hesitated before slaughtering livestock. Pallas had ended many
lives, but he was not a killer.

The esteemed builder had made his way through the hills
close to the city's edge by mid-morning. The sun was already in full
bloom. In the distance, there was a youngster trying to sell fruit to
wealthy merchants. Pallas looked on as several carts blazed past
the budding entrepreneur. The engineer recalled the beatings he
had received as a boy when he came home empty-handed from
town. The memories flashed with amazing clarity as he made his
way down the dusty hill. Pallas came from a small town in the

northern hills of Greece. It is hard to sell to the poor.

The prospective customer stopped in the road and turned to face the scrawny Roman. The boy assessed the poorly dressed man with long white hair and a heavily whiskered face. He was surprised that this peasant was interested in his supply.

"This fruit is very expensive, sir," the youngster warned.

The wanderer spoke, "What are you doing out here alone, boy? The first group of delinquents that heads down the hill will beat you black and blue. Then they'll feast on your hard-earned baskets." The youngster was noticeably offended by this drifter's critical assessment of his operation.

"I'd like to see them try," he fired back, nodding toward a nearby bush, where lay a bullish man. The lump snored with an empty jug of wine at his side.

"I see," his client replied with a grin, motioning toward the heap. "Your father, I take it."

"It's a piece for the apples. Two for the pears," the little salesman answered, remaining in the shade. He did not want to haul the heavy baskets out to the road for some haggling wanderer.

"I wouldn't pay two coppers for the basket, boy. Does a laying hen come with that pear?"

"No, sir."

The foreigner assessed the slightly built, brown-haired kid. He could tell the child had probably spent his entire life in the hills surrounding the city. The lad had a very Roman way about him—a certain misplaced confidence. Pallas strolled over and began rummaging through the baskets. The common grunt tossed a few of the lesser apples he came across into the dirt.

"What are you doing, old man?"

"No one in their right mind would pay a piece for a rotten apple, boy. You should know better than to put them on the top."

"Rotten? They're barely even bruised," the youngster huffed, scrambling to pick up all the fruit. When the lad looked up, his ill-mannered customer was holding a glistening orb.

"You know, the last time I was in the markets, I saw lesser apples going for two pieces." Pallas tested the pint-sized salesman.

"We can't afford a table at the markets." The boy sighed. "We stand by our prices, sir—one piece, as advertised."

Satisfied, Pallas pulled his coins from his cloak. The boy was very surprised by the bulging sack the peasant held in his weathered hands. He thought it was probably filled with snacks—pistachio nuts possibly. No doubt, the lad was hungry. When he heard the clinking, he knew better.

The unlikely customer's hand emerged holding a gold piece. The young one's eyes doubled in size; he could count on one hand the number of times he had seen a gold coin. Pallas flicked it high into the air for the stunned boy to catch. At that moment, the merchant's incapacitated father groaned and belched. The youngster glanced over in shame. Pallas looked in the massive man's direction, glimpsing a mark on the oaf's arm.

"I see your father bares the mark of the Roman Masons."
The boy's embarrassment vanished as his elder knew it would.

"Yes sir, he set stones before his back went out. He worked under the Master Engineer, Lord Pallas," the small salesman stated with a renewed sense of self-worth.

"I thought I recognized him."

The little Roman gazed up at the wealthy peasant as his quick mind churned. Remembering his father's many stories, the stunned merchant analyzed the tattered noble before him. His eyes caught a glimpse of the iron bar at his customer's hip; it clicked.

"Lord—Pallas?"

"I never understood where people got all that *lord* nonsense from. If any of them ever met my father, they'd know what I mean," he stated, before chomping off a huge hunk of his apple.

"Thank you, Master Pallas," the scrawny lad belted out. His eyes fixed on the gold coin being crushed between his small fingers.

"Be careful with that, boy—the more one has, the more one wants." Pallas set off toward the city's edge, apple in hand.

The engineer's mind wandered as he paced through the bustling city. Shouting merchants and caged livestock from all over the world were at every turn. Everything and everyone was for sale. Fortunes changed hands daily. The aroma of perfectly cooked lamb filled one street; the scent of horse dung filled the next. It was a sensory explosion; bright colors, loud conversations in multiple languages, music, artwork, and hundreds of aromas clamored for one's attention. Wagons creaked through narrow alleyways, flocks of pigeons fluttered through the air. Gorgeous, well-tanned, brown-haired women dressed in bright colors filled the streets. Many were laughing and chasing after their young children. All the while, the pounding hammers of the blacksmiths kept a steady beat, fashioning the weaponry that protected the flow of goods and resources throughout the empire.

Hardship in the north and wars to the east had driven up the costs of raw materials. The price of salt was also quickly on the rise due to a meager wheat harvest; however, the hardship had not made its way into the Roman markets just yet. There were still many coppers in the purses of the citizens. They freely spent them in excess.

Pallas arrived at the base of the Capitol. Pigeons dispersed as he ascended the steps confidently, ready to trade in his hammer and ledger for a deep glass and good company. No more cracking whips across the backs of slaves.

My time has come, the builder thought as he entered the massive hall.

— V —

ETERMINED DARK EYES GAZED ACROSS END-
less miles of rolling snow-covered farmlands. The man
behind this insidious glare was surrounded by opulence taken
from every corner of the known world. From his elevated fortress
the commander watched over his massive slice of Germania; like
a hawk soaring over an open field, his shadow alone struck fear
into the hearts of the conquered. This was Pallas's friend, Alexander.

The lord's father, Artemis, had left the bulk of the family's
fortune to Estor—Alexander's much younger half-brother, the
product of his father's final marriage. Alexander did not sulk; he
used his much smaller inheritance to build a fortune of his own.
Meanwhile, Estor used his family's wealth to manipulate the Roman Senate for personal gain whenever the opportunity presented itself. Both brothers had a knack for the art of corruption. The
estranged siblings often sought to ruin, defame, or outwit one
another by any means available.

A great rebellion had erupted in Germania a few years earlier. The barbarian horde had been better supplied than anyone
could have imagined. The former general immediately suspected

his brother's involvement. Alexander squashed the rebellion, but it took two years of costly bloodshed. Soon afterward, all the prize horses in Estor's stables died from an inexplicable plague—swift retribution. It did not stop there: since the rebellion ended, most of Estor's trade convoys never returned from the North. The attacks continued until he finally shut down all operations in his brother's corner of the world. This did not stop Alexander from spending a small fortune every year trying to disrupt his brother's other business endeavors.

Family was not the former general's strong suit. Alexander had four wives: two in Rome and two in the North. Between them he had seventeen children, not to mention twelve illegitimates fathered with servant girls over the years. These were just the offspring he knew about. He did not see his children often because of the distance, although it was mostly due to the fact that their mothers could not stand the sight of him. Truth told, the children were not very fond of their father either.

Greed was not the man's principle; wealth in and of itself meant nothing to him. Once he was too old for battle, he needed another avenue to channel his competitive spirit. It was the power and respect behind his wealth that motivated the lord. Alexander would melt down every gold coin in his chests to burn his competition. Would-be adversaries knew this, so they treaded lightly and never kept anything from him. The titan ruled with an iron fist, controlling all the goods and, most importantly, all the information in his domain.

Lord Alexander was an imposing figure; he had hard, dark eyes and thick, jet-black hair splashed with gray streaks. The Roman sat like a statue, taking in the motionless snowcapped mountains that commanded the horizon. He ruled North Country—he had once even looked the part. In his youth he had been a powerful, well-kept man. Now, the tired soul who sat on this windblown veranda wearing a bearskin cloak was old, fat, and gray.

It began to snow; the blustery whirlwind stirred deep-rooted memories. The old man recalled a distant winter morning from his early years in the Roman Infantry, a memory so intense that it was forever seared into his prideful mind. When his heavy eyes closed, *he was there again, in his dreams. . . .*

Long ago, Alexander had been part of a tracking mission to corner a particularly illusive group of thieves. The bandits had been stealing weapons and precious metals. Instability was the enemy, so the Vandals had to be brought to justice—killed. The raiders had mastered their craft. They wielded Roman steel taken from the many soldiers they killed; they were hardened men adorned in bear and wolf hides. They would always attack at dusk. At the day's end, the merchants would demobilize. The cart horses would be unhooked, grazed, and watered. Once the travelers busied themselves with making camp and preparing their evening meal, the barbarians emerged from the forest. As a rule, they left no survivors; nightfall covered their retreat back into the wilderness. If not for the lost goods, there would be no proof of their existence at all. For a time they went about their business with impunity. By passing up on goods owned by hefty Roman purses, the criminals avoided pursuit. The prosperous times ended when the raiders unknowingly killed an Imperial Courier—a man who happened to be distantly related to newly crowned Emperor Commodus. Overnight, they became highly sought-after outlaws. Eager for recognition, Alexander vowed to annihilate them.

The strike force tracked this murderous group deep into the mountains. The Northerners were on foot, but they knew the country well. The Romans struggled to weave their heavily laden beasts through the treacherous mountain passes. When the terrain became impossible to traverse from horseback, they left the animals behind with two soldiers and continued on foot. It was not long before the men were exhausted; Alexander was pushing forward too quickly for most to keep pace.

"General Alexander," a soldier addressed his commander directly as the two were trudging up a steep incline. The general did not acknowledge him. The foreigner addressed his commander once more, "General Alexander, *sir.*"

"What is it now, Pallas?" he snapped, turning around to face his associate.

"Sir, we should turn back."

"Ridiculous. We have been able to see the Vandals' campfire every night. We have been gaining on them. Only a cowardly fool would turn back now."

"Rest assured, General, they have been able to see our fires at night as well," Pallas replied. The Roman's eyes flickered.

"What are you getting at?"

"Don't play a fool, General. I know the thought has crossed your mind. Not to mention, sir—I shouldn't have to tell you how ridiculous it looks when a general leaves his horse behind. Your intensity is commendable, but you have no business soldiering on foot."

"I have my suspicions," Alexander said, looking off into the distance. An endless circle of towering peaks surrounded them.

"We could barely keep up with them when we were on horseback. Now we are on foot, and we are gaining on them," Pallas spoke fiercely. The general's eyes were fixed on the horizon, searching for words in the ocean of pines.

"Yes, I have had my suspicions," Alexander repeated. He was becoming a little uneasy now. Even still, he could not hide how annoyed he was at being confronted by a low-ranking commoner.

"Look how spread out we are. What if we stumbled upon their group over this next hill? What are we going to do? Charge them on our own?"

"Watch your tone, Pallas," Alexander sneered so that a few of the men who were closer behind could hear. The Roman turned to assess his strike force. Half the men were a good quarter-mile behind, fumbling through the deep snow.

The young man resented the foreigner, even if his advice was sound. The general was aware that Pallas had been in the

North for many years. This powerfully built Greek seemed disinterested in battle and unconvincing in his training habits. To Alexander, this made him the worst kind of soldier. It set a bad example when someone the men respected took formal drills lightly.

More careful with his approach, Pallas continued, "As fanned out as we are, all they would have to do is wait for us from an elevated position. A decent bowman could pick us off, one by one."

"I agree. We should regroup—since the worthless dogs can't keep pace," Alexander huffed. The cold was getting to him. They had only stopped moving for a moment; with the sun falling it did not take long for the frost to set in. Steam from the men's breath hung in persistent clouds around them; all dreaded the unforgiving darkness.

"Sir, I fear we are walking into a trap. We are risking a great deal to catch a small group of thieves. You know they will be replaced by another squad of rebels as quickly as we eliminate them."

"We have not come this far to turn back. Another word and I will have you flogged when we return to camp." That was the end of the debate. Given his recent promotion, it had been too long since the general had seen battle; he was eager to engage.

After two arduous days, they came within a mile of the bandits. The soldiers had drawn straws the night before to determine which man would remain behind to set a false fire in the distance.

It was a ruse meant to trick the enemy into thinking they were a safe distance from Roman pursuit.

In the middle of the night, with their false fire burning in the distance, they crept silently across the snow-covered forest floor. The anxiousness before battle did little to block out the miserable cold. In time, the enemy's flickering campfire came into view. The shivering soldiers fanned out to surround the encampment. The flames cast long shadows across the snow. Most of the men were more eager to reach the blazing logs than anything else. The outlaws had made camp on a ledge at the base of the hillside. The legionaries crept through a dense pine forest that gave way to the clearing. With a cliff at their back, the villains would have nowhere to run.

The wind was fierce out on the elevated ledge; a strong gust ripped down the hillside, silencing their approach. The warmth of the fire drew them toward the enemy. The general noticed Pallas outpacing the rest. His temper flared; he preferred to keep the cowards toward the back. Fearing he too would fall behind the foreigner, Alexander rushed out in front.

The sprinting general gave the signal, and his men stormed the sleeping barbarians. They aggressively tore through the motionless bundles, only to discover that here was not a soul to be found. Unnerved, the men went silent.

While the others huddled around the fire, Pallas remained alert. He was analyzing every shred of the encampment. There were about a dozen bundles, yet only one sleeping fur. The harsh snow-blown wind roared. A few of the younger soldiers added several nearby logs to the fire then held flat open palms over the tumbling flames. Even through the storm their silhouettes around the increased blaze could be seen from afar.

"No—put that out," Pallas demanded.

"Are you mad? We will freeze," a shivering soldier huffed.

"They must have heard us coming," another stated.

"Put that fire out now!" Pallas locked eyes with Alexander; the young commander was less than prepared for the intensity that met him there.

"Extinguish the fire," the general ordered.

A few soldiers began reluctantly kicking snow onto the flames. It was a large fire; their efforts did little to extinguish the blaze. A heavy snow began to fall—it was total whiteness all at once. The tree line was barely discernible from the fifty-foot drop beyond the ledge. Following his instincts, Pallas jogged toward the forest.

"Men, make for the tree line," he called back to the others.

"Absolutely not. We will hold this ground," Alexander shouted. Pallas looked imploringly at the commander.

"Shields linked—*now!*" The soldier was forced to return to the storm-battered group. Their shield wall did little to lessen the effects of the wind tearing across the ledge. Their hands were losing sensation; all eyes were fixed on the dark forest.

"We should take cover in the pines," a shaking young man insisted.

It was too late. The tall trees began cackling all around them. Nearly fifty torches lit simultaneously in a U-shape around the cornered Romans. Howling and roaring soon replaced the deviant laughter. The fearsome sounds echoed through the wilderness for miles; wild howls filled the pine forest.

"War hounds," a young Roman groaned, and gulped.

"Daggers ready," Alexander roared.

"Daggers ready," the soldiers echoed in unison.

The windblown snow was cascading down on them all as the roaring barbarians' footfalls intensified. The torches did not move with the sounds of the impending onslaught. When the soldiers saw the barrage of flaming arrows fill the dark snow-blown sky, they understood why. Conveniently, all the archers had to do was aim for the falsified encampment's large glowing fire through the storm.

"Testudo! Shields high—die fighting," Pallas commanded.

"Die fighting!" the men roared. The soldiers formed an impenetrable dome with their shields resembling a tortoise shell. Facing imminent death, Alexander witnessed his men rallying behind the unruly foreigner; his rage swelled. Lethal balls of fire rained down on the band of legionaries. The roars drew closer as the wild howling ceased. The hounds were close.

The pack of dogs arrived amidst the third wave of falling arrows; they leapt ferociously from the blinding whiteness. Some thirty beasts attacked from all sides, clawing through the snow-filled gap at the base of the shield-shell. They ripped between the exterior soldiers' exposed shins and pounced on the defenseless men holding their shields high at the dome's interior. The beasts were fearless in ways men could only dream of. Many of the soldiers were too focused on blocking the volley of flaming missiles to adjust; the man-eaters showed no mercy. They viciously pounced on their distracted victims, gnashing and clawing relentlessly. Frantic daggers were used to subdue the snarling beasts. As the men scrambled to fight off the bloodthirsty hounds, the testudo failed momentarily, several falling arrows found openings in legionaries' armor.

It was a well-conceived assault. The beasts and consecutive rounds of flaming arrows kept the Romans pinned down, huddled together with shields high to ward off the steady barrage. With the cliff at their backs, they had nowhere to run.

That dark morning, when Alexander saw the swarm of barbarians flowing through the tall pines, he was, for the first time, afraid. All had heard of skirmishes wherein the Vandals left no survivors. His mind played with the notion that this could be one of those moments and one of his last.

Spears thrust from the shield wall with deathly accuracy, but the bloodthirsty horde kept flowing through the tree line. Under duress, the cornered soldiers turned to their short javelins. They slammed their shields into the nomads, then pelted them with these missiles. Well trained, the men kept formation, fighting in pairs to limit their exposure. For a time, they began pushing the enemy back toward the forest. After exhausting their spears and arrows, the dome became indefensible. They were forced to turn to their swords. At once, the barbarians' numbers became overwhelming. The arrows kept falling. Alexander knew his testudo formation would prove useless against the constant deluge of fire—especially against a downhill assault with a cliff at their backs. Their only hope was to push into the forest.

Alexander bellowed the order, *"Charge!"*

The soldiers broke formation to plow into the enemy's ranks. The Roman force was outnumbered, caught in a terrifying swarm of clubs and sickles. Better weaponry, armor, and formal training barely settled the score. The whiteness was so intense that barbarians appeared and vanished as the legionaries surged through the pine forest. Amidst the chaos, Alexander noticed another soldier out in front of him, though he could not determine the man's identity through the turbulent blur of heavy snow and bloodshed. Then the realization came—it was Pallas, but it was not the soldier he knew. This was a man transformed, a warrior.

The soldier out ahead was a blank-faced scourge. His sword was death and he wielded it with ease. Expressionless and maddeningly formulaic, every lunge was lethal, consisting only of well-aimed strikes to arteries, vitals, and tendons. His silence made the tall pines shake as he weaved through the swarm. The foreigner was not a passionate fighter; he was a flawless executioner. Alexander had spent a lifetime developing his style, becoming an artist of battle. He was forced to witness the finality of a warrior whose every movement was lethal. There was no showboating, no drawn out combat, just death. Clubs narrowly missed his expressionless face as he plowed through the storm. Always resourceful, Pallas used the trees around him as pawns. Their trunks would absorb blows meant for his evading shadow. The ghost would vanish behind a tall pine then appear from the shadow of another, using the blinding snowfall to his every advantage.

Even through the storm, Alexander could see that the man he knew was merely a shadow, a fraud. Any rational fear of death had been replaced by an overwhelming prideful need. This commoner would not outshine him. The general grew more furious as Pallas continued to extend his lead.

"Regroup," Alexander ordered into the swirling snow.

What was left of his men rallied around him; Pallas was not among them. Throngs of raiders collapsed on the slow-moving legionaries. The son of Artemis hacked and roared in his attempt to outmatch the Greek warrior. Unlike the mangled corpses he left in his wake, the commoner's kills were clean. Pallas was a silent plague drifting through the storm. He moved across the snow like a scorpion over sand, stinging oncoming assailants with cold sharpened steel.

As the sounds of battle began to taper off, the exhausted general could once again hear the fresh snow crunching beneath his boots. Corpses littered the forest floor. Wind flexed the branches above, dumping heavy loads of white powder. It was the intermittent horrifying cries that drew him farther into the pines. He waded through the drifts cautiously; the enemy's numbers were dwindling. Alexander had lost track of the foreign renegade. Soaked in sweat and blood, his damp cloak began freezing at his knees. Fighting against the storm, he trudged on, following the dreadful sounds deeper into the unending forest. All of his men lay slain behind him; he debated returning to the beckoning fire in the distance.

The stubborn Roman boldly called out into the storm, "Pallas—fall back!"

What was left of the enemy was retreating in terror; something was hunting the fleeing barbarians. Alexander struggled to locate the foreigner as he pushed through the towering pines. The warrior was no more than a shadow in the blinding storm—existing only in the muffled cries of his dying victims.

"Greek," Alexander roared with fury.

At the top of the incline, a lone figure came into view, slain archers were strewn all around him. What remained of the enemy had fled—convinced that a white-haired ghost haunted this forest. The torches that the Vandals had used to ignite their firepower were still scattered on the trees around them.

The general paused a safe distance from the warrior ahead. He called out to him fiercely, "Greek—did you not hear my commands? Fall back!" The shadowy figure did not respond; he stood entranced in the torchlight.

Alexander's deflated pride was dragging through the snow at his feet. His stubborn mind refused to accept that this commoner was the better warrior. The very idea of this man was unfathomable; his ego could not handle the affront. The sharp, cold air stung his lungs as his heart raced wildly—his mind went blank with jealous rage. Succumbing to his pride, Alexander let out a lion-like battle cry. He charged through the bloodied snow at the lone wolf. Subconsciously, Pallas was counting the thuds as his commander drew down on him. He was going to give the Roman the opportunity to take heed on his own accord.

The fact that the foreign brute had ignored his fiery charge was the ultimate insult to the noble swordsman. He leapt into the air in preparation to cut the unruly Greek down. Pallas side-stepped—avoiding the blow. It was then that Alexander got his first good look at the dead-eyed assassin. He could see the freshly frozen blood on his face, through which channels of warm tears had recently flowed.

The silent warrior turned to face his prey. No sadness remained in Pallas's cold eyes—blankness had washed over them. The foreigner had gone gray at an early age; blood coated his white hair and whiskered face. The wolf's breathing was controlled, his heartbeat stable.

"You insubordinate wretch—you left us to die!"

Pallas did not respond. Instead, he dropped his dagger from his right hand and wrenched a blunt club from a fallen barbarian's frozen death grip. The noble's rage swelled at the commoner's indifference; he charged again.

The defenseless counters were over. Pallas blocked the strike and backhanded his attacker with the butt of his sword.

The blow sent Alexander wobbling into the drifts. The towering general was sent reeling like a slave boy, backhanded by his master. The snow fell in heaps around them, eager to hide the shamefulness of the carnage that the men had left in the otherwise whitewashed woodland floor. There was a distant sun cranking into position, illuminating the eastern horizon.

The Roman scrambled to his feet in absolute fury to face the man who dared to disgrace him. This overwhelming feeling of insignificance was the worst pain he had ever known. His mind blamed his failure on the Greek's left-handedness. He would have to adjust; he had been trained to battle sinistra. His enemy had vanished into the snowstorm. The general's eyes darted across the forest trying to find the gray's footprints. There were none; the ghost had vanished.

"Sinistra—face me, you coward!"

There was no reply. Only steam from his exasperated gasps filled the frozen air around him. Without warning, he felt a hard kick to his back. Cruelly accurate, the blow shocked the fuming soldier's left kidney, as intended. The wind was instantly knocked out of his chest. Alexander was forced to his hands and knees, gasping for air. A second swift kick landed across the bridge of his nose; he heard it break. Warm blood ran freely from his broken face as he crawled through the snow.

Strong-willed, Alexander retained consciousness. He could not resign himself to the fact that another warrior could beat him so completely. The injured man rose slowly to face his enemy.

His assailant still had not uttered a word; he had not even made a sound. The frustrated noble ripped his dented helmet from his head.

"Greek, you lowly slave. I am going to paint the snow red with your blood."

Alexander did not show it, but doubt had invaded his psyche. He was worried he would end up like the Vandals that littered the snow-covered forest floor, prey to a single mortal wound to his neck or gut. That he, the son of Artemis, would die at the hands of this ghostly wolf.

Like a wild predator, Pallas could sense his fear. The once-silent assassin let out a roar that shattered every fragment of confidence his opponent had left. The general was bleeding profusely from his nose. Both eyes were bruising, and his left kidney was throbbing. He stood shivering in his icy armor, bracing against the ensuing storm. As tireless as the frigid gusts, Pallas continuously heaved his sword at his fading foe. The son of Artemis fought bravely, but he was truly outmatched. His attacker had replaced his dagger with a club. Every failed lunge by the general resulted in a painful whack from this unforgiving wooden scepter.

Struggling to gain an edge, Alexander sacrificed his view when he raised his shield to block a powerful overhand blow from his assailant's sword. The strike never came. In that momentary lapse in combat, the commander sensed that he had been played. In one fluid motion, Pallas slid through the snow and dropped his sword. Wielding the club with two hands, the Greek swung mercilessly into the Roman's exposed left shin. Both men heard the bone crack. It was a powerful strike; the tremendous jolt brought Alexander to his knees. Desperate to remain in contention, he lifted his now heavy sword feebly to defend himself.

The Greek had vanished into the storm. The predator let him kneel for what seemed an eternity, tortured by his own dreaded thoughts. Finally, the wolf appeared from the whiteness. He stood undetected behind his watery-eyed, disheveled foe. Without a word, Pallas swung his club at the general's right forearm. It too snapped; his victim's ornate sword fell into the red snow. Alexander's right arm crumpled uselessly to his side as he stared blankly out into the constant snowfall.

A determined sun was steadily rising through the storm. With eyes locked on the distant mountains, the general exhaled his fear of defeat. Pallas kicked the shield off the fallen warrior's left arm. The noble inhaled what he thought would be his last breath. In that gasp, his prideful fear had been replaced by a strange sense of freedom. For the first time, he had been unchained from the burden of his own greatness. Pallas drove his elbow hard across his victim's brow.

Alexander woke with a start, an old man once again, in front of a warm fire on his veranda. The Roman's dark eyes gazed proudly across his domain.

— VI —

PALLAS'S ANNOUNCEMENT OF RETIREMENT HAD not gone over well, but he refused to dwell on Emperor Septimius Severus's threats. After all, he was free. Unchained from the tediousness of construction—the mundane, the repetitive— all of it was in the past now. He took a powerful swig from his jug. The lukewarm liquid stained his grin blood red before he plunged at Lucinda to steal a loving kiss. A flustered smile flashed across her pleasantly plump face; she was an eye-catching beauty.

Lucinda glared at him and jabbed, "The sun has barely been up for an hour. You are a drunkard. Maybe we should just lock you up and ship you back to the Greeks who made such a fool."

They were preparing to travel to Germania with the spring shipment of weaponry and supplies for the Northern Legion. This was a slow-moving, well-guarded supply train; two thousand armed men defended the shipment between its many checkpoints. The wealthier merchants employed additional mercenaries to guard their more extravagant cargo. These hired swords defended their employer's goods as much from the Roman soldiers as any would-be ambushers. The Northern Rebellion had been over for nearly two years, yet many rebel groups remained. These nomadic outlaws existed on plundered goods. Many men who did not pay the fee, or opted to ride alone, lost their fortunes and their lives to outlaws on their journey north.

Pallas chuckled and smiled at his woman as she brushed the hounds off her. "How are your pups doing, my love?" he asked. She could not help rolling her eyes at him.

"They are as eager to get back to their home in the North as I am. I don't have to tell you how much I miss my homeland." Her eyes shifted. "Now, why on earth are you bringing all that nonsense?"

Lucinda was noting the carts overflowing with mirrors, pillows, and trinkets. Pallas assumed she was referring to his tool chest. He had packed all of his favorite hand tools. The instruments had not been fussed over; however, they were very well organized. The engineer did not waste time polishing his tools or any of his possessions. He possessed things to improve his life; he thought it ridiculous to waste time obsessing.

"As always, you are right, my dear," he replied with a tolerable hint of sarcasm. "Just the bare necessities," Pallas bellowed.

The Greek hurled several expensive measuring devices out of his chest onto the dirt in his courtyard. Servants rushed over to wipe them off and put them back in his warehouse. When he was finished, only a small bundle of rudimentary hand tools remained, so he flung the carrying chest off the cart as well. He grabbed a nearby bucket used to catch horse dung while traveling through wealthier sections of the city. He dumped out the contents and threw in his tools. A recently hired servant looked on in stunned disbelief. Those more used to his oddities just turned away and chuckled at their vulgar master. Lucinda shook her head and a few more servants laughed.

"Now I only have what's required to make repairs to the carts. That is as it should be. More importantly, we now have room for the pups on our cart. Leave that extra cart behind. We will not have to pay as much to the guard. Leave those other three behind as well," he ordered, motioning to the large carts carrying a wide array of luxurious trinkets. The servants looked to Lucinda to authorize the addendum. She nodded in agreement, then they quickly began offloading and redistributing the goods.

The esteemed engineer could afford to pay the fee for a hundred carts, but he had never been one to flaunt his wealth. Those who did not know Pallas—upon seeing the three carts carrying mostly wine, spices, and dogs—would assume he was a moderately successful merchant. They would also blend in better with the other carts en route to the North, which was advantageous. Besides, he had not wanted to bring all that useless nonsense to begin with. Lucinda would not miss the heaps of luxury either. After all, she had been happy enough to sleep on dirt for the first half of her life. She had been a servant before she met Pallas. The old man still could not get her to stop cleaning. Lucinda, like the hounds, was from Germania. Many years ago, she was sold to Roman merchants after her village fell prey to starving rebels. She was barely a woman then. Her early years had been cruel; it was a wonder that she maintained such a positive outlook.

Pallas's trusted house warden was busy helping the others get everything offloaded and resituated. Under his breath, he mockingly muttered what Pallas had told him the night before, "Take everything."

Icarus and his wife Aurora had raised their master's daughter, Adriana, along with their nine children as if she was their own. The engineer was forever indebted to them for doing such an excellent job. Icarus had no formal training in any area of money management, but he had been blessed with a great deal of common sense. Pallas was certain his estate would be managed flawlessly by Icarus in his absence; the man was like a brother to him.

"Where is that good-for-nothing fool Antonius?" the builder barked. "Can he not even see his uncle off?" Icarus could tell something was eating at his master, and he knew that it was not Antonius's absence. Pallas took a long draw from his jug while his eyes wandered off down the road ahead.

"Make sure that little rodent stays out of trouble while I am gone, Icarus. He's good enough for an in-law; I don't want his blood on my hands anyway. Besides, he's like a brother to Adriana."

Icarus noted how the aging wolf's voice faltered as he said his daughter's name. He was sure it was Adriana's absence that had him wound up. The servant stopped fiddling with the horse bridles and turned to face a sullen Pallas. His normally quick mind struggled to think of something to say to his old friend. His master was a good man; this was hard for him.

Pallas hugged Aurora, then sighed. "Adriana could not make it to see us off?"

"Unfortunately, she has still not forgiven you for missing her wedding," replied Icarus, before his wife could answer.

"There was a fire at my jobsite. The entire city could have burned to the ground," Pallas retorted. Then he downed another swig as he began to pace back and forth.

"I know, we have explained the situation. She is still as stubborn as ever," Icarus replied.

"Just like her mother," Pallas muttered, clinging to his jug for support.

Aurora chimed in, barely able to contain herself, "She is with child, Pallas. Word of it arrived mid-afternoon yesterday. I would have told you right away, but—" She paused. Pallas stopped pacing immediately; the beginnings of a grin began to form on his whiskered face. Not wanting to upset her master any further, Aurora continued cautiously, "But I had hoped that maybe she would surprise you, by coming to tell you herself before you left."

Lucinda was happily moving all the pups to their cart. She casually entered into the conversation, "These are the only pillows I will need. You aren't as crazy as you look, old man. There is nothing here that we can't find in the North—nothing we need anyway." After setting down the balls of fur, she got a look at the excuse for a smile stamped on her lover's face. "What's *this one* so happy about?"

"Adriana is pregnant," Aurora blurted. Lucinda's bright blue eyes ignited.

"That is wonderful. We will have to return next spring after all. Well, it's about time, though, isn't it?" In mid-sentence, her eyes fell on the jug in Pallas's hands. Oblivious, he drank deeply.

"Put that *infernal jug* away," Lucinda snapped. "Shame on you. You have a lot to be thankful for, you no-good ingrate. I'm not going to have you sulking around with that stupid jug all the way to Germania." Everyone struggled to muffle their chuckles; the former servant kept her man on a very short leash. It was a good thing, too.

"Alright, alright. Clearly I should've kept you on the payroll," Pallas jabbed, handing the wine over to his unruly woman.

"I will keep you informed as best I can," Aurora said, barely able to contain her excitement. After all, Adriana was as much her daughter as anyone else's.

"Once made equal to man, a woman becomes his superior," Pallas joked, snatching Lucinda and pulling her close.

"That's enough babbling; there's work to do," she huffed, wiggling free.

Pallas addressed the group, "That settles it. Icarus, I will see you all in a year's time. Tell Adriana she may have anything she needs. My door has always been open to her. Now that I am gone, I'm sure she will visit her old home often. Aurora, see to it that my daughter wants for nothing."

The engineer and his daughter had always been distant. Still, he was proud of the woman she had become. Years ago, after his late wife's death, Pallas had lost touch with the notion of family. In the dark times that followed, women and wine had helped maintain some form of sanity for the builder. Had he not found Lucinda, he would never have made it out of that hole. Now, despite his power and greatness, his daughter's disapproval could bring him to his knees. He considered his absence from Adriana's childhood an inexcusable failure. It would haunt the old man until death relieved him of his burden.

By mid-morning, they were packed and headed toward the meeting point for the caravan. Pallas snatched back his booze after his woman drifted off to sleep in the rumbling cart. He took a long swig from his jug as his old bones propelled him down the rocky slope. He ducked his head into the wagon where Lucinda napped to pluck out one of the pups. The animal slept peacefully in his arms. Its mother had been following the cart very closely. Now she was at his heels, keeping a dutiful eye on her little one. The engineer looked at the soft ball of fur in his hands; it barely had teeth protruding from its gums. It kept its eyes closed to avoid the sun's blinding rays. He assessed the fragile creature in disbelief, thinking of the ravenous beast it could become. If trained properly, this pup could be made into a man-eater—a war hound bent on destruction, willing to die to inflict pain. The engineer looked up. A peasant and his son were standing in the roadway just ahead. Unfortunately, the boy's father seemed very excited to see him. The portly man had a ridiculous smile stamped on his round face.

"Pallas. Ah, Lord Pallas, sir, how are you?" the man babbled as he blundered toward the famed builder to shake hands vigorously.

"Good morning," the engineer replied. "I am well, but I will be much better soon. I hope you are not waiting here for me, my friend." With a wave, he let the crew leader know to keep going.

The peasant squirmed in his sandals. "Actually yes, we are here to—"

Pallas interjected, "I am going to stop you right there. Sir, I can only assume that this young man is your son, and that he wants to be a great builder someday. Maybe he could not care less about building, and the dream is yours."

"Yes, well I—" The builder spoke and the peasant kept quiet.

"You want your son to travel with me as my servant, and in return you hope I will impart on him some fraction of my *infinite* wisdom," Pallas joked in a scripted fashion. The portly peasant was oblivious; his son could tell that the lord had accommodated many similar conversations in his time.

"Yes, that is exactly why we are here," the man blabbered as his son rubbed his brow in embarrassment.

"Gentlemen, I am retired from the trade. Now, young man," Pallas said, addressing the lad at his side. "If you are ever going to build anything, you cannot have your father doing all the talking for you. You are still quite young, so I don't fault you for letting your elders speak. But know this, my young friend—if you really want to build, there is no man that can stop you. Especially not a washed-up bag of bones like me. You understand that, right lad?"

The boy put on a very determined face and belted out, "Yes sir, Lord Pallas." This quick affirmative response made his father proud.

"So you see, gentlemen, it is nothing personal. I have turned in my hammer and ledger. I am finished. Another ambitious young man will, no doubt, aptly fill the void I have left behind. Who knows, maybe he is standing before me right now," he said with a toothy grin. "Good day, my friends."

Pallas had mentored only four apprentices in his twenty years as the Master Engineer of Rome; all had gone on to become great builders in their own right. As such, an apprenticeship with Pallas was a highly sought-after position. Nobles had often tried to buy in, but he only accepted pupils with raw talent. It was true that two of his four apprentices had come from wealthy families, but it was not their status that had garnered them the position. These young men possessed the same fire and intelligence that had propelled their families forward in previous generations. The other apprentices came from humble beginnings, but similarly hard-working families. One's father was a blacksmith and the other's a millwright; as such, they had established mechanical thinking skills at an early age working under their fathers' guidance.

By now the carts were about fifty yards up the road. Pallas tucked the snoring pup under his arm and hustled after them. As he bustled along, his mind left the hills. He began to dream of the buildings he could design for his friend Alexander while on retreat in the North. He imagined flawless arches and sky-scraping towers. Soon afterward, his right foot landed in a large pile of horse droppings.

"Infernal beasts," he barked. "Doggone mules." The dung was quite fresh and potent. He looked to the heavens to address the gods. "Well, that's right. I'm not supposed to be thinking about that shit anymore either, am I?"

The traveler stopped and set his pup down to wipe off his sandal on a nearby rock. Its mother licked the ball of fur clean, while he tended to his footwear. The dog's ears raised, then her tail went still. Pallas heard the pounding of galloping horses drawing near. He looked toward the hilltop; the blazing sun hindered his view. Seven dark horsemen were charging down the hill toward him. The beasts came to a halt a few yards from where he stood. The pup's mother was growling and barking at this heavily armed band of Imperial horsemen. For a moment, the engineer feared he was about to be detained for leaving Rome against the emperor's wishes.

Then he recognized the leader of the pack—Estor. Alexander and his much younger half-brother shared a father, but not much else. Pallas had never met their father, the notorious former general named Artemis. It was said that Estor was an exact replica of the man. The horsemen surrounded the wealthy foreigner, swords unsheathed. Pallas snapped his fingers. The hound stopped defending her master and trotted toward the distant carts with her pup nestled between gentle fangs.

Estor, adorned in dark decorative armor, adroitly dismounted from his steed. The noble stood a full head taller than Pallas. He removed his helmet and stared loathingly at the commoner. Estor was an imposing figure; he bore an uncanny resemblance to his brother. The man had inherited most all of his father's faults: arrogance, pride, and envy. Unlike Alexander, Estor had not inherited Artemis's fearlessness. He hid this well.

"Good morning, Estor. How *thoughtful* of you to see me off," Pallas badgered.

"That was quite a stunt you pulled, old man. The emperor should have taken that lowly head for your *disrespect*," Estor snapped. A great cloud of slowly settling dust surrounded the encircled horsemen.

"Emperor Severus knows I meant no harm. I am done. I am too old to serve him aptly. He deserves a younger, more ambitious man to lead his projects. I did what I did for the future of the empire." Estor spat into the dirt in objection.

"Careful, old man, you are bordering on insinuating that the emperor needs your advice. You don't really think we need your help to further *our* empire, do you? After all, we were dominating this world long before you graced us with your presence, *Greek*," he finished, pointing his sword at Pallas's chest.

"Put away your sword, Estor. I know enough to be more afraid of the coin purse at your side than that blade in your hand."

"You really are something, old man. Lord Pallas, the prized gem of the emperor's court."

"What do you want, you sniveling shit? I don't have all day to play soldier with you in the hot sun," Pallas growled, highly annoyed by the noble's pungent arrogance.

"Know this," Estor raged, "if not for your association with my dimwit brother, the emperor would have made an example of you."

"Is that all?" the foreigner replied, as obnoxiously as possible. Estor approached the much smaller old man. Hateful flames burned in his dark eyes. Pallas did not succumb to the elitist's intimidation tactics.

"This is for my brother. A message, from the emperor himself, for the *great* Alexander," he seethed. The lord dropped the sealed scroll into the dirt and kicked up dust toward the foreigner. Estor slammed his decorative war helmet back on as he headed toward his horse. Keeping a watchful eye on the soldiers, the elder knelt to retrieve the discarded roll of parchment.

Rising to his feet, Pallas felt propelled to offer his friend's brother a lesson. "Estor, we are all born ignorant—but one must work hard to remain stupid."

The Roman yanked himself effortlessly up onto his great beast. Estor's henchmen rallied around their fuming master. Before turning to leave, the noble paused. His eyes locked with his elder's through the plumes of dust. The Roman called down hatefully, "Old man, do you really want to do what is *best* for the empire? Then hurry up and die. Tell my brother to do the same."

Estor's sycophantic horde chuckled in unison.

— VII —

AFTER WEEKS OF TRAVERSING SNOW-BLOWN mountain passes and stopping at dozens of small villages along the way, Pallas's carts rumbled toward the outskirts of Alexander's estate. The slow-moving supply convoy was constantly exchanging goods with the many armies that bound the North. Much of the supplies from the shipment were also destined for the baron's compound; as such, heavily armed guards traveled with them for the entirety of their journey. Signs of the recently quelled rebellion became increasingly evident as they pushed deeper into the mountains—razed townships and storehouses littered the rugged trail.

The rumbling supply caravan drew all sorts of onlookers and beggars out of the woodwork. Villagers watched the great band of legionaries marching past with blank faces. The ground shook as the endless stream of open carts overflowing with shields, spears, armor, and swords rattled by these bewildered onlookers. Their number consisted mostly of women and young ones; the able-bodied men had fallen prey to Roman steel in the rebellion. The children had witnessed the destruction. Now they watched helplessly as the unending stream of glimmering metal continued to flow northward. All knew they were conquered.

It was a dreary, wind-bitten afternoon when the towers finally came into view—prime barbarian raiding weather. The scent of the pines was familiar to Pallas as they rode toward the great structure; the compound commanded the horizon. The builder was taken aback by its enormity. The architecture and craftsmanship were not particularly impressive; nonetheless, the mountainous structure's intrinsic cost demanded respect.

As soon as they entered the gates, Alexander greeted his guest, "By gods, look at the old fool!"

Pallas turned to face the familiar voice. It was Alexander, but not the man he had last seen seven years earlier. His friend had gained a considerable amount of weight, was limping, and looked tired. As the Lord of the North got closer, Pallas could smell the wine.

"Hello, old friend. I see the welcoming party has already started."

"It never stops. Come here, you old dog," Alexander demanded. He lunged forward to violently hug his brother-in-arms. While the baron looked weak, Pallas quickly realized he had retained a good portion of his former strength.

The Roman jabbed on drunkenly, "Getting a little frail there, aren't you, old man?"

"You're one to talk. Look at you—too much beef and pork, I take it."

"No, mostly hens," he growled, eyeing a passing servant

girl. Alexander winked and nudged his friend. The young girl scurried past and took off down the corridor. The lord roared with deviant laughter. Lucinda glared at the hopeless pig.

"Ah, Alexander. This is Lucinda," Pallas said, proudly introducing his fair-haired accompaniment.

"Excellent, it's a pleasure to finally meet you," he swooned.

"Thank you, my lord," Lucinda replied. She bowed and Alexander caught a glimpse of Pallas's Germanic hounds.

"What are those wretched beasts doing in my house?" the baron bellowed.

Lucinda blocked him from going near the cart of puppies. "You will leave my poor babies be!"

"Babies? They are murderous monsters," Alexander objected. "If you only knew how the Vandals use those godless mongrels."

"You will not lay a finger on them," she snapped.

Upon seeing the furious look on Lucinda's cute face, the burly lord burst out laughing. He teased Pallas while looking into the woman's fiery eyes, "Ooh, she's a feisty one. I see why you kept this one around all these years. I'm with you —*I like a little fight.*"

"By gods, pull it together, Alexander," Pallas demanded as Lucinda tended to the rattled puppies.

Alexander laughed it off. "I apologize, my lady. The girls will take you to your quarters. This wretched Greek and I have a lot of catching up to do." With that, he threw his arm tightly around Pallas's neck and led him down the corridor. Lucinda shot furious glances at her lover as he was ushered away by their crude host.

The monumental conglomeration of mismatched towers was a testament to Alexander's greatness. Once inside, endless corridors streamed every which way, stringing together the many grand halls. This compound had clearly been built in phases. No real scheme or underlying theme was present. Its many halls were cavernous and empty; strong gusts often ripped through the corridors. The massive stone structure was sparsely furnished; it was, in essence, a colossal manmade cave.

The lord led his guest to the highest tower. At its peak, they came upon a young man that Pallas thought he recognized. The brooding noble was standing on the patio looking out across the countryside. Alexander stopped his nonsensical chatter about his most recent encounters; the climb had left him winded. The rain had turned into a windblown mist; it was cold, but bearable.

The baron addressed the curiously familiar man, "Nicodemus, you *scheming rat*—what in the world are you doing up here? Is this where you are when I can't find you?"

"I just needed a minute," Nicodemus replied.

"Listen to the sorry little shit," Alexander jabbed. "Doesn't do a wretched thing all day, and he *needs a minute*." The lumbering lord smacked his friend painfully on the back and chuckled.

"I would hardly call overseeing the entirety of this region's affairs *nothing*, cousin," the young man sneered.

"Nicodemus," Pallas said, astonished, "I hardly recognized

you."

"Yeah, little runt is all grown up," Alexander added, still struggling to catch his breath.

"Pallas, I hope your journey north was comfortable," Nicodemus replied.

"It was great. I needed the exercise."

"Look how thin the old wolf is," Alexander blabbered. "We need to fatten him up." The gasping lord began coughing violently; he had to grab the parapet wall to steady himself.

Noticing the worried look on Pallas's face, Nicodemus whispered, "My cousin has been told time and time again to take it easy. Nonetheless, he keeps bucking around, stirring up trouble. He is healthy enough for now, although I admit it is of growing concern. After all, his father died at fifty, and he's nearly there." The baron tugged at his chest, still struggling to get his bearings.

"Chest pains?" Pallas asked.

"It's nothing. I'm fine." It seemed the stairs were more than Alexander had bargained for.

"Did you look over the recent correspondences from the capital?" Nicodemus asked with unsettling smugness.

"You whining wretch. Do I look like I am in any condition to deal with that nonsense?"

Shoving him aside, the lord approached the ledge. "Pallas, everything you see before you belongs to me." The tyrant shamelessly roared out into the majestic, snow-covered hills, *"Everything is mine!"*

"It's a beautiful country, Alexander. I do not doubt that you command it well." Pallas reached into his cloak. "Before I forget, I must mention that I carried a letter from Emperor Severus." The builder handed the sealed scroll to Alexander.

The baron glared at the unbroken red seal. "Is it from the emperor, or his council?" he asked, ready to crumple the parchment and throw it off the tower.

"The emperor," Pallas insisted. The lord now looked even more annoyed.

"Well, I guess I will have to read it then."

The baron began fumbling with the twine that bound the scroll. Nicodemus came over with a small dagger and cut the binding adroitly. The young man was lingering, craning his neck to get a look at the correspondence. Alexander shoved his cousin aside, then kicked him in his leg for good measure. The lord broke the seal and analyzed the document for authenticity—it was genuine.

As Alexander read, his mood shifted considerably. The man stared hard into his friend's stone gray eyes. "Who gave you this?"

"Estor."

"Estor, right—*Estor*. As in my shit-eating brother, Estor?" Alexander sighed.

"Yes, your brother gave it to me the day I left Rome."

The lord looked furiously across his domain. "I cannot believe no one has killed that insolent bastard. By gods, eventually someone has to do it—that scheming, conniving *scum*."

Nicodemus could hardly contain his curiosity. "What did it say?"

"That is none of your concern. This letter is of no concern to either of you." The lord held the scroll over a flaming torch. The weathered parchment disintegrated in the fire.

"You are leaving for Rome tomorrow," Alexander told Nicodemus.

"By gods, the winter is still strong."

"It hasn't snowed for weeks, boy. Regardless, I have urgent correspondence to deliver to the capital."

"Since when?"

"*Since now*, you good-for-nothing scavenger. Pack your shit; you leave at dawn."

"How long will I be staying?" the noble asked, inspecting his nails for imperfections.

"Maybe a day. I expect a speedy reply," the master answered with a toothy grin.

"What?" Nicodemus fumed. "That's ridiculous."

Alexander chuckled at the twisted pain on his cousin's well-groomed face. "You are an ungrateful little mule, you know that? We will discuss the conditions of your stay tomorrow morning before you leave."

"Which horses am I taking?" Nicodemus inquired, gradually warming up to the idea of a visit home.

"Enough questions—get moving, boy." The young man

scowled at them both before storming away.

Once his cousin was gone, Alexander spoke, "Little rodent acts like he rules this land. If he only knew the wars we fought at his age—the warriors we stood against."

"What was in the letter?"

Alexander looked his friend squarely in the eyes. "Pallas, I swear on my life that if that letter had anything to do with you, I would tell you. Do not worry—the correspondence did not concern you. This is between Estor and I; it is no concern of yours. You are done with Rome—*enjoy it*."

A mischievous grin crept across Pallas's face as he looked across Alexander's endless domain; he could not help himself. "Your brother seemed well," he stated.

"That boy is a disgrace. At every turn, I run into his pathetic pawns and fiendish schemes. I swear that snake was behind the rebellion. He instigated it. By gods, I think he even supplied it. You should have seen the barbarians' weaponry. All smuggled north from Estor's personal smiths. There's not a doubt in my mind. He wanted to ruin me. I could have died in the struggle. He wants me dead, you know—my own brother, my own blood!"

"At least you have Nicodemus looking out for you now."

"You saw him up here—assessing his inheritance. No doubt, Estor will be the first person he meets with when he arrives in Rome. Here I am, crawling out of debt from the rebellion and that little runt is up here—*stargazing*."

"Family is difficult."

"Power and money are what muddies the waters." Alexander sighed heavily, staring out across his domain. "Pray we die before we become too weak to defend ourselves."

"Pray and work, my friend, that's all you can do."

"Pallas, they are like wolves circling around me, waiting for any sign of weakness. Then they will pounce, rip me limb from limb, and take what they think is theirs." The engineer noted the very real pain in his friend's eyes.

Aging is hardest on the strong.

— VIII —

S PRING HAD GIVEN WAY TO AN UNUSUALLY WARM summer. The valley was in full bloom when Nicodemus finally arrived back from Rome that afternoon. His stay in the capital had been much longer than expected. The self-satisfied aristocrat swung down from his horse to approach his elders. The limping courier had a fresh cut healing above his left eye.

"What the hell happened to you, boy?" Alexander boomed.

"Little trouble, that's all," Nicodemus answered. He was dodgy and withholding. No matter—the young man did not appear to be badly injured.

The baron poked fun at his cousin, "The barbarians had their way with you then, huh, boy?"

"The lowly roaches begged for death," Nicodemus sneered.

"Did they now? Well then, seems you finally figured out how to use that pretty sword of yours. You may be worth your salt after all," Alexander badgered.

"You should dress more plainly so that you are not such an obvious target," Pallas advised the staggering noble.

The young man ignored the foreigner's advice and addressed his cousin, "Your answer has arrived, my lord."

"I see. Well, give it here then. Although you could just tell me what the damn thing says; I'm sure you have already poked your nose into it." Alexander snatched the scroll from his cousin and sped through it. A great smile stretched across his full face.

"Good news?" Nicodemus sneered.

"Excellent news."

The lord held the scroll out over a nearby torch, letting it crumple and disintegrate in the fire. Ever since he had received word from the capital, all the old dog wanted to do was drink and chase servant girls. He slaughtered some choice livestock and threw a feast to celebrate his cousin's successful journey.

As a result of the festivities, Pallas had gotten out for his evening stroll later than usual. The retired engineer had made a routine of long evening walks around the grounds. These strolls worked up his appetite and cleared his mind. All week long, he had been modifying Alexander's catapults. He improved their accuracy and increased their range considerably, which left his friend very pleased. The Roman would occasionally invite rich landowners to his grounds to launch stones at mock structures in the distance. He employed six men to build and rebuild this playground. In the face of such lavish displays of wealth, Pallas had to chuckle, recalling his friend's recent complaints about *crawling out of debt*. While he was not one for such indulgences, he had to admit there was a good bit of fun in organized destruction.

The engineer just had to avoid thinking about how these machines were used in the outside world, for he was no stranger to ingenuity's proclivity for violence. Military inventions drew off forces used in construction—tension, leverage, and torque. Cranes, pulleys, and hoists—machines that placed ornate marble carvings effortlessly into position—were reconfigured into weapons capable of nearly effortless destruction. A common dreg with no conceptual knowledge of the machinery could be taught to crank the lever into position, load the projectile, and trigger the mechanism. There was some fine-tuning involved, of course. Even still, with about a week of training, just about any fool could use these war machines to bring down structures in a fraction of the time that it took skilled artisans to create them. Lifetimes were spent building towering monuments, which these weapons reduced to rubble in moments. In his youth, Pallas himself had taught siege crews how to target structural elements.

Unhindered by the dark clouds invading the westward sky, the Greek set out on his evening walk. Midway through his stroll, rain began to fall. The wanderer trudged through the increasing storm, barring his eyes as he made his way through the wind. He had always reveled in a summer storm's thunder and lightning. White light shot across the horizon. The bright flash revealed a large lone tree blown to bits in a distant clearing. The accompanying thunder shook the earth and sent a shockwave across the valley. Pallas halted, staring at the mangled tree smoking and steaming in the fast falling rain.

"Incredible," he said into the storm. "Absolutely incredible."

The wild man laughed and wrenched his goatskin from his

side; he was quickly becoming drenched. A second blast and subsequent quake of thunder sent him running for cover. The engineer jogged toward a dilapidated building in the distance. He had passed this vine-covered structure on the far side of the westward horizon several times that summer. It was only visible during the last leg of his daily loop around the grounds. As he got closer, something commanded his full attention. Lightning flashed again, illuminating the building's edges.

Pallas was usually quite intoxicated by this final leg of his evening walk. Also, the glare of the falling sun along the westward horizon often hid the structure within the tree line. Many times over the preceding months he had stumbled down this very hill. The builder had never given the neglected stable a second glance. Whatever it was, the structure stood forgotten. Abandoned—left to rot on the outskirts of barbarian territory. The closer he got, the more taken aback he became with its shapeliness. His pace slowed. He approached the overgrown farmhouse for the first time. Intrigued, his eyes moved across the forgotten building's edges, analyzing its construction.

Heavy rain doused the wanderer as he fought through the thicket of bushes and tall grasses surrounding the shelter. He was soaked to the bone but took no notice. Curiosity pulled him through the storm. The heavy overcast blocked out the setting sun; darkness was collapsing on the valley. Pallas hacked his way toward the stable, snapping any branches that snagged on his cloak. A blinding flash revealed the inspiring arched entryway; it had been formed seamlessly. As he lifted the latch and entered, thunder crashed, reverberating off the mountains. Darkness hid the mastery within, but he could feel it all around him. Lightning flashed, illuminating the columns and angled trusses—brief glimpses of flawlessness. Rain pounded on the roof above; the wind roared against the walls. Thunder erupted.

Even in its neglected state, the building stood strong against the storm. Pallas's eyes flashed from wall to wall. Even to his critical eye the structure appeared to be flawless. Rubbing his tired eyes with calloused hands, he began scrambling around the woodwork. The storm was subsiding; the engineer knew the lightning would no longer aid him in his discovery. Darkness seemed determined to hide the building's contents from view. From the brief glimpses the storm allowed, the structure appeared to be an effortless work of art. Without his instruments, sober wits, and the light of day, he could make no accurate judgments. His bare feet moved across the smooth wooden floor; its seamlessness was inconceivable.

The fateful storm had moved on. Pallas watched the distant torches of the main house being lit one by one. Out of sight, invisible servants rushed about illuminating the grounds—a multitude of small flames lit miraculously. The engineer was overwhelmingly intrigued. A creeping nervousness hung over him as he exited into the passing winds and light rainfall following the storm. He hobbled through the darkness, re-analyzing what he had seen. Questions and thoughts swirled through the wise man's foggy consciousness.

Pallas had never seen wood manipulated in such ways. It had been molded and shaped like clay. Lumber was not his preferred medium; stone, brick, and marble construction were the Roman way. Wood was used mostly for high-end furniture and flooring. Admittedly, Roman carpenters were highly skilled; their scaffoldings and temporary supports were essential to the monuments they erected. Lightweight and cost effective, timber was used mostly by commoners. Regardless, the engineer had never seen the medium mastered so completely. From a fundamental standpoint, the structure was built better than anything he had ever thought to build in his life. This thought left him both excited and—strangely enough—*terrified.*

The tormented builder hardly slept. The next morning he rose early, eager to return to the neglected farmhouse on the far side of the grounds. He made quite a ruckus as he got himself and his instruments together in the early morning darkness.

"Have you finally lost your mind?" his woman jabbed as he scrambled around the poorly lit room.

"My dear, I have no time to talk. Get some rest. I love you— I'm fine, I just have to do something this morning—but yes, I may be completely insane. Just get some rest."

"Alright, just be careful. A drunk has no business wandering off into the dark. Don't lose your way."

"Lucinda, I'm not a bumbling idiot."

"No, you're an intelligent idiot—that's the worst kind, dear."

Pallas rushed through the shadows and slammed his toe into the table leg. "Argh—by gods. Where are the hounds?" he barked.

"Don't take your foolishness out on me. I let them out. Just call for them, they'll come. Heaven knows you need them; you can barely navigate this room. I would hate to see you try to get anywhere out there in the darkness. It's best you take a couple extra pairs of eyes with you."

"Of course," he grumbled.

"Bring yourself something other than that dreadful jug. Some bread is on the table. I don't need you passing out in the woods. Take your time."

"I'm in no hurry," he said as he took off in a rush. About halfway down the staircase he missed a step and rolled the rest of the way. The sound of his falling echoed throughout the guesthouse.

A panic-stricken Lucinda was out of bed and at the top of the staircase in an instant. She called out frightfully into the darkness, "Pallas, are you alright?"

Her lover lay at the bottom of the steps in a ball of cloak and instruments. There were a few large knots already forming on his gray head. He rubbed a particularly painful one throbbing over his eyes and answered, "Damn these northern bastards. They couldn't build a decent staircase to save their lives."

"Come back to bed, you fool. You can go wherever you think you *need to be* at daybreak."

"No, I'll be fine. Go back to bed, Lucinda, I'm alright."

"You are right—wise men know nothing," she snapped as she threw her hands in the air. Then she stomped her dainty feet with all her might across the wood floor so that Pallas could hear her frustration. She hopped back into bed in a huff and closed her eyes.

Pallas took the bread off the table. He knew his woman would be unapproachable later on if she woke to find the loaf left behind. The builder was out the front door in a flash. He let out a light whistle; the hounds answered with some soft early morning woofs. Lucinda heard the hounds and smiled. She knew the beasts would keep a close eye on her old fool. This comforting thought allowed her to drift off into a peaceful sleep once again. The master dropped some scraps of lamb on the ground for the animals, which they gobbled down, barely stopping to breathe. The largest of the three, a male named Thor, remained behind to watch over the entryway. Pallas knew his woman was well protected. Even as he slept Thor's ears remained engaged; any misplaced sound would stir him.

The engineer set off, picking at the crisp loaf. The two female hounds were making large investigative loops around him as he made his way down the trail. They bounded through the thickets that surrounded the path, excited to be out in the crisp early morning air, hard at work with their master. After about an hour of walking, Pallas could see the forgotten farmhouse in the distance. The sky was getting a bit lighter now. It was turning from black to a revealing blue-gray. The moon was still visible; it shone very bright that morning. The welcomed moonlight made navigating the rocky trail much easier for the hungover adventurer.

It was still quite dark when Pallas arrived at the front door of the abandoned building. He was prepared for this; he reached into his bundle and grabbed out several torches. He stuffed the last piece of bread into his mouth and chomped on it as he used his striker to light some hay and twigs in the dirt. He lit his torch in the small fire, then stomped it out with his sandal. Holding the flame away from himself, the old man stood in the seemingly modest structure's menacing shadow. An unsettling nervousness came over him in the early morning fog. He entertained a sudden impulse to burn it, to snuff out the mystery then and there. The builder was familiar with pride, but envy was still new to him.

Restraining himself, Pallas entered and placed the torches in several holders conveniently carved into the columns that supported the rafters above. This lit the room enough for him to prepare his instruments while he waited for the sun to rise. He glared at the bucket of rudimentary tools he had brought with him to Germania, silently cursing the fool who had neglected to bring the entire set. When the sun began to rise, the building's true beauty was revealed. Beneath a heavy coat of dust lay the mesmerizing woodwork. As the soft morning light filled the space, an awe-inspiring utilitarian design became evident. The windows were situated perfectly in order to take full advantage of the rising sun. Pallas refused to dwell on his pathetic assortment of tools. He knew how to make the most of them. It would take longer, but he would manage.

This stable was functionally flawless; not an inch of space had been wasted. Structural elements were conveniently positioned to allow for the influx and egress of beasts and workers. Every edge, every knot in the wood, every notch, every peg—nothing was out of place. Pallas began searching for errors; he found none. Even the inherent flaws in the wood seemed purposefully dispersed. He worked hard to sweep up the dust and remove the cobwebs. The more he uncovered, the more impressed he became. The more measurements he took and formulas he worked, the more convinced he became. This was true architectural mastery, to a degree the engineer had not dreamed possible. The floor was flatter than he thought timber's tolerances allowed. The ornate carved archways defied gravity. The perfectly formed bends in the wood made him question its properties. This small forgotten structure stood in defiance of everything the master thought he knew of his craft.

The master's fear of jealousy melted away as his investigation intensified. Hours passed like minutes as the wise engineer tirelessly delved further into the case. He inspected the stairs that rose to the storage rafters. No nails were used to form this breathtaking spiral column, only notches. The wood was toothed together seamlessly, molded and shaped like a blacksmith's red-hot iron. The spindles had been hand turned and honed. Aside from the wood's integral swirls, they were all identical, as if they had been molded from clay with a pot maker's casting. Pallas was still hard at work analyzing the structure when the sun began to set in the westward sky. The last of his torches were nearly exhausted. He had not eaten; he had barely touched his jug. His fire for construction had been reignited by the mastery that surrounded him. A part of him even began to doubt whether this structure was manmade at all.

For the final test, Pallas took a pouch of round marbles from his things. He placed the smooth orbs randomly around the edges of the structure's seamless floor. The planks had been shined and smoothed in a way that would incite the envy of the greatest marble worker's discerning eye. Then he ascended the spiral staircase again with a large sack he had filled with dirt that afternoon. The old man knew, had he brought his entire chest of tools, he would not have had to dig at all—no matter. Standing on the crossbeams, the builder dropped the heavy sack down to the floor below. The sound of the impact boomed and echoed throughout the rafters. Not a single marble rolled. The building's bones were as well constructed as its finishes. Pallas's heart was racing. He yanked his jug from his side and chugged it deeply. Dumbfounded, he stared down at the masterpiece beneath him. The flickering torchlight danced menacingly across the woodwork. The building was teeming with confidence.

The builder began to make his way back to the stairs. All at once he found himself covered in silky strands. In the midst of flailing at the spider webs, he lunged for the trusses to avoid falling from the rafters. In doing so, his calloused fingers dragged across an out-of-place roughness on the timber's hidden edge. Pallas frantically rubbed the cobwebs off his face and hair then brushed the spiders off his arms.

"Easy now, you fool," he growled. Regaining his composure, he held his torch up to inspect the apparent flaw on the truss's hidden edge. A lone word had been expertly seared into the central king post. It appeared to be a skillfully etched signature, a brand:

CITIUS

Pallas was shaken. He had only eaten a loaf of bread since daybreak, and most of his jug's fiery contents now occupied his empty stomach. In a daze, he watched his torches burn themselves out slowly, one by one. Once the darkness hid the building's flawless interior, he was freed from its hypnotic powers. More carefully this time, he made his way down from the rafters. Frustrated and tormented, the engineer left his instruments strewn haphazardly about the woodwork. Then he set out into the cool night air, toward the torches of the main house, overwhelmed by the masterpiece left to rot on the outskirts of barbarian territory. There was a part of him that wished he had never walked through its doors at all. Had he never entered the forgotten building, he could have died supremely confident in his own abilities. Now he hobbled through the fields in a daze, not bothering with the path.

One word consumed him—*Citius.*

— IX —

DESPERATE FOR ANSWERS, PALLAS BARGED INTO Alexander's quarters to find Nicodemus quarreling with him over taxation policy. The engineer cut in, "Who built the stables on the edge of the westward clearing?"

"Greek, are you drunk? Or have you finally gone completely mad?" Alexander asked, looking to his cousin for support.

"That abandoned farmhouse on the outskirts of the grounds—who built it?"

"Wait—you're serious?"

"Alexander, this is no time for games. I need to find the builder."

"By gods, Pallas, what is it? Did you rip your tunic on a loose nail in there?" the lord badgered. His friend was wearing what amounted to rags. Nicodemus snorted; the way he laughed almost looked painful.

"Names!"

Nicodemus's eyes flashed with anger. "Watch your tongue, Greek."

"The last thing I need is you growing accustomed to giving orders," Alexander barked at his young cousin.

"Who built it?" Pallas demanded.

"By gods, I have to say, it's good to see you adjusting to retirement so well. You loony wretch. Take a seat, old man," Alexander commanded. He handed a jug of wine to his guest and insisted, "Here, have a drink."

"No thanks, not in the mood," Pallas said as he handed the bottle back to his friend. Nicodemus took notice of this uncharacteristic behavior.

"Alright then. I'll have to send for the documents. A farmhouse, you say? I can recall a project in the clearing, but it was some time ago. No matter, I'm sure the records are tucked away in my archives somewhere. It has only been about five years since I had that stable built. We never even used the damn thing, but maybe it would be better if I called for a nurse. Are you sure you don't need a drink?"

"Just give me the damn bottle. I'll drink the entire thing right now if you would just get me what I need."

Pallas snatched the jug back from his friend and guzzled it greedily. The wine calmed him considerably. He hammered on, "Right, that's better. Now send for the records. I must meet the man who built that masterpiece."

"It's a glorified pigpen, you old fool," the gregarious lord responded with a chuckle, looking to Nicodemus for confirmation.

"Alexander, the structure is flawless. The wood was worked like clay, manipulated like a blacksmith bends hot iron. A true master crafted that structure. I have never built like that." Pallas spoke with a rare pain behind his warm gray eyes.

"Very well—we will find this mysterious *hog house builder*. This way, you can finally meet your equal. Hopefully his hammer and measure can humble you. I remember a blizzard many years ago, when a lowly Greek humbled my warrior spirit."

"Yes, and I'll humble it again if you do not for once make good use of all your power and influence. Find me this wise craftsman who has been hiding his greatness from the world. I wish to speak to him, to discover who trained him; maybe I know his maker."

"Do not make the same mistake I made with you, Pallas. Often greatness is not learned—it is born into this world. A lowly common bastard like you should know this," Alexander cracked. Lost in thought, his old friend was unresponsive. The engineer was still reeling from what he had seen.

Alexander kept at him. "A wise man once told me that explaining fire is difficult."

Pallas finished the sentiment; it was a lesson he often preached. "Yes—sometimes we just need to see it burn."

"Yes, you old Greek. Well put."

"I wish to go beyond the fire that burns me. It will not be long before this master is found. By gods, a man like that has no business building stables," Pallas declared.

"War has torn this country apart. So many were killed that most of the men who built these grounds are dead. So few remain; it may be difficult to locate this carpenter."

"I believe his name was *Citius*," Pallas said, undeterred by the odds stacked against him.

"Ah, so this grandmaster has a name now, eh?"

"I can't be sure. The word was etched into the rafters. It appeared to be a signature."

"Well, I can't recall a builder by that name. No matter, rest assured that means nothing. With all the artisans who've built on this compound over the years, I'd be hard-pressed to remember a handful of their names. That said, if the man's alive we'll find him," Alexander said with his back to the others. The lord stood before a great window, staring into the distant mountains.

— X —

"CITIUS, THE TIMBER'S SPLIT."

"The beam, or the post?"

"The beam."

"Damn—don't drive the post again, Petrarch."

"I won't."

"Give me the torch," Citius ordered.

The leader was climbing down the other side of the cavern. The miners had been beating posts into position under a sizable crossbeam. Failure to hammer in sync could cause a cave in. The determined young man came into view in the faint torchlight, black-eyed and confident. He expertly tossed a knotted rope, like a grappling hook, up over the beam where the cavern peaked. The heavy knot fell to the ground on the other side. His helper took hold of the knotted end and braced himself against the cave wall. Citius began climbing; he pulled himself up on top of the timber to inspect the situation. An imperfection in the cavern ceiling happened to land near the midpoint of the beam. This lack in foresight had caused the wood to split.

"Remind me to never let Babar locate the posts again."

"What is it?"

"I should have double-checked his layout," Citius replied, more to himself than to Petrarch. Then he called down to his friend, "We are going to have to lug two more posts, and another beam down here."

"Are you serious?"

"We can't leave it like this."

"No matter, our days are all the same," the bright-eyed helper added.

"More or less. But still, even Babar should do better than this." Citius paused to inspect the damage; the timber was marred and splintering, but salvageable.

Looking up, Petrarch decided to pose a nagging question. The helper shouted up to his boss, "Is what the others say true? Did you slay a giant?"

"Throw me the sledge and bar; I want to see if I can clean this up," Citius replied, ignoring the inquiry.

"We have a bucket. Why don't you hoist them up?"

"Come on, *scrap*, throw the damn things up here," the veteran badgered.

The inexperienced miner struggled to gauge the distance from below. It took him a few tries to get the hammer up to his leader. The chisel was more balanced and easier to loft upward. After throwing the tools to his boss, he kept talking; although, he barely got a word in before Citius began chiseling out the imperfection.

While the worker struggled, his helper continued to preach

his never-ending sermon, taking up right where he had left off before the beam split. Petrarch shouted over the hammering, "So he said to them, 'Blessed rather are those who hear the word of God and keep it.'"

Brushing the sweat and gravel from his forehead, Citius stopped working momentarily. He spoke over the booms that echoed from down the shaft, "You know, you really need to spend some time with a woman. Your priorities are questionable at best. I'm telling you, Archer will never reward a daydreamer."

"A shortcut to riches is to subtract from our desires," Petrarch replied.

"And religion is what keeps the poor from murdering the rich."

Citius went back to hammering as loudly as possible before his friend could reply. The stubborn rock did not want to break free. When he stopped to catch his breath, Petrarch was ready; he thought aloud from below.

"You know, if you could slay a giant, then you could probably rid us all of Archer as well."

Citius shot his helper a disapproving glance. He knew his friend was joking, so he decided to allow him some slack. To avoid the topic of Archer, he gave in to Petrarch's initial inquiry. "It was not a giant, just a man. He was fat and slow. It helped that he was fairly stupid. The truth is that I didn't slay him; I killed him."

"What's the difference?"

"No one slays anyone. This isn't one of your stories. They

just kill them. You need to realize that if Archer hears you spouting off about your almighty Father, he'll kill you. After all, that's how this prophet, this Jesus, got himself killed, right? By talking about himself too much, right?" Petrarch struggled to form a clever response. The scowl that followed was out of character for the humble slave. The gadfly looming above smiled triumphantly.

"Right—well, whenever God is ready. We must trust in the Lord," the believer huffed.

The overseer was highly amused with his friend's hardheaded response. Instead of pushing him any further, he went back to working as loudly as possible to block out his helper's voice. He did not want to be tempted to offer his usual spattering of counter examples or to interrupt his colleague's sermon with a challenging question. The bright-eyed young man continued to preach from below. Not surprisingly, he was babbling about a mustard seed for what could have easily been the third time that week. His leader could only make out bits and pieces of the parable over the steady beat of his hammer. As Petrarch was closing in on the well-versed punch line, the rock broke free from the ceiling. It crashed down a few feet from his imaginary pulpit.

The unsuspecting missionary jumped and turned a shade paler. "What are you trying to do? Kill me?" he shouted, touting the most furious glare he could manage.

His leader smiled mischievously. "Trust in the Lord, my friend, for through him all things are made."

"To hell with you, and here I am trying to save your cursed

soul."

Upon hearing his noble friend finally condemn him to hell, Citius howled with laughter. An infuriated Petrarch knew how to get him back. He returned fire, "Just so you know, the others say that you did slay a giant. And that's not all they believe. They say that you have been sent here by God to kill Archer. They say that you will free us all from this dreadful prison."

The leader's laughter ceased, for he was well aware that the lord had begun to see him as less of an asset and more of a possible future adversary. Citius could see it in Archer's eyes; the Lord of the Mine was far beyond paranoid. The last thing he needed was that madman thinking he aimed to seize control of the mine. Even worse, for him to think he aimed to usurp power with the help of the Christians.

"Not another word," he growled. Petrarch gulped and took a step back; he had heard of Citius's temper, but he had never witnessed it until now. The finality of the veteran's tone was undeniable, but that was not the worst of it. There was an unmistakable ruthlessness buried beneath his indifferent façade.

"I understand, but—"

"Forget it all—every word, every story, every lie—all of it. You don't need it, and you don't need them. Stop trying to save my soul, and focus on your own for a change. I know better than to fill my head with *lies!*"

The last word was nearly drowned out as the entire cavern rattled and a great panic burst forth from down the shaft. Miners hard at work below cried out. The bulk of the work crew was just out of sight, though within earshot. The eruption was followed by indiscernible clamoring and howling from the depths. The beam began vibrating menacingly beneath the miner's feet.

"Take hold of the rope," Citius commanded.

"What?" Petrarch asked nervously. Well aware of the gravity of the situation, he snatched up the rope and braced himself with all his strength. His master swung down from atop the beam. The coarse rope skidded in Petrarch's hands, burning them terribly. The slightly built believer refused to loosen his grip. Citius rolled to his feet. His wild eyes flashed.

"Run!"

The entire cavern was shaking now. Citius shoved a dumbfounded Petrarch out in front of him as they sprinted together toward the nearest hollow. The hollows were emergency shelters—dome-shaped enclaves carved into the cavern walls for use in dire situations like these. The miners hugged the cave wall as they darted forward, scurrying like helpless mice across the damp cavern floor. They did not make it far; large rocks began to rain down all around them. An enormous boulder was about to crush Petrarch in stride. Citius yanked him by his cloak and dove headlong into a pitch-black split in the cave floor. The mine's many chasms were unpredictable—some cracks were five feet deep with sandy bottoms, whereas others were forty feet deep with jagged rock floors. The miners had no time to investigate now.

The men plunged violently into the darkness; several large

rocks fell behind them into the narrow gorge. Stones impacted all around the falling salt miners as their bodies bounced and skidded painfully down the walls of the chasm. Without warning, they slammed hard into the sandy floor. Despite the tremendous pain, Citius did not hesitate. He rolled instinctively when he hit the sand, taking cover under a concave rock formation. Rocks thudded fatefully into the salty gravel and echoes reverberated throughout the gorge. Petrarch screamed out in agony. A massive boom followed his horrifying cry when a boulder slammed into the opening above. This prevented their section of the fissure from being filled completely with jagged stones. The muffled rumbling slowly came to a halt.

The veteran coughed up blood, groaning in misery. It hurt to breathe. Citius must have broken half of his ribs in the fall. His hip was badly cut; he felt his right hand with his left. Two of his fingers were grotesquely out of line. An intense heat and coinciding throbbing pain told him his right forearm was fractured. The young man was still functional—albeit, barely.

"Petrarch?" he inquired hoarsely, fearing there would be no reply. He called out again, much louder. Great plumes of salt dust filled the air around him, stinging his lungs and biting at his wounds.

"*Citius.*" A pained whimper found his ears. "Citius, I can't move. *I can't move.*"

"Stop trying—breathe slowly!"

"I'm thirsty, Citius." Petrarch began sobbing inconsolably.

He panicked and began calling out; he was going into shock. "*Help me, Citius*—I need water! I can't move—*help me!*"

"I'm coming, Petrarch. Hang on."

The survivor could feel the thick, swirling dust rolling around him in the blackness. He kept his mouth closed and struggled to breathe. At wit's end, he roared out in preparation. Then with all his strength, he jerked his mangled fingers back into position. Clinging to sanity, he rolled around on the sandy cave floor, gasping for air. The pain had made his lungs fail temporarily. It was so intense that he vomited violently, coughing into the briny sand. The strong-willed miner began crawling toward his hysterical friend; nothingness surrounded him. A maze of jagged stones protruded from the sand; he weaved between them. Citius was disoriented and nauseous, likely from a concussion sustained in the fall. He could hear his helper choking on the salted air.

"Citius, I'm so thirsty. I need water. Please give me water." The injured young man knew his friend carried a flask.

Petrarch would be dead within an hour. The slave was bleeding internally and had sustained spinal injury. He could not be moved; a large rock had fallen on his lifeless legs, pinning him to the sand-covered floor. Death by dehydration was a common fear for the slaves, who constantly inhaled the unforgiving salt dust. Salt poisoning was a slow death; the mine was determined to pickle one's organs. Trapped beings entertain a different mindset than their freed counterparts. The hardened miner's emotions were shutting down. Citius's humanity was fleeting with every painful breath he labored in the dust-filled darkness.

"Citius, water—please." A long silence followed; tension and frustration were suspended in the dark space between them. The dust stung Citius's eyes as they flickered blindly in the abyss.

Compassion, a long-forgotten impulse, swelled and knotted in his throat. Against instinct, he pulled his flask from his side. After carefully gauging its weight, he unplugged the vessel to pour the cool liquid into his friend's mouth. Negative thoughts swelled; he feared he was now pouring out his only hope for survival. While offering water to his dying friend, his black eyes stared blankly into the nothingness. He knew better than to seek meaning as he stopped the flow of water. Petrarch gasped, choking as he inhaled the salt-filled air. The crippled slave was in dire condition but very grateful for the refreshingly cool drink. Since childhood, he had feared the thought of dying thirsty.

With his left hand Citius slowly put the flask back into his cloak. This same generous hand emerged with a well-sharpened dagger. The blade had slit his leg in the fall; no matter, he was thankful he had it now. The young man exhaled calmly. He felt words were not necessary. Still, the knot in his throat remained. Mistaking the feeling for weakness, he struggled to choke it down, but it persisted. Petrarch was gasping on the salted air. The leader could feel the fallen man's fear; it drew strength from the darkness. He found the words.

"Remember that you are dust, and to dust you shall return," Citius prayed.

Petrarch exhaled steadily as his fear began to fall away. Without a sound, the leader slit his dying friend's throat, releasing him from torment. Afterward, he sat motionless in the sand for some time. He cursed God for making his friend suffer. Hardship—*this* is the fate of a believer. *This* is the fate of a man who preaches the word of God. Despite his anger, he was grateful that his friend's words had come to mind when he needed them.

A determined survival instinct took hold. Self-reliance had always been his salvation. Citius made a sling for his arm from Petrarch's bloodied cloak then risked a small sip of his water. He figured the crevice was roughly thirty feet deep. He made this judgment based on the duration of their fall. The frustrated miner spat blood into the rocks. It was all an adrenaline-infused blur. He knew the way they had skidded and bounced down the crater's walls could have allowed them to survive a considerable fall.

The young man's broken ribs would make his ascent torturous. His mind was playing tricks on him; he thought he could hear the out-of-place sound of flowing water. Negativity was relentless; it took everything he had to begin forcing his way through the rocks. Choking on the slowly swirling salt clouds, he pushed forward, clinging to consciousness. He was startled when cold water began raining down all around him. The icy water removed his drowsiness. The miner turned his face upward to taste the rain. He spat immediately; it was brine. No doubt the salt water would, in time, fill the entire chasm.

The trickling water soothed and stung Citius's many cuts

and bruises. After traversing nearly fifty yards, he made his way to the narrowest point of the gash in the earth. Unable to see, he had to feel around to navigate. He reached a dead end. If rocks were blocking the opening above, he would have nothing left to do but wait to die. The rock formation's V-shape would allow him to maintain three points of contact as he shimmied upward. A skilled climber, he balanced himself by maintaining equal pressure on both feet. His one free hand investigated for footholds in advance as he ascended blindly.

The salt miner had worked hard labor since childhood, so he was used to physical exhaustion. The pain was also bearable; it brought back memories of the many beatings sustained throughout his lifetime of servitude. The determined slave even had the nerve to chuckle in the blackness.

"Citius, it doesn't get much worse than this," he groaned. The survivor shut out his pain and climbed through the salted rain.

The slave's meager diet kept him rail thin. He was wiry but deceptively strong. Both attributes made him an excellent climber. Athletically, he propelled himself upward, determined to continue his miserable existence, trapped in the depths of the frozen mountain. He lived only for the challenges of the mine, where adversity was dispensed at random. Without hardship, there would be nothing to differentiate him from the other lost souls doomed to die in darkness.

Citius remembered his arrival at the mines. This had also

been the day he had realized the source of Archer's power. *In the uncertain darkness, the memory's clarity intensified. . . .*

The new arrivals stood for their initial inspection. Several henchmen were patrolling the crowd, grabbing at the younger-looking slaves, boldly inspecting the loin cloths of any who lacked whiskered faces. Everyone was still draped in the filthy, layered rags that had kept them from freezing to death as they marched through the mountains to reach the mines. Archer gave the black-eyed newcomer before him a curious look. He pointed at Citius and a massive guard attempted to grab at him.

With stunning ferocity, the slave sidestepped then whipped his hanging chains across the giant's brow, busting his nose wide open. The massive man groaned and hid his battered face in his hands. Archer's brutally scarred face twisted violently as he cackled at his henchman's misfortune.

The injured giant winced in pain. "That's no damn wench!"

"Surely not," Archer replied, struggling to contain his amusement. The master almost never laughed. Indeed, his position was dependent on his ruthless image.

After regaining his bearings, the thug's furious eyes searched for his fast-moving assailant. He saw Citius wielding the slack from his chains defensively. "I am going to crush every bone in your body, boy."

"That's enough, *Mule*," Archer commanded. The brute dared to offer his master a threatening glance.

"I am going to kill this—"

"I said that's *enough*," Archer commanded. In the blink of an eye, the master had his dagger at the giant's throat. There was not an ounce of indecision in the disfigured man's piercing stare. He kept this unruly dog on a short leash.

"Your time is near, boy," the lumbering oaf sneered through gnashed teeth.

"I am expecting two. *Now find them*," the lord snapped. Mule gave Citius a long, hard look, memorizing the scrapper's face. No doubt when his chance came he would strangle the life out of this disrespectful fool. The brute forced his way through the herd of dumbfounded newcomers.

Archer liked what he saw—the fearsome little scrap that the outside world had banished to his domain. He spoke in formal Latin to find out what he was dealing with. "No, boy, you certainly are no wench. What's your name?"

"Citius," the slave replied. The lord gave the newcomer a discerning look; men willing to stand up to Mule were hard to come by. Foolishness aside, there was value in boldness.

"Ah, yet another barbarian bastard with a Roman name. Well then, welcome to my world. Try not to let Mule kill you before the week is up." With a broad grin spanning his gruesomely branded face, the Lord of the Mine unlocked his prisoner's chains and handed him a pick. Something made him pause; his eyes sharpened. He tested the fighter, "If you who are wicked know how to give good gifts to your children, how much more will the

Father in heaven give of the Holy Spirit to those who ask him?"

Citius looked at the tyrant blankly, questioning the man's sanity.

"I see. You are not one of them. Maybe you'll last. I'll warn you, my dog is good with faces, but this should keep things interesting." Archer slipped the bold new arrival his dagger and preached, "Seek and you will find."

"Here they are, Archer. I found them," Mule bellowed from across the cave.

The brutal henchman was grabbing and sniffing at what appeared to be two scrawny young boys. They wrenched away, and he became violent. The slaves were dainty; their cropped heads were pathetic looking and disheveled. There was a certain beauty hidden beneath their smudged faces. Citius realized the terrible truth; two young women, draped in rags, had been smuggled into this hellhole. Archer noted the anger in the slave's eyes; he mistook it for manly hunger and smacked the newcomer on the back.

"Don't worry, boy. Produce for me, and you'll get your shot at them."

There was no time for Citius to respond. The master jogged over and whacked his unruly servant with his club. "Hands off the merchandise, Mule," he shouted as he beat the giant back. The massive man cowered away from his scar-faced leader. Archer undid the girls' chains and began inspecting them gently with lingering hands.

"Water," he shouted.

Another oaf rushed over with a ready jug. Archer allowed the women as much as they wanted to drink. The rest of the new arrivals were parched, but they were given no nourishment. Instead, they were ushered deep into the shaft to begin their lives as salt miners. This was how Archer maintained order. He controlled all of the weaponry, liquor, and women. As such, he controlled the strongest of the men. His operation hinged on exchanging small fortunes of salt with the guards who defended the entry ledge. In exchange, they smuggled in the three keys to Archer's reign— pain, addiction, and pleasure. Top producers avoided the first and enjoyed the rest.

The mine was ancient. Germanic nomads had worked its salted caverns for thousands of years, long before the Romans seized control of the highly lucrative operation. Citius had arrived in the mountain at the age of fifteen; he was barely a man during that first arduous year. Banished from the civilized world, he found himself among society's dreaded exiles: the insane, the sociopathic murderous scum, common thieves, dregs, and Christians from every dark corner of the known world. The mine was no place for a good-willed man. The situation was simple: adapt or die. He quickly realized he had to forget all the kindness a select few had shown him in the outside world. Goodness would die with all those who clung to it in the depths. This was a cruel world wherein only the ruthless excelled. If evil were determined to surround him, he would match it step-for-step in severity. If blood were to be spilled, he would let it flow. Once the others realized this truth, Citius excelled.

The salt miner's life was hard. Everyone was nameless; only the brand on your back distinguished you from the other lost souls destined to die in darkness. Dates, days, time—none of these existed in the depths. Cave-ins were a common occurrence; death was constant. Casualties had been accounted for; slaves and prisoners from all over the empire arrived in droves to die for the precious mineral. Salt was a life-giving force that brought stability to the outside world and fostered civilization. Yet, to the human tools who mined it, salt was a dreadful, unforgiving compound.

In time, Citius grew strong and experienced. By his second year, he had become a top producer. He had arrived with a strong background in carpentry; this knowledge served him well. The slave had worked wood for as long as he could remember. It was his love for this work that sustained him. In this produce-or-die world, the value of a great mind was compounded exponentially. The young exile became an expert in every facet of the salt mining process. He excelled in bracing the shafts, general construction, and rigging. Those who worked with him reveled in the extent of his mastery; few died on his watch. He identified poorly crafted timbers, neutralizing future collapses. His developing mind was relentlessly sharpened by his daily struggle to survive. The carpenter had become a great leader, one who led by example.

The newcomer's skills did not go unnoticed. The Lord of the Mine was kept well informed of all the goings-on within his domain. The talented slave was eventually given access to three times the typical miner's daily water allowance and twice the food. This was a tremendous advantage in a world where salt poisoning, a slow death by dehydration and starvation, plagued its inhabitants. Once Citius had come under Archer's wing, he was untouchable. To defy the lord meant death; this was the only law.

The mine's security system had evolved over the centuries. At present, guards defended the entrance, which was also the only known exit. It was a narrow spiraling passageway about seventy-five yards long. Entrants were forced to crawl through the snaking tunnel to the Main Cavern one by one. Even if every miner tried to rush through the narrow opening, the guards would only have to face them individually. It would not be long before a pile of their corpses blocked the exit.

After crawling single-file through the entry tunnel, the slaves came to an elevated ledge. New arrivals stood in awe, beholding the massive Main Cavern sprawled out before them. From the surface above, the shaft's enormity would have been inconceivable. The endless cavern was filled with magnificent ancient rock formations formed by thousands of years of slow-flowing water. The cavern's true beauty remained hidden by the darkness; torchlight was poor and often nonexistent. To make matters worse, a horrible smell of excrement stung the arriving miners' nostrils—the welcoming scent of their newfound hell.

Once new prisoners arrived at the ledge, a guard would lower a rope fifty feet down toward the base of the shaft. The lifeline ended twelve feet shy of the cavern floor, so prisoners had to dangle and drop the rest of the way. The older, less physically capable captives were often fortunate enough to die at this stage of the journey. They would lose their grip and their feeble bodies would fall to the rocks below. This was the extent of the mine's sympathy. Those afraid of heights would at times cling to the rope. In the event of this unfortunate delay, barrels filled with arrows were kept on hand. Usually, the mere threat of being shot was enough to make the slave descend. Yet, it was occasionally necessary to shoot the coward down.

In the mine's early days, a great scaffolding staircase had connected the entrance ledge to the cavern floor; it had long since been destroyed. If a miner was too volatile for a small crew of guards to handle, he would be separated from the rest. The warden would not put the handful of men who guarded the entry ledge at risk. Instead, the slave would be lowered by the lift with the rations. Indeed, Mule had entered the shafts of Saltz Mountain this way.

As custom dictated, new miners would be assessed at face value by Archer. Men's hands were checked for calluses; their height and muscularity were inspected. Then their toughness was tested by the scalding-hot brand seared into their backs. Those deemed too weak or pathetic by the lord's discerning eye were slain. The reason: food dispensation was dependent on salt production. Citius realized the totality of his exile; a part of him died watching the weak among them slaughtered like cattle. Many of these victims prayed aloud to their God before the spear points pierced their chests. Archer had a knack for identifying Christians early; although, if one proved to be an exceptional worker then he might last a short while longer.

Being from the North, Citius had never met a Christian; he had only heard others complain about their growing numbers throughout the known world. Plague and rebellion had been chiseling away at the empire. Christianity thrived in these uncertain times when those in power could not find answers that God provided. Disease and infection spread like wildfire through the cities and trade centers. The bodies were heaped into great mounds on the outskirts of towns and burned. All could smell the stink of hellfire. A keen awareness of mortality primed the disenchanted masses for the Christian promise—*eternity*. The powers that be feared the idea of a swarm of believers indifferent to the empire. A wave of persecution followed, but martyrdom only strengthened the message's validity.

The great plague eventually passed, but this foreign cult persisted. Persecution intensified; the feud between the empire and the faithful began to span multiple generations. Thousands of the persecuted were banished to the mines. Citius's friend Petrarch had been among their number. The believer had a sharp mind and a knack for storytelling. He spent long hours explaining the intricacies of his faith to his hard-working barbarian leader. It was hard enough hiding Petrarch's faith from Archer, so the miner heard but refused to listen to his friend's words.

Archer's disdain for religion was deep-rooted. He had been banished to the mines because of his family's faith. He had witnessed the pain in his father's eyes when his only son denied God. His mother was cut down. His sisters were beaten, abused, and sold into slavery. Soon afterward, he was rounded up with a group of others who had similarly agreed to renounce their faith in exchange for their lives. He was just a boy, but he had learned how dangerous God could be. He began to hate his father and all those like him willing to risk their families and their lives for God.

In mining, efficiency is the name of the game. Initially, Roman soldiers oversaw mining operations, which were performed by local contractors skilled in the craft of salt mining. Soon demand swelled and these contractors were given slave laborers to meet their new quotas. Now, more soldiers were required to prevent mutiny and escape plots. To the avaricious wardens, this increased expenditure was an unfortunate consequence of the otherwise ideal concept of slave labor. During the first two hundred years of the mine's existence, many Roman soldiers lost their lives at the hands of barbarian slaves armed with tools—pickaxes, hammers, and wooden stakes. After riots, the prisoners held all the cards, holding a fortune of salt ransom for weeks at a time. Change came when a brutally wise, viciously intelligent mining warden named Pyranus arrived.

The son of a wealthy commoner, Pyranus had been educated with the sons of nobles. The best teachers Rome had to offer fashioned his powerful mind; the young man came to the mountain teeming with determination. During his first year as Warden of the Mine, he analyzed the costly process of pulling salt from the depths. The soldiers were very expensive to maintain. He was quick to realize that the entire operation could be halted by mutiny. The fortune of salt below would be held captive by slaves until out of starvation they negotiated new terms of work. This was unacceptable and yet, to a keen observer like Pyranus, beautifully predictable.

Miners had been shocked to see the warden walking through the shafts watching them work—watching everything. Of course, the young Roman had been wise enough to give the men extra rations in the weeks before he entered the shafts. Pyranus personally reviewed the Northern Shaft. The journey around the mountain was costly, and the mine was too far from the bulk of his forces. Uprisings were more prevalent on the northern side of the mountain—a drawback of the shaft's more accessible design. The main problem was that its salt deposits were not nearly as rich as those found in the Southern Shaft. After review, the warden boldly consolidated his efforts; the Northern Shaft was deemed a losing investment and abandoned.

The commoner's son was industrious.

Pyranus carved a hole into the ceiling of the Main Cavern. He burned the rickety wooden scaffolding that connected the shaft's entrance ledge to the floor below. The fifty-foot tall staircase was replaced with the aforementioned rope. This became the only way in and out of the mine, except for the newly developed Main Pulley. The arrangement was simple and cost effective. Once a week, the pulley would lower from the opening carved into the cavern's ceiling. Soldiers armed with bows manned the entry ledge. They would oversee the miners from this vantage point as they loaded freshly mined rock salt onto the lift's circular platform. When hoisted upward, the platform would spin slowly, which made it even harder for an escaping slave to remain out of sight. If a miner managed to hide behind the pile of rock salt to avoid the guards' arrows, they would sound the horn three times. Pyranus had accounted for every scenario, so the pulley never slowed.

There was a massive cave that led into the mountainside. This is where the Main Pulley exited the mine; the cave served as a weighing station and storehouse. Pyranus constructed a building at the cave's entrance in order to conceal its true enormity. Once a week, the lift hoisted the platform filled with rock salt into a multistory, fortified stone cylinder—*the tower*. It was a tight squeeze; even if a slave were strong enough to cling to the bottom of the platform, he would never escape. The critical dimension between the platform's circular outer edge and the silo's walls was merely inches wide.

This fortification was the product of Pyranus's dreadful imagination—a nightmare, born into this world. The tower had nine small openings, located four feet above the storehouse floor.

These access doors encircled the entire stonework at consistent intervals. If the horn sounded, alerting an escape, soldiers armed with long spears would man these ports. Two archers would stand at the top of the stone silo. The pulley would stop briefly to allow the spearmen to repeatedly pulverize the escapee through the access ports at the base of the tower. Meanwhile, the archers rained arrows down on the helpless miner. This was an intentionally brutal slaughter, meant to deter escape. The slave's torn, arrow-ridden body would be weighed against the water earned by the salt and lowered in its place. Escape attempts up the pulley became rare. The slaves loading salt onto the platform would try to kill an escaping miner long before the guards had the chance. They were desperate not to lose out on their hard-earned fresh water.

Pyranus had concluded that if starvation fostered negotiations, then it should be the general state of things. The arrangement was simple: mine salt or starve. The strongest miners, men like Archer, maintained their own conception of order, while the weak and sick were eliminated. If a man did not produce, a man would not eat. It was no longer necessary to maintain an army in case of mutiny. Most of the Roman soldiers were soon replaced by much cheaper local mercenaries. The warden oversaw the mining operation for thirty years until the time of his death. His legacy was the masterpiece he had created—an efficient salt-producing machine that practically ran itself. Slaves in one end, salt out the other.

For efficiency's sake, Pyranus had petitioned to build a refinery in his storehouse, where the Main Pulley exited the tower. After all, the unrefined rock was far heavier and more costly to transport than the finished product. The Roman rulers never gave the commoner's son permission. The salt from the mine was directly taxed by the emperor. There was a weighing station to the south run by the emperor's men, who also oversaw the entire refining process. This separation of powers was a safeguard against unscrupulous pilfering of the lightweight finished product. During Pyranus's reign, the mountain was inspected annually to ensure that no refinery was present. A close eye was kept on the commoner, for he had proved himself much wiser than anyone could have imagined.

This was the world to which Citius arrived at the age of fifteen. Pyranus had died fifty years before the young man took his first steps on the dingy cavern floor. Three new mining wardens had come and gone since the wise man's death, but none had dared to alter his foolproof system.

Difficult times had come to the empire. With the price of salt nearly matching that of gold, priorities were changing on the mountain. The current Warden of the Mine, Nero, was an exceptionally greedy man. Given the high price of salt, he began to demand more from the mountain than Pyranus's system could sustain.

— XI —

THE DETERMINED SURVIVOR CLAWED HIS WAY
upward through the dust-filled darkness. The thick cloud of
salt dust persisted. It stung his lungs and burned his dry mouth.
The sound of running water was gaining momentum. What
had begun as a slow trickle was becoming a steady stream. He
fought to pull his battered form onto the flat surface above. Had
he made his way to shelter in one of the many hollows, he would
have drowned. That great split in the earth and the boulders that
blocked it had saved his life. Petrarch had borne the cost of his
safe passage—blood is sometimes necessary to keep fate at bay.

The great pile of rocks behind him was straining to hold
back what was becoming a raging torrent. Feeling the ice-cold water rising at his feet, he took off up the shaft as fast as his broken
body allowed. He could hear other panic-stricken miners sprinting past him as he staggered up the rugged terrain. The dust was
blinding as he made his way into the Main Cavern. When he exited the shaft he saw everyone fighting for elevated sections of
the cavern floor. In his weakened state, he did not bother trying
to secure high ground. Instead, he leaned against the cave wall to
assess the extent of his injuries in the dim torchlight. He watched

the herd of slaves scrambling for the rocks scattered about the cavern floor.

Pandemonium was gaining momentum as the draft from the depths intensified. Archer was there, shouting at the others to keep back. Half a dozen frightened women were huddled behind him. His trophies were adorned in luxurious silk garments and jewelry. His entire force was armed with spears, desperate to hold the high ground. The true frailty of Archer's reign was being exposed as the seconds passed. He and his twenty well-armed henchmen were surrounded by close to two hundred starving salt miners. The tyrant had always used fear to keep the horde at bay; it had worked when they had nothing to fear other than his wrath. The threat of the rising water far outweighed that of sharpened steel. The mob began deliberately pacing toward the high ground; even the perfumed harem could not mask their stench. Upon seeing the whites of the slaves' eyes, Archer hurled his spear.

Feeling the pressure, the lord's henchmen turned to violence. They cut down the largest of the rebels. This forced the mob back momentarily. It was unprecedented to see all the women together. Citius searched for Arielle—a young girl from Iberia. In his first years trapped in the mine, whenever Archer had rewarded him with a woman, he had chosen her. When the lord decided to keep her for himself, the talented miner got to know the rest. Over four hundred men worked the mine; of them, fewer than thirty were ever given the opportunity to get to know Archer's girls. Even his henchmen were rarely rewarded. Most slaves did not last longer than a year, so they never felt the true pain of a world without women. The master gave his inner circle just enough to keep them sane, nothing more; the lord loved his women.

Through the clouds of dust, Citius could see fear in Arielle's movements. He was forced to realize that he could not save her—that Archer was her best hope for survival. This was a truth she had realized years ago, when she begged Archer not to let any of the others touch her. She knew that in doing so she would never see Citius again. Her crystal-blue eyes searched the raging mob, looking for her lover's face in the masses. He was not there. She prayed that he had died quickly in the collapse. Arielle had not forgotten her father's faith; she knelt to pray for a swift end to the chaos.

A deafening blast shook the mountain. Out of sight, the boulders that strained to hold back the gushing brine were blown into the shaft's walls. A massive pressurized slug of ground water had been unleashed from the depths. They all could hear yowls of mortal terror coming from below as the water ripped through the darkness. Many miners, hard at work in the adjacent caverns, had been unaware of the impending disaster. Their faint screams echoed toward the herd of slaves huddled together on the towering rocks.

The black wave—laced with gravel, splintered timber, and stone—surged through the shafts. The deluge swallowed the lost souls it encountered indiscriminately. The hopeless cries sent a chill through the salted air. The crowd went silent, all were enraptured in dreadful anticipation.

Archer's eyes were fixed down the shaft. He could hear the crashing waves echoing menacingly out of sight. A great wind was coming from the depths as the rush of water displaced the dust-filled air below. Terror set in as plumes of salt dust filled the cavern. The weak were trampled; able-bodied men began scrambling up the cave walls. Fearing the worst, the guards sounded the alarm for rebellion. Overwhelmed, the bowmen began raining arrows down on the crowd below. Archer fought to hold the high ground, slaying all those who came within the range of his spear.

From the edge of the brawl, Citius watched in disbelief as the series of torches several hundred yards down the narrow shaft began to be snuffed out in rapid succession. The ominous gust intensified; salt dust was emitted in great plumes from the depths. The water was moments away. Fueled by adrenaline, he shed his sling to climb the cave wall. The guards on the ledge could feel the wind but did not understand the magnitude of the situation. They continued firing arrows at the mob as the panicked slaves scaled the walls.

Battle raged as the great mass of water rushed into the cavern. The floodwaters spat and roared, wielding a great swarm of projectiles. Hundreds of miners swirled in the mighty wave. The pressurized water drove boulders into the cave walls, shaking the great hall. The rumbling caused spears of rock to rain down on the struggling masses. The guards watched in horror as the water continued to rise, swallowing the climbing miners by the handful until all the torches below were snuffed out.

As he climbed, Citius could hear the muffled screams of the others as they were gobbled up by the turbulent waves. The miner scrambled as best he could, but soon he too was swallowed by the rushing tide. He was yanked and thrown violently by the powerful surge. It was total darkness all at once. He could feel splintered timbers and corpses rushing past him. He stole a breath of air whenever the waves allowed. The blackness made it hard to determine which way was up once the current forced the slaves under. Many died because they swam down for air. Most of the miners being swirled around him could not swim. Their bodies were buoyant in the highly concentrated brine, so they too swirled about at the surface. The flood was slowly losing momentum; the swirling slaves fought to keep their heads above water.

Without the waves bouncing them up into the air, the remaining survivors panicked. They lashed out, attempting to stay afloat by clawing over their fellow prisoners. The insanity turned violent; Citius was caught in a swarm of desperate souls fighting to survive. A drowning man flung his arms around his neck and forced him under. He was able to shrug off the first attacker, but he had barely taken a breath when two more grabbed hold of him. They climbed up his weakened form, forcing him under as they bit at the air above. The slave was crippled by his injuries sustained during the cave-in. His broken ribs sent shooting pains down his spine as he fought to squirm free. The surface was a blur of biting, kicking, clawing madness. The drowning young man's lungs screamed as he ripped at his attackers. The frigid water was already taking its toll on the sickly slaves.

Amidst the struggle, Citius recognized a familiar voice. It was Archer—a salt miner since childhood, he had become the most powerful slave in the mine. The indiscriminate floodwaters did not care who Archer was, and at that moment neither did the prisoners. All were losing strength, battling to keep their heads above water. Two more drowning miners became entangled in the brawl. The tower's hatch opened, sending light across the frothing flood. The platform lowered rapidly. Light from the portal above allowed the guards manning the entry ledge to see that the brine had risen nearly forty feet; it would soon rise above their post. Nero's men began firing at the slaves brawling in the swirling saltwater. This well-aimed barrage of arrows struck several of the men forcing Citius under.

As the turbulent flood continued to steadily rise, the guards remembered their training. They cut the age-old rope and ran from the ledge into the tunnel. The fleeing guards labored forward on their hands and knees until they reached the first hollowed-out cavern. The perspiring thugs frantically swung sledgehammers at the wooden posts that suspended several tons of loose stones above the tunnel's opening. This was Rebellion Protocol. Never, since the institution of Pyranus's System, had anyone had to knock down these posts. As such, they were well set by decades of gravity; the timber would not give. The larger guard snatched the better hammer from his associate. Without argument, the smaller man took off up the tunnel. The ancient hammer snapped in two after just a few swings. The determined oaf took out his battle axe to hack at the posts. The man was drenched in sweat, terrified by the thought of what Nero would do if any slaves escaped on his watch. He heaved his axe with all his might and the weakened post gave way. The loose stones collapsed, crushing him mercilessly.

Beneath the ledge, Citius was losing his battle against the others. He stole only one breath for their every three. A great crash boomed from the direction of the ledge. Archer knew the guards had sealed the exit. Citius's chest was collapsing in on itself; he managed to steal what he feared would be his last breath. Again, he was forced under; his lungs clung to the breath of air within. He was beginning to slip away when a great crash rocked the water. A huge log smashed into the waves; the impact forced him deep into the brine as it disposed of several of his attackers. More logs continued to fall from the tower's opening, which was now only fifty feet from the water's surface. The heavy lengths of timber slammed into the turbulent swarm killing any miners who happened to be battling below. The logs were meant to serve as buoys; instead, they acted as missiles, bombarding the foaming waves.

The drowning miners fought to get out of harm's way. Citius's arms were finally freed; he bit at the salted air as logs crashed down all around him. Archer forced him under again.

With his free hand, the young man reached into his cloak, searching for his dagger. It was gone. It had been lost to the dark water in his struggle. Fighting to the surface, he caught a glimpse of a long, splintered wooden stake in the faint light cast by the tower's circular opening. Frantically, he lunged for it as Archer repeatedly pushed him under. His hand closed around the splintered shank. As his fingers wrapped around it, the disfigured lord forced him below the surface for the last time.

The master was surprised at how easily his subject had gone under. He soon realized why, when he felt the jagged stake impale his stomach. The barbarian drove the weapon into his attacker and twisted it up into his rib cage. The tyrant's grasp failed as he choked on the salted air. Freed from Archer's death grip, the survivor blasted out of the water. Logs continued to crash around them. Taking hold of the shank, Citius's eyes met Archer's.

The fighter felt compelled to offer a piece of wisdom to his dying leader. "All those who exalt themselves shall be humbled," he shouted over the crashing waves. Without another word, he yanked the wooden stake out of his victim's gut, letting blood spill into the brine.

Upon hearing his father's words, Archer stopped fighting death and died calmly in the black water. Able to breathe freely, Citius now fought the cold. He prayed his failing limbs had the strength to climb. He let go of the fallen ruler and swam toward the cavern wall.

The logs stopped falling; freezing refugees clinging to the

floating timber cried out for help, but none came. In the hours that followed, many more slaves succumbed to the icy floodwaters. Bodies would continue to surface from the buoyant brine for days. The young man knew Arielle was among them. The half-frozen miner took refuge on a narrow ledge about ten feet above swirling sea of brine. Air pockets from below would bubble to the surface for weeks after the Great Flood. The shivering miner lay his head on the rocks and passed out from exhaustion.

— XII —

THE ROOM WAS DARK AND COLD; NERO SAT EE-
rily still. The tall, balding Roman was brooding. His breath steamed as he stared into the failing fire at his feet, oblivious to the plummeting temperature of his personal quarters.

There was a slave pretending to sleep in his bed of furs. She was bundled up in animal skins but still could not stop shivering. Emboldened by the cold, the girl sat up and nervously addressed her master.

"Lord Nero—are we finished, sir?" The sulking noble did not notice the small voice. His dark eyes were fixed on the hypnotic smoldering coals at his feet.

"Master—are you finished?" she dared to ask again.

"Are you cold, girl? I thought you people were supposed to be used to this endless winter."

"Yes, sir. I am very cold," the barbarian whimpered, in broken Latin.

"Very well, *slave.* Leave me be."

The golden-haired girl rose from Nero's bed. She dressed herself hurriedly, not daring to even glance at her master. She flinched when an urgent fist slammed on the warden's chamber door.

A breathless guard called out Nero's name, "The mine has flooded! Open the door, sir!"

Another chubbier guard caught up with his associate. Gasping for air, he blabbered, "What are you doing, you fool? What are you thinking, banging on the warden's door like that? Are you trying to get yourself killed?"

On the other side, Nero took a deep, furious breath and exhaled steam slowly through his nostrils. He rose to his feet with a foreboding calmness. The slave must have sensed his rage; she had stopped dressing. She balled up defensively in a dark corner of the room, wincing at the spider's every move. The towering man's long arm reached down to grab a stool that rested by the entryway. With long, cold, bony fingers he unlatched the door but did not open it.

"Gentlemen, please join me," he beckoned.

The exasperated guard stepped away from the door and shook his head at the other, a warning. The guard gave his little associate a smug, disappointed look as he pushed the door open. Torchlight spilled through the entryway into the dark room. The master's quarters appeared to be empty. The messenger's eyes struggled to adjust. He caught a glimpse of a young slave in the far corner of the room. The faint torchlight exposed her teary eyes and scratched face. He ignored her.

Assuming the warden was in his bed under the animal skins, the guard made his way toward the furs. There was a loud creak and sudden boom; the door slammed shut. The soldier reached for the hilt of his sword and spun around toward the entryway. His face turned directly into the apex of Nero's long, powerful swing. The spider's lean arms accelerated the stool through the burly man's bearded face. The chair shattered. The warden released his grip, sending shards of timber across the room.

A brief silence followed. Only the faint sound of smoldering coals from the failing fire could be heard. The soldier dropped to the cold pine floor with a hard thud. Without hesitation, Nero drove his bony heel into the man's face. The merciless blow was surely fatal. The lord stood in the dark fuming, basking in his brutality. The cornered slave screamed in terror. The guard on the other side drew his sword but did not dare enter.

"Wench," Nero seethed, "what did I tell you?" The trapped girl was sobbing and whimpering uncontrollably in the corner of the warden's room.

"What did I tell you?" he roared.

The gangly spider was drawing down on her. Amidst it all, the plump soldier on the other side was debating whether or not to intervene. He desperately wanted to just walk away from the dreadful screams. "By gods," he sighed. Against his better judgment, he kicked the door open.

"Lord Nero, sir," the cowering guard shouted in the most convincing voice he could muster.

The master slowly turned to see what fool had the nerve to enter unannounced. It was Dimitri. The weary guard's eyes fell on his murdered associate's lifeless form. Then his stare drifted back and fixed on the towering animal that was Nero. The warden assessed the fear and horror in his personal attendant's eyes. He had no remorse but was oddly embarrassed to have unnerved his little friend. The Roman's keen beady eyes flashed on Dimitri's polished sword. The servant hurriedly returned the glimmering blade to the sheath at his side.

"What did you plan to do with that?" Nero inquired of the well-kept weapon with a deviant grin.

"Not a thing, sir. Just a precaution," Dimitri stammered.

"You should be ashamed of how *pretty* that blade is," he jabbed, poking fun at Dimitri's virgin sword. Nero wiped the blood spatter from his gaunt face then gave the girl at his feet a nudging kick. Her face was buried between her arms and knees.

"Get out," he commanded.

The slave crawled past him, clutching to her tattered garments. Once out of reach, she leapt to her feet and bolted toward the doorway, brushing by Dimitri as she fled. The guard could barely look at Nero; he felt ashamed for how badly the girl had been beaten. He gulped down his disapproval and entered his master's quarters.

"Sir, like Albus said, the mine is flooded."

"I have been clear with the men that my personal hours are not to be interrupted. Have I not?"

"Right, sir. Well, it was an emergency. He was new, nobody will miss him. All that aside, this is no small matter; we should send word to Lord Alexander."

"Emergency? Have we not had floods before?" Nero chastised.

"This is different."

"Well, how bad is it?"

Dimitri grimaced at Albus's broken face and gulped. "The water rose above the entry ledge, sir," the cringing servant responded.

"Impossible."

"Saw it myself, sir. Unbelievable, I know, but true."

"Did any escape?"

"We blocked the exit."

"Well done. Any survivors?"

"Hard to say, my lord," the servant replied as he made his way across the room in conversation. He began snacking on some cold bacon he found by the fire. The shivering guard added a log to the failing embers and continued, "After we collapsed the exit, we dropped a few loads of wood down from the tower. I doubt if any of those wretched fools can swim. Tomorrow we will assess the situation. Maybe a slave or two will be bobbing on the logs. Hopefully, they can tell us what happened."

"This is a disaster," Nero fumed.

"Absolute disaster," Dimitri added. Catching his master's glare, he scrambled. "We will have to act fast." The guard was standing close to the fire to warm his hands.

"Anything else I should know?"

"It's salt water, sir."

"Explain."

"The water that flooded the mine: it's brine, sir. The guards who inspected the tunnel said the stuff was stronger than seawater," Dimitri said. Nero glared at the flames—quickly analyzing the information, trying to find the best way to navigate his newfound circumstances.

"Are there any outsiders at camp?"

"Well—let me think."

"Get on with it," Nero roared.

"Yes, a few merchants arrived the day before yesterday. They brought pigs and chickens mostly. A little booze too, the strong stuff," Dimitri belted out, practically tasting the vendors' goods. The servant avoided his master's empty stare.

"We will make certain that any and all outsiders are dead by sunrise. No word of this flood is to leave camp. *Understood?*"

"Yes, sir."

Taking hold of his spear, Nero spoke forcibly, "I will need your loyalty more now than ever, Dimitri."

— XIII —

N O WORD HAD COME BACK ON THE FARM-
house's supposed mystery builder. Pallas had traveled
to interrogate several local artisans. He asked them all about this
man called Citius, but none had heard of anyone by that name.
Lucinda's natural accent helped considerably. These people were
suspicious of their conquerors. With Lucinda's blond hair and
blue eyes at his side, trust was easier to come by. Still, those questioned seemed confused as to why anyone would be seeking out
a specific carpenter; to most, builders were as replaceable as the
trees they worked with. The peasants often recommended local
contractors for whatever job they supposed the wealthy foreigner
had in mind. When Pallas tried to explain his motives were not of
that nature, he was met with skepticism. The Northerners concluded that this Citius character was of the worst variety—a murder, thief, or philanderer.

"How many did he kill?" some would ask.

"Fill me in—what kinds of horses does he target?" others
would inquire.

"I'll keep an eye out for that Citius," they would say with
a self-assured nod. As if they believed the man was going to kill

their grandchildren as they slept. Then again, it did not help that Pallas had the look and feel of a bounty hunter.

The engineer had to chuckle because he had inadvertently done a swell job of ruining Citius's good name. Maybe now the man would be better off dead. Despite its fruitlessness, his quest was much too important for him to fail. He had dedicated his life to construction, so it disturbed him in a profound sense that this great talent had gone undiscovered. Setbacks and dead ends aside, the adventure was more appealing than stumbling around the halls of Alexander's compound. The wolf smiled; maybe in the next village, he would try a different angle—tell the peasants that he was in search of a murderer named Citius.

No one was happier to be touring the countryside than Lucinda. The aging beauty was very useful indeed. As a child, she had hunted with her father until her village was raided by a neighboring tribe. As fate would have it, she had been sold four times since that dreadful day. Owners never kept her long; she had too much fight in her to make a good slave. She suffered a great deal before she caught the Greek's eye in the marketplace. As they traveled, Lucinda provided most of the meals with her bow. In the wilderness, the kind woman felt close to her family again.

They spent the entire summer galloping all over the province with their pack of hounds at their heels. They managed to sell off several of their dogs as they traveled. The pups had already grown strong. Northern families were eager to purchase Lucinda's well-trained hounds; so many of the wolfish shepherds had been slain during the rebellion.

Alexander's record-keeping system was limited; it proved to be useless. Pallas decided to tour every recently built structure since the construction of the forgotten stables. Still, they found no evidence of the undiscovered builder's mastery. Most all of the leads brought them to fatherless homes, orphans and widows at every turn.

Although the rebellion had been quelled two years earlier, evidence of the struggle was still strewn about the countryside. Their pursuit led them through razed villages; the charred remains of once-bustling trade centers. Galloping across disheveled fields, they stumbled upon clusters of skeletons. There was still a great distaste for Roman occupation. The Greek could see the suffering in his woman's eyes; these were her countrymen's bones in the mud.

Rome had brought its technology and industry to the North. Many of the fields that had allowed the local population to swell would never have been cleared had it not been for occupation. As with many things, without one there could not be another. The North's economy grew strong, and its people grew tired of Roman control. Wherever it cast its shadow, the empire created an economy that revolved around taxation—fields were cleared, ore was mined, goods were sold, and everything was taxed. All the while, a large military presence provided enough fear to keep the locals in line. News of the uprising had made it to Rome years earlier. Pallas had stayed current with the wild tales from the North; his supply lines had been plagued during the war. The Senate eventually sent a great wave northward to crush the rebellion. The empire coerced the mob to crumble from within. Deep-rooted local divisions were exploited; in the end, the rebels turned on each other.

The engineer visited many structures, but none bore the mark of greatness he sought. Throughout the summer, he interrogated dozens of architects, suppliers, and laborers. Most had done work for Alexander in some fashion over the years, but none had any information about the stables. No one knew anyone by the name of Citius. In every town it was more of the same, most of the individuals he spoke with were surprised that he was out looking for a particular carpenter. Several peasants asked if this man called Citius was a thief or a killer. Time and again, Pallas reassured them that it was nothing criminal; although, he realized he was unintentionally creating a notorious villain.

Every now and then, his woman would say, "I do not understand. Why do you have to meet the man who beat you?"

Lucinda's angle was well played; she knew this question drove Pallas into a fit. The last thing she wanted to do was return to Alexander's estate. She knew that if she nagged him, he would rebel and press deeper into the countryside on his wild goose chase. To her, this country jaunt was heaven, and she had a growing secret that made it all the sweeter.

After the occasional bout with Lucinda, the Greek would gallop ahead on his horse. The pounding hooves helped him to clear his thoughts. He would reassure himself of his well-intentioned journey. Truth told, Pallas did not know what feeling made him continue to dig deeper and ride farther; it was not envy nor was it his competitive nature. There was something in the man that needed to struggle—to sweat and bleed. The engineer could not truly believe a man had built the farmhouse, until he met the man who did. Doubt made him seek the truth.

As weeks became months, Pallas noticed a difference in Lucinda. The leaves changed from a rich green to an assortment of fiery shades, and his woman changed as well. She was sleeping later than usual and moving slower. She wore baggy clothes and refused to ride any faster than a steady trot. Her appetite was sporadic and she struggled with nausea. The old dog could see it in her eyes that she had something to tell him.

It was a brisk morning for that time of year. They were bundled up near a small fire. Pallas decided to break the early silence with a joke. "With my luck, tales of a raping, murdering, horse-thief, carpenter named Citius have already spread throughout the whole of Germania by now."

"You're probably right. I'm waiting for a passerby to warn us to look out for him. It's a small world. It's bound to happen if we keep at it." The Greek chuckled; he knew his woman had something on the tip of her tongue. He did not want to ask. He prided himself on figuring her out. Holding her close, he had a pretty good idea already.

Toward the end of their breakfast, he finally asked, "How

far along are you?" His timing was a little off; she had just re-turned from a mid-meal vomit break.

"How long did it take you to put all that together? You've never been able to outride me," she quipped as she groggily stumbled back through the brush. Her master laughed jovially at her ways.

"Well, I always give you the better horse."

Returning to the warm blankets, Lucinda's eyes met his. She was scared. "Going on six months, I think. And don't act so surprised. You've been pawing at my hips for months, you no-good scoundrel. When have I ever been this heavy?"

"It seems the northern air was all you needed."

Joyful tears began trickling down her full cheeks. "I am so happy, I can't believe it." This was the longest she had ever gone without miscarrying.

"A child and a grandchild born in the same year. Well now, the gods are good. I should abandon this ridiculousness. We need to get you home."

"Absolutely not," Lucinda insisted. "Like you said, it could be the northern air. My homeland's food and water have taken us this far. My son needs northern nourishment," she said, rubbing her belly.

"So it's a boy?"

"Yes, a mother knows. He has been moving for weeks. He's strong."

"It's about time. You deserve a decent man in your life."

"Isn't that the truth," she teased. "One thing is for sure—you need to start taking better care of yourself. You will be sixty by the time my son is ten."

"Which means you would be fifty. Don't worry, my love, I will have thrown you out by then," he said with a whiskered grin.

"As if my son would ever let you." Pallas laughed and pulled her close.

The journey took on a slower pace after their discussion. They relaxed and enjoyed the peacefulness of the rolling countryside. Most of the hamlets they drifted through were occupied by women and children. Only men too old to work the fields or too young to lift a club remained. The rebellion had destroyed the local economy. It would be many years before these people recovered. Rome did not rebuild the North. The battered townships would stand as a deterrent for decades to come. The young who remained would know what happened when one defied the empire. All the men were dead. Pallas was beginning to fear Citius was among them.

That is, if he ever existed at all.

Nearly two months had passed since Lucinda shared the news. Winter was setting in; the weather was getting colder with each passing day. They were moving slower than ever. Pallas had bought a wagon as soon as he realized his woman's status. His priorities were well-grounded; he no longer felt frustrated when his search for information proved fruitless and the trail of names ran cold. They clunked through the wilderness at a breezy pace, enjoying the scenery and each other's company. His sense of urgency deflated as his companion's belly swelled.

Their adventure had taken them full circle; Alexander's estate was only a week away. Pallas was eager to get his pregnant lover to the compound; Citius had become an afterthought. They approached a modest trade center that sat alongside a mighty river. Not surprisingly, not a single builder lived in this rickety fishing village. The engineer had assumed this was the case as they trotted toward the town. Even from a distance, he could see that the walls of the structures were out of plumb. There was no doubt about it, the buildings had been slapped together by amateurs—farmers, merchants, and fishermen.

Children barreled through the town center, pelting one another with snowballs. Lucinda watched them with great joy. Pallas had not seen freshly fallen snow in over twenty years. As a soldier, he had learned to dread the white powder, but now he enjoyed its company. This town, like so many others, had been decimated in the rebellion. It was not difficult to find shelter, because his northern woman was clearly with child. The locals were eager to help.

Having finished his usual barrage of questioning strangers at random, Pallas entered a local inn. As usual, his interrogations led nowhere. Once within the lodging he enjoyed several servings of wine while he savored a large, juicy filet of fresh fish pulled from the river that same morning. His hefty purse was a welcome sight to the impoverished peasants. When the innkeeper's daughter tempted him with more than a meal, he knew he had better leave before he woke up on the wrong side of town.

It was nearing dusk when the old man left the lodge for an evening stroll. He walked along the river's edge; a good meal and wine had calmed him considerably. His worries over his second bout with fatherhood were set aside. The engineer relaxed as he watched several fishermen loading their boats, preparing to pursue the evening's catch. These men seemed unaware of the cold. Their routine was well organized; no time or step was wasted.

The men rowed in unison drawing closer to Pallas, who marveled at them in the evening light. The vessels sliced through the choppy water effortlessly. Their planks were curved, shaped, and joined flawlessly. Every knot in the wood had been placed with purpose. The engineer's eyes left the river to fix on the empty trees, which appeared to be rooted in the fading horizon.

Images from the stables stirred as Pallas reveled in his unlikely discovery. He thought better than to approach the fishermen in the darkness. Instead, he decided to meet them at daybreak when they set out for their morning catch, hoping they would be more likely to talk in the light of day. The wanderer reluctantly left the riverbank; Lucinda was probably already wondering what he had gotten himself into.

At dawn the following morning, Pallas left his woman in a well-warmed bed and set out for the docks. What he thought was early turned out to be late. The fishermen had already shoved off;

they were far out on the water, hard at work. In the long hours that followed, the tired engineer paced up and down the riverbank to keep warm. He could not help thinking about the innkeeper's daughter—her bright smile and full breasts. One more instance to add to his extensive list of regrettable accomplishments. Lucinda had steadied him; a former version of himself would not have had the strength to walk away. Looking out across the water, he imagined his woman holding his unborn son and found peace on the river's edge.

A few hours after sunrise the four boats finally rowed back in his direction; Pallas watched them cut through the current with wonder. The beautifully formed vessels glided across the wind-whipped whitecaps. Pallas remained on the riverbank until the crew reached the pier then he approached with caution.

All of the fishermen were surprised to see a white-haired man standing in the determined gusts that raced across the river. They assumed the wanderer had come to beg for fish. His garments were foreign and tattered; he had a somewhat Roman look to him. Most of these commoners had lost sons in the rebellion. Only their grandchildren and sons' widows remained to evidence what they had lost. Witnessing the grief and loathing on their weathered faces, Pallas realized a Mediterranean man was not welcome. As the men began to unload, one of their number walked along the dock toward this outsider. The Northerner determined the well-built foreigner was no beggar. Indeed, Pallas had the look of a workingman, and his piercing blue eyes did not look at all out of place on the river's edge. The fisherman decided this loner was not to be feared.

The peasant addressed the outsider in broken Latin. "Good morning, sir. Are you hungry?"

"No, my friend. I am here to ask you about those vessels," Pallas boomed for all to hear. His confident, well-versed northern tongue was a surprise to all. Thanks to Lucinda, and his years spent building in Germania, he spoke several dialects with proficiency.

"Ah, you know the water?" the fisherman asked, with a subtle smirk.

"No—not water. I know wood, I know people, and I know talent when it jumps up and smacks me in the face," Pallas said, grinning at the motley crew before him. Several of the old men chuckled. This odd foreigner spoke their language well. He was comically out of place, but completely unfazed.

"Unfortunately, they are not for sale, sir. You cannot find ships like these anymore."

"Why is that?" Pallas demanded. The men were a bit startled by the jovial foreigner's sudden intensity.

"Argon's son Darius is in charge now—that's why," one of the lot replied.

"Did Argon build these boats?"

"Yes, it took him twenty years of average junk to finally master his craft. Then about seven years ago, his vessels changed. We have never seen ships like these. Now they are unavailable.

You understand why we cannot sell. These boats are our livelihood."

Several young ones sprinted across the dock from the village; no doubt, these were this lot's kin. The old men left the eager lads to do the unloading. Several of the crew members curiously approached the outsider. A few others simply walked past him toward the village unamused. It seemed the foreigner's features were more than they could bear.

"I am not here to purchase ships, my friends, although I am very impressed by these. I came in search of this man you call Argon. Where can I find his shop?" Pallas inquired.

"His shop is a day's journey upriver. If you have a horse, you can get there before nightfall, but you will not find Argon at his bench."

"Why is that?" Pallas asked the group, a bit annoyed that he had to.

"The old man died about five winters ago. His son has taken over the business," the leader said. His tone told Pallas that this man had known Argon well.

One of the others spoke up. "Ay, Argon's boy's name is Darius. My brother bought a boat from him this spring. The damn thing sunk two months later. That boy has a long way to go."

A gruff voice spoke out from beyond the group. "Argon was a hopeless fool, just like that dimwitted boy of his." When the men heard the weathered voice, they all began to chuckle. They made way for their elder to hobble toward the outsider. He gestured for the others to quiet down; it appeared their guest wanted to speak.

Intrigued, Pallas asked, "If Argon was such a fool, then who built these vessels?"

The elder was quite a character; he had a charming, misplaced swagger. He spoke freely, "Well, old man, everybody knows Argon was a damn fool. His boats were overpriced. You were lucky to get two seasons out of his best. Not surprisingly, his son's crafts are also barely worthy of crows' shit."

A few men chuckled and the rabble-rouser continued, "Now, these ships here are of a different breed entirely." He waved an open palm proudly in the direction of the fleet at the dock. The elder was happy to see Pallas hanging on his every word. "You see, Argon had a stroke about ten years back. That old man could barely wipe his ass, let alone build ships like these." Several of the men laughed as they helped the children unload the day's catch.

Expressionless against the cold wind, Pallas asked, "Then who built them?"

"Can't say for sure—can only speculate. See, when the old man fell ill, he took on several helpers."

Another man chimed in, "Those bastards didn't know a damn thing."

The elder waved the other off. "I'm getting there, you idiot. Right, so Argon couldn't get a good day's work out of any of these *hired hands*." He paused to glare at the other for cutting in. Then he let his keen eyes fix on Pallas. "But you see, my friend, it was around that time that Argon bought a young slave from a drifting

Roman merchant."

"Yeah, an old Roman drunk," a crew member added.

The weathered Northerner shot this interrupter a disapproving look for a second time. "As I was saying, rumor has it that this boy built every ship, including these here. It's been over half a decade, yet these ships still ride the water as well as they did the day we purchased them."

"What was the slave's name?" Pallas asked in stunned disbelief. He could not come to grips with the idea that a young man had fashioned the boats before him, or worse yet, the masterful stables.

The elder paused to stare out across the choppy river. "Argon's father was a Roman. The man was obsessed with all things Roman. That son of his is even worse. Darius warned us that someone might come through these parts, looking for that lad." The old man looked hard at the outsider. "I doubt if the slave had a name when he got here, but Argon called the boy *Citius*." The others went silent as the elder hobbled briskly toward the village.

Pallas noticed a handful of the fishermen shy away. They kept their heads down and avoided his pale eyes. Unhindered, he continued his questioning. "Where is this slave now?" he called. The elder kept walking.

One of the others answered, "Not sure, my friend. You'd have to ask Argon's son, Darius."

The obnoxious man who had interrupted the elder spoke out of turn yet again. "Rumor has it, Darius got in an *argument* with the slave. Word around the river is, the slave and Darius's wife—well, you know." At this, all the men chuckled.

Another chimed in, "I thought it was his daughter."

"Thanks, Norde. But *wife* is funnier than daughter, so would you just stay the hell out of my damn story?"

"You're one to talk, Haus," Norde rebuked, glaring at his much smaller associate.

"You never knew when to keep your mouth shut, Norde."

"No, but I can teach you how." A stocky man stepped between the two.

"Stay out of this, Oden," both old men said in unison to the peacemaker.

"Where is this slave now?" Pallas shouted. His deep voice boomed across the frigid breeze, startling the squabbling villagers. There was more to this foreigner than met the eye. This lone wanderer was not a man to be trifled with.

"Easy now, my friend. I apologize. These numbskulls have a way of interrupting each other to the point where not a damn thing gets accomplished." Oden glared at the others then continued, "Before the war I heard the slave was sold to the salt mines. It's a damn shame. To think, a young man who could build ships like these was sent to the mines."

"Nobody lasts long in the mines," Haus chimed in. "Besides, if he wasn't sent to the mine, he probably found death in the rebellion."

The stocky man lost it. "Since you are such a chit-chatty little dimwit today, you can scrub all the decks and mop the bloody dock after we are done cleaning today's catch."

It occurred to Pallas that Oden owned the entire operation. Also, Haus had to have been his younger brother; their voices were nearly identical and they fought like family. The bold Northerner turned and addressed the outsider, "Old man, if you want to find Darius, head upriver. As for Citius, don't bother. The rebellion aside, Saltz Mountain is where a man goes to die. The mines are hell on earth."

"So, what's this all about?" Haus questioned. "Did the slave steal some horses?"

"No, it's nothing like that."

"He killed somebody, didn't he?" The others nodded in agreement.

"I knew he was a bounty hunter," Norde confidently announced to the others. "As soon as I saw him, I knew."

"Shut your mouth, Norde," Haus said over his brother's shoulder.

"No, it's nothing like that," Pallas assured them, shaking his head. He could barely hide his annoyance with this familiar line of counter-questioning. The fishermen were growing skeptical of this foreigner's true motives. By now, the old man was accustomed to this. The captain ushered his younger brother toward the boats; there was work to do.

Haus turned to a handful of others and spoke in a low voice so that the outsider could not hear, "Well, we all know the boy's history with wives and daughters." The men laughed; Pallas ignored their guessing games.

"Well, good day, my friend. We have work to do," Oden said.

"How did Darius know I'd be coming?"

"That is not for me to say, sir," Oden responded, obviously finished with the discussion.

"Not a problem. Thank you, gentlemen."

As Pallas stepped down the rickety dock, his thoughts swirled. *A young man had built the stables.* All this time, he had been imagining a wise master with many years invested in the craft. For a time, he had even doubted whether the structure was man-made at all. The engineer was more eager than ever to find this lost prodigy.

— XIV —

I T HAD BEEN MONTHS SINCE THE GREAT FLOOD
destroyed the mining operation. With Archer's world washed
away, Citius and the others were now setting posts and beams
from one of several floating workstations. The mining warden
had called in outside help. Nero hired Flavius, a local builder with
a reputation for quality workmanship. A Roman citizen, Flavius
had been sent north during the rebellion to oversee the construction of several outposts for Lord Alexander. Nero had lured him to
Saltz Mountain with a promise to pay handsomely in salt.

The engineer arrived with twenty of his most trusted carpenters. At first, he had impressed all involved with his all-or-
nothing attitude. His crew adopted the handful of former miners
who had somehow survived the flood. The slaves worked day and
night to get the floating work platforms in place. The undertaking
was getting off to a great start until it came time for Flavius to
perform the actual task at hand. The Roman was a well-trained
builder of traditional structures. He was hard-wired for formulaic construction practices on even soil, with good lighting and
ample room for error. In other words, he was a well-renowned,
glorified box-builder. Four sturdy walls and a roof was his bench-

mark. Flavius was far from incompetent; he just lacked the raw talent the task demanded.

It only took the engineer a week to recognize Citius as an asset. As the days became months, more and more of his duties began to pass to the veteran miner. The slave's background in shipbuilding was instrumental in the successful completion of the floating work platforms. Flavius's crew had great respect for its leader; it pained them to see him out of his element.

The inherent danger of the endeavor weighed heavily on Flavius. The builder knew enough to know better. The proposed network of Archimedean screws was a sound design; it was the mine's parameters that made his stomach turn. This scheme was originally used to transport large amounts of water up a mountainside. Under the design's conditions, there was ample room for error. Namely, if the enchained network of screw pumps failed at one link, the end result would be a somewhat harmless spillage of water down the mountainside. Here lay the grave danger, for in the mine if any one link in the chain failed, the lower portion of the network would flood. There was nowhere else for the water to go. Meaning the men building the upcoming link at the base of the network would drown. Worse yet, Flavius knew the nature of his position required that he spend the bulk of his time at the base of the network. He would be one false step away from a watery grave for the duration of the project.

As the engineer struggled, Citius was also having a hard time grasping the task at hand. All he had to work from were

Flavius's sketches. They were rendered from what he prayed was an original, much better set of plans. For if these sketches were indeed accurate, the young man feared they were all doomed. The Roman's renderings were conflicting, often lacked key details, and hardly came close to portraying any kind of conceptual understanding. Citius was desperate to analyze the original copy with his own eyes because relying on Flavius's inconsistent sketches could prove fatal. Unfortunately, out of fear of losing his only hope for success, Nero kept the project's plans under lock and key in his personal quarters.

Flavius was very caught up in the dimensions of each specific link in the chain. However, much of the design had to be reconfigured, which nullified all of the original dimensions. Still, he clung to them. What Nero was asking of him required a complex engineering background. The stick-builder could not visualize how everything was supposed to be pieced together. The concept was not foreign to Flavius; Romans often used water power in order to wash away soil and uncover precious ore. His mind was just incapable of the necessary divergent thinking required to adapt to the cavern. Out of frustration, he was desperately trying to force the original scheme to work in the depths. In doing so, he was dooming them all.

Not surprisingly, the project began to fall behind schedule. Nero's most trusted guard, Dimitri, had been ordered to spy on Flavius. He would visit the jobsite often under the guise of wanting to gamble with the Roman work crew. During his visits, he watched the engineer fumble with his sketches and witnessed multiple setbacks. Flavius would spend a week having his men build an item; then he would spend the next week having them take it all apart. Furious with the lack of progress, Nero stopped letting the carpenters leave the mine at the end of each workday. Flavius's men were allowed to surface only once a week; morale quickly began to deteriorate.

Soon after, Nero ordered that Flavius report his progress in person, weekly. In the coming month, all the carpenters noticed a change in their leader; he would snap and lash out at his crew over trivialities. The men began to grumble amongst themselves. Most wanted to leave the mountain; they were tired of being worked like slaves. Meanwhile, supplies were piling up outside the mine. Large beams, massive spools of rope, and hundreds of drums of tar lay in the yard waiting to be installed. Nero was growing more restless as he watched the materials pile up. They were occupying ever-growing sections of his compound. His anxiety was warranted; after all, it was hardly a covert operation with such massive stockpiles on display.

As the clock ticked, Dimitri watched on. He witnessed the engineer becoming more useless with each passing week. The agent's reports to Nero worsened; the warden's plump sidekick remained in the mine for weeks at a time, keeping a close eye on the operation. Completely out of touch, Flavius began to reveal to Dimitri that he relied strongly on one of the slaves. The spy watched the Roman builder continually confide in one young man in particular. More importantly, he noticed the more often Flavius was seen discussing the project with this slave, the more work was done that week. The pattern became undeniable; this slave was the key element that progressed the project. Flavius was actually slowing the job down because this slave was dependent on his renderings of the construction drawings. The Roman spent most of his time out of the shaft painstakingly sketching details from the plans to show this slave.

Dimitri was a keen observer, with an uncanny knack for reading between the lines. Flavius's men did not even realize they were being interrogated. Dimitri listened to their responses, but he also drew accurate conclusions from what they did not say. It was no wonder that Nero placed so much trust in his associate. Even still, the lord refused to believe that a slave was leading the Roman carpenters in constructing his complex network of screw pumps. He explained to his loyal servant that, more likely than not, Flavius was explaining his sketches to this slave. As the weeks passed, his spy's reports continued to state otherwise. Meanwhile, the warden's weekly meetings with the engineer were becoming increasingly redundant. Flavius struggled with specific details and avoided fixed schedules at all costs.

Coming apart at the seams, Flavius confided in Citius, "I am going to quit. I cannot build this. I am losing my mind—working in torchlight, the cold, the echoes. I can't take another day of it."

"You cannot quit, sir," the slave responded.

"I know it will be difficult for all of you moving forward. Unfortunately, no amount of riches could convince me to pass another month locked away in this prison. This project is simply not buildable. The plans do not account for any of the conditions we are toiling with down here. By gods, if one link in this chain fails, we will all be killed. This job is a *death sentence*."

"That's not what I mean, sir." The builder gave his helper a fearful look. The determined miner continued, "That overseer, Dimitri—he has been watching our every move. Your men mentioned a new guard found his way down here a month back. Nero had him killed that day. The level of secrecy with this project is—"

"I know," Flavius blurted, "but I have no choice. I just have to convince the warden that his secret is safe with my crew."

"Sir, you may have a chance, but believe me when I say this: your crew now shares my fate." Flavius looked so defeated and broken; it was difficult for Citius to watch him crumble. The engineer was well aware that the warden had not let his men leave the mine for two weeks.

"I have to try. If I do not plead with Nero, we will all die. This design cannot tolerate these conditions. It will fail, and we will all be drowned or crushed when it does. I did not come here to die, boy."

"You need to get me the drawings," Citius demanded.

"Damn it! Haven't I told you? Nero won't let the documents out of his sight. We have to try to reason with the man."

"Then we are all dead men, because there is no reasoning with Nero."

"Citius, you have been trapped down here for too long. Your paranoia is understandable, but—"

"Believe me, Flavius—that man is only loyal to *salt*. You share no banner; he is not a Roman. He is barely even a man. Even if we do successfully drain the mine, he will kill us all. We have to take action."

"Listen to yourself. What are you proposing—rebellion? Conspiring to kill a Roman nobleman? Do not put me in a position—"

"By gods, Flavius, understand this: whatever amount of salt you have been promised, it is too much. A single grain is more than Nero could ever stand to part with. Believe me, he would cut you down for a handful. If you think you are going to help him steal this sea of salt and then walk out of this rock alive, *then you are a fool*."

"Another disrespectful word and I will turn you over to the warden myself," Flavius snapped.

"As soon as Nero discovers that he does not need you, he will kill you."

"No doubt, this rebellious attitude of yours is what damned you to this salted tomb. You are wrong, boy. I had considered bargaining to purchase you. Now that you have shown what an ungrateful little beast you truly are, I see that I was mistaken. I have no use for a man like you."

"Flavius, wait—," Citius pleaded, regretting he had let his temper get the better of him.

"That's enough, slave. Get back to work," the Roman roared for all the others to hear. Although out of earshot, Dimitri had watched the entire exchange unfold. The spy did not need to hear a word to know what he had just witnessed.

The next time the pulley lowered the platform to the work-station with materials, Dimitri was sure to ride the lift back up to the outside world. When the hoist jerked the circular platform off the raft, the floating work deck swayed in the dark water beneath its expanding shadow. Returning to the surface, the lift carried scrap lumber and empty tar drums out of the depths. As Dimitri emerged, his eyes strained to adjust to the torchlight. When the hoist's cranking ceased, Nero's trusted agent rushed off to tell his master about this argument between Flavius and the barbarian.

Later in the workday, the Main Pulley lowered again. Roughly fifteen guards descended on the clamoring worksite. It caught everyone's attention when the platform stopped a little over ten feet from the water's surface. A brief silence followed, during which the guards lowered a wood-rung rope ladder down to the floating work deck. This was unprecedented. Immediately, a great tension swelled in the still air.

"Flavius," the largest guard barked, "Nero wants to meet with you."

"I will report to Nero at my scheduled weekly meeting. If he ever wants this job to be finished, *he needs to stop interrupting*," the engineer shouted. The tone in his voice was strangely defensive; the men stopped working. All eyes turned to the suspended platform.

The guards drew their swords. This rallied Flavius's loyal crew; they armed themselves with sledgehammers and picks. The workers huddled around their leader; they jeered and stomped, rocking the floating workstation in the dark water. The guards were well aware that they were greatly outnumbered. Fortunately, from their elevated position, the crew's numbers meant nothing.

"You will come to meet with Nero—*now*," the overseer snapped.

"If that bastard wants to meet with me, he can come down here himself," Flavius roared back.

A particularly enraged carpenter began hurling stones at the guards. There was plenty of debris on the rafts from chiseling out footings for the crossbeams. Four or five more of Flavius's crew followed suit. The guards used their shields to remain out of harm's way as they pulled the rope ladder back up onto the platform. Stone after stone slammed against their shields. The mob below was becoming unpredictable. Citius took the opportunity to make his way toward the stored food and fresh water.

"Flavius, stop this madness at once," spat the lead guard.

"Damn you all to hell," roared one of the builder's loyal subjects.

"To hell with Nero," barked another.

The Roman carpenters had not seen the light of day in over two weeks. They were ready to fight. Citius could feel the rage in the air; he had hoped to convince Flavius to escape. He wanted to rebel, but not like this. The young man knew all of the cards were on the table now. He took cover and filled his flask with drinking water.

Flavius grabbed hold of a nearby torch and hurled it up onto the suspended platform. Unlike the stones, the torch was a real threat. The lift's deck was slick with tar from hauling the drums of black slurry down to the worksite. On impact, a section of the hoist burst into flames. Several guards fought to stomp out the fire. When one of the workers reached for a second torch to hurl at the soldiers, Nero's archers were ready. They fired with deathly accuracy into the brazen man's chest. The arrow-ridden carpenter fell backward off the work raft into the pitch-black brine.

The smoldering mob erupted; anything and everything was hurled at the swaying guards. A volley of torches bombarded the tar-slicked platform, and the blackened timber ignited. All at once, the overseers were engulfed in violent flames. Several guards instinctively leapt from the burning lift to escape the well-fueled fire. The fallen were mercilessly bludgeoned to death by the enraged swarm churning below. Wild cries echoed up into the storehouse, shaking the great stone walls. The lead guard had been in many battles; he did not panic. The former soldier gave the signal to raise the platform and instructed his men to stand on their shields to snuff out the flames.

Many of the stones and tools flung at the henchmen hit their mark as the lift cranked the defenseless guards to safety. Several were struck in the head by makeshift projectiles. Their injured bodies either collapsed into the flames, or they lost consciousness and fell into the bloodthirsty mob raging below. The workers cheered victoriously as the pulley cranked the platform upward. A great wave of madness swept through the rebellious crowd. The roars thundered throughout the cavern as the handful of guards who remained standing were slowly cranked out of range. The light from the tower above was blocked as the lift rose. The platform was hoisted up out of the portal in a cloud of black smoke; Nero's storehouse filled with the stink of simmering tar.

Swaying on the deck with the rest, Citius was forced to realize the painful truth—the lift would never touch down on the work raft again. They would never escape. His plan to coerce Flavius into seizing control of the lift station was no longer an option. Ahead of the curve, while the others celebrated, the veteran robbed their stores. He drank as much fresh water as he could and snatched whatever food he could find. Staring into the dark water, the young man thought of Arielle and Petrarch. At least they were free.

The victory was short-lived; during the week that followed, no food or drinking water was lowered to the imprisoned workers. Nero, like his predecessor Pyranus, understood that starvation and compromise often went hand in hand.

— XV —

AFTER LEAVING LUCINDA BEHIND AT THE FISH-
ing village, Pallas rode his horse hard. As instructed, he
followed the river north through the forest. He arrived at the
man called Darius's establishment by late afternoon. The engineer assessed the make of the buildings. They were of sound construction but lacked what he was searching for. Undeterred, the
foreigner approached the house and rapped on the door. A mid-
dle-aged man, who certainly appeared to be of Roman descent,
answered.

The landowner was annoyed with how this wanderer had
hammered on his door. "Who are you?" he asked in a gruff voice.

"I am here to purchase a boat, my friend," the outsider replied.

The man was unconvinced. "I have never seen you before."

"Does that matter? Is this a shipwright's establishment or
not?" Pallas pressed. With that, his hand reached into his cloak
and emerged with a bulging sack of coins. The oaf's eyes lit up.

"Like I said, I am here to make a purchase. Now—are you
Darius?" the wealthy drifter asked. The merchant's eyes were
fixed on the straining coin purse. He snatched his cloak and

stepped out of his house in a hurry.

"Yes, sir—that I am. Let's head out to the shop and have a look, eh?" he answered with a winning smile.

"Of course, that's why I am here."

The proprietor escorted his customer out to the workshop. The prodigal salesman stood by impatiently as the indecisive foreigner looked over the some three dozen boats. The crafts varied in size and quality. Most were ancient, covered in dust and cobwebs. The newer-looking vessels were by far the worst; all were haphazardly slapped together. Pallas was limping feebly around the shop. Feigning disability, he required Darius's assistance from time to time.

The shop was a disorganized, neglected mess. Sawdust lay all across the floor and birds were nestled in the rafters. It seemed the men were correct in their summation of Darius's operation, for he had certainly let his father's business decline. The shop's aisles were overcrowded with crates and barrels; none of the tools had been cared for. As the old man limped through the mess, one dust-covered boat caught his eye. He ran his open palm across the smooth-finished planks and brushed off a few cobwebs.

The merchant took notice and piped up, "Ah, I see you have taken a liking to that one. That is the last ship my father built before he died." Darius lumbered over to his slow-moving customer. The rickety floorboards strained under his massive form.

"Yes, this is a very fine ship, indeed," Pallas replied, inspecting the craft. "Your father built this?"

"That's right, my old man was renowned for his craftsmanship," Darius replied. He took a long, assessing look at the outsider. "I hadn't planned on selling this boat, it being my father's last."

Pallas realized the oaf was simply attempting to drive up the price; he played along to keep the man talking. The hobbling drifter set his coins down loudly on the table at his side and said, "Merchants can't afford to be sentimental."

"She is the last of her kind in the valley. You will not find another like her," Darius assured him.

"So I hear."

"Last of its kind," he blabbered on shamelessly.

"What does a craft like this typically go for?"

"It all depends," the owner said, beaming ear to ear. The hulking salesman was dusting the boat vigorously to expose the well-formed woodwork. He lifted it up with ease; Pallas took note of his strength.

"That's understandable, Darius. But of course, I must inspect the piece for flaws before I make an offer."

While in conversation, the hefty shipwright carried the boat over to the display stand. The days had gotten shorter and the sun was already setting. The bullish merchant was scrambling around to light a few torches. He was careful to avoid touching all the bird droppings that speckled the workbenches. Once he had situated the boat so his guest could inspect its spine for integrity, he took a step back. Finally, the boat's true beauty was revealed by the torchlight.

"Come, see the seamless construction," Darius beckoned. "I assure you—my father out-did himself with this final piece." He eagerly helped his crippled customer over to the workbench. Leaning forward, he blew a thick coat of dust off the finely honed timber. The dust swirled and plumed in the torchlight.

Amidst the turbulence, Pallas's eyes moved over the vessel. There it was, that single word, burned into the boat's spine:

CITIUS

Darius noticed his customer was staring at the brand etched into the wood. With two meaty fingers he attempted to rub the letters off, only to discover they had been seared into the woodwork. He had not known of the brand's existence until now.

"Well, it seems my old man already named this one for you," Darius said with a nervous chuckle. "*Citius*, that's right—fast. She's ready to hit the water, my friend." Pallas ran his fingers across the black seared letters, inspecting their authenticity. The outsider knew the mark; he turned to face Darius. The oaf stood a full head taller than his guest. The Greek's eyes turned to stone. Beneath his cloak his left hand grasped the iron bar.

"Where is Citius?" Pallas demanded. A bewildered expression crept across the merchant's face. Then there was fear. Cursing his foolishness, he sized up the outsider. Darius glanced at the sack of gold, then lunged for the drifter's throat.

A lamb became a lion. In a violent upward burst, Pallas broke the massive man's outstretched forearm with a powerful blow from his iron bar. In one fluid motion he ducked then drove a hard right hand into the Roman's rib cage. In an instant, the wolf had snatched a wood chisel off the workbench. A moment later, the rusted blade was firmly placed at his victim's throat. The gasping bull stopped dead in his tracks. Pallas grabbed a fistful of the brute's hair and forced him to stare at the single word etched into the vessel's spine.

"Where is Citius?" he roared.

"I—I—," Darius scrambled for words.

"You, you—what? Spit it out, boy—before I rip out your throat."

"That slave had no business—"

"Listen closely, you fool. That slave should have been your master. You are going to tell me everything I need to know to find this *slave*. Rest assured, if the young man is dead, I will return. In the end, you will beg for death."

"I sold that ungrateful little runt. The boy spent more time fishing and swimming in the river than building boats. What good is a lazy slave?"

"A lazy man did not build *this*," Pallas shouted, slamming his hand on the pristine woodwork.

"I had to chain the boy to his bench to get him to work. My father had spoiled the little bastard rotten by the time I inherited him."

"I know when a man is lying, Darius. Only a no-good, talentless excuse for a man like you would sell that kind of talent to the mines."

"Who said I sold him to the mines? I did no such thing."

Desperate to control his fury, Pallas clenched his wrought-iron bar. Remorseless, he smashed his captive's outstretched fingers with the blunt weapon. "I'm asking the questions, you insignificant roach."

"Please—please—," Darius slobbered. The oaf's mangled fingers were instantly torn and bleeding.

"If not the mines, then where?"

"That little shit was shaming my house—my own daughter. They were in need of carpenters. I unloaded the scoundrel." He choked the words out with his eyes fixed on his brutalized hand.

The Greek pushed the rusted chisel into the roll of fat on the back of his victim's neck. "Give me a reason not to kill you, boy. I assure you—nothing less than the truth can save you now." There was no remorse in his dead eyes. The shaking oaf prepared to speak.

"Most all who knew the young man died in the rebellion. I alone am left to give testament. I figured Alexander would send someone to kill me—and here you are."

"You know Alexander?"

"Of course I know him," Darius spat. "You should ask that fat tyrant where the boy is; he owned him longer than I did." The merchant watched as the outsider's face went blank.

"He controls all the information in his domain," Pallas muttered.

"The fuck he does," Darius sneered. Without warning, the snarling wolf slammed his captive's head onto a chop block strewn with bird droppings. He grabbed a mallet and held it threateningly over the Roman's head.

"Tell me everything."

The squirming merchant was stunned by the old man's inconceivable power. Wracked with pitiful sobs, he choked out his words gasping and spitting for air. "He probably even knows you are here now. A man would have his heart cut out for talking. Alexander does not tolerate betrayal."

Without a word, Pallas began to press the shank into Darius's neck. The drifter's ghostly silence was terrifying.

"Alexander himself banished that boy to the mines! That's right—he caught that barbarian bastard with his prized servant girl. Alexander is a jealous man," the pitiful heap finished, sobbing hysterically into the filthy chop block.

— XVI —

WHEN THE MAIN PULLEY finally lowered just over a week later, the once-fearsome mob had been reduced to a dumbfounded flock of sheep. The starving slaves stood in silence watching the platform fall. The crank echoed through the silent cavern. The prisoners had only one torch left; it burned pathetically at the work raft's edge.

Light from the tower's portal fanned out across the crowded raft. The lift's shadow slowly tightened, focusing in on the gaunt-faced workers huddled below. This time, the lift stopped twenty-five feet above the floating work deck. The guards remained out of sight. They had learned from the riot. There was no longer an angle to hit them with a thrown stone. As the suspended platform swayed, a longer version of the wood-rung rope ladder that had been lowered a week earlier was provided.

"Flavius—Nero wants to meet with you," said a voice from above. The man did not bother to yell, his words echoed across the dark water.

The defeated engineer addressed his crew, "Men—you have all served me well. There is no sense in prolonging this any further. I fear I have destroyed us all. Forgive me." No one replied;

all of them understood that they were now doomed to die in the mountain.

Flavius's feeble, starving muscles barely had the strength to cling to the rungs. The rope ladder swayed as he climbed. When he finally reached the top, the workers watched a couple guards pull his shadow onto the platform. There was a brief scuffle. Soon after, his lifeless body fell from the platform. The corpse slammed hard into the floating work deck; the raft rocked in the dark water. A few carpenters rushed over; their master's throat was cut. All eyes moved to the rope ladder looming above.

"Nero wants to meet with the slave called *Citius*," the guard shouted over their murmurs.

The young man's name rang out in the cavern. Citius gave the others no parting words. He walked across the deck to take hold of the ladder. The men watched in silence; no one envied his position. When he reached the platform, the guards yanked him up. The workers below heard a great disturbance; the suspended lift swayed violently as the barbarian was beaten into submission. The rope ladder was reeled in as the pulley's ropes drew taut.

The great ropes whined as the massive gears cranked the lift toward the light. The prisoner was chained at the wrists and ankles. No slave had seen the light of day since the institution of Pyranus's system. Well aware of this, Citius feared the worst. The guards joked rudely amongst themselves as the pulley cranked the platform up into the tower. Upon witnessing the stone silo's construction, the young man realized why so few dared to try escaping on the hoist.

The emaciated slave fell when the lift came to an abrupt halt.

"Ay! What the hell was that for? You bumbling donkey—a little warning next time would be nice," the largest guard shouted at the operators.

"Up, bitch. On your feet," another grunted at Citius. The brutes kicked the slave to get him to stand.

Four archers appeared above with bows drawn and aimed squarely at the prisoner. Citius jerked in dreadful anticipation. The thugs yanked his chains as all the access ports surrounding the tower swung open simultaneously. The barbarian could see heavily armed soldiers at each window. Long spears slowly emerged from the murder holes. The guards stepped aside to allow the spears to surround the prisoner. The slave's chains were drawn taut; the rambunctious guards went silent. The sharpened spearheads stopped inches from him as he heard the flexed bows creak into holding position.

An unidentified man outside the towering entry silo shouted, "Is the slave secure?"

"The prisoner is secure, sir," a guard shouted back.

Flogs dropped from above; the instruments thudded onto the great wooden platform. The shrill voice seethed, "Let him know whose mine this is."

The spears withdrew from the prisoner. The guards reached down and grabbed the whips. The hooks and shards had been removed; even still, the flogging that followed was tremendous. They alternated lashings methodically. All involved were waiting for the order to stop long before it came.

"That's enough," the maniacal voice finally called out. The guards loosened their grip on the chains and Citius collapsed to the floor. The miner hit the platform hard then passed out from exhaustion.

"Get the little cuss cleaned up. I can smell his stench from here," the voice called out. The bowmen above the platform chuckled. The sinister voice continued, "Toss him in the brine so his wounds don't fester. Minimal food and water shall be provided. I have something to take care of in my quarters. I should be finished by the time he's been tended to."

"Yes, sir—Lord Nero, sir."

The unconscious barbarian was thrown into the dark pool of brine in the storehouse. The slave awoke immediately, thrashing about in the shockingly cold water. The guards' laughter erupted, echoing throughout the empty cave.

"Ah, hell. The little shit can swim," one of them grumbled.

"Little cockroach can float," another growled.

Despite the cold, Citius became calm floating on the surface of the deep pool. The salt water was soothing, but it stung the fresh wounds on his back. The guards tugged his chains to pull him to the pool's edge. The bread he was given was stale but excellent. He was also allowed a small bowl of drinking water before the guards took hold of his chains. They escorted the prisoner through the large double doors that concealed the storehouse. From the outside world, it would have been impossible to realize the enormity of the cave hidden behind those walls. When the great doors opened, the light of day shocked the prisoner's eyes. The brightness was intense given his years spent in darkness. The guards chuckled at him stumbling blindly through the snow.

The brute manning the chains to Citius's left was particularly obnoxious. He kicked and shoved the prisoner to keep him pacing. "Come on, little girl. Get moving," he sneered.

It was cold but warm enough that the sun was melting the white powder. The icy path was freezing the slave's bare feet. Eventually, his eyes adjusted to the bright light cast by the sun's reflection off the dwindling layer of snow. They were leading him up the mountain toward a small building in the distance. Just then, the door to the dwelling swung open. A fair-haired girl stumbled out. She hobbled toward them. Her clothes were disheveled. As she drew closer, her condition became apparent. She had a fresh black eye and a cut lip. When she noticed the soldiers, she kept her head down.

The obnoxious guard could not help himself. "Ah, you're lucky, boy. It seems Nero is in a good mood today; the little bitch only has one black eye." The others snorted, trying not to laugh openly at the poor soul.

The girl, broken and battered, looked up in shame at the man who mocked her. She reminded Citius of the women who cared for him as a child. She reminded him of so many others he had chased in his youth. The stumbling woman's defeated eyes met with his; they ignited a violent rage within the staggering prisoner.

The cruel guard felt the chain in his hands snap. In an instant, he found himself yanked toward the barbarian. Citius drove his elbow mercilessly across the bridge of the cruel jester's nose. The blow was well aimed and powerful. The brute collapsed into the slushy mud, bleeding profusely from his shattered face. The outburst had taken the others by surprise. They all rushed to secure the man's chains as he kicked and lashed out viciously.

The broken woman looked on as the burly guards struggled to corral the emaciated savage in the slippery slush. She drew strength from her countryman's relentlessness. The slave wiped the tears from her battered face and held her head high as she made her way past the pandemonium.

— XVII —

AFTER HAVING A BITE TO EAT, NERO STOOD AND paced around the room, drinking his wine. He seemed distant, locked away in his own thoughts. Suddenly he spoke from behind Citius's wooden chair, "Boy, you speak my language like someone who knows how to read it."

"Yes, I can read Latin. I—"

"Spare me, *slave.* I don't need your life story. Short confirmatory answers will more than suffice."

The looming spider was noticeably pleased with the barbarian's response. In passing, he handed him a bundle of scrolls. Then he leaned on the table across from his guest, savoring the contents of his glass. A pair of wolfish beasts stood guard, watching the slave's every move. Citius unraveled the parchment as the towering Roman spoke.

"Introductions are not necessary. You know that I am Lord Nero, the Warden of the Mine. As for you—who you are has never mattered to anyone. As such, you sit here." The host was very comfortable talking down to his guest. Citius recognized his voice; this was the man who had ordered his prolonged beating in the entry tower. His anger was well hidden behind the documents.

After he felt the young man had taken enough time to view the drawings, Nero spoke again. "This network was designed for the gold mines at Las Medulas. It was there, *with this design*, that Roman engineers transported enough water to wash away a mountain. In doing so, all the gold buried within was revealed. Far from buckets, is it not?"

The prisoner did not answer right away. He was too focused on the documents, beyond impressed with the plan's intricate details. Finally, he responded, "This is where Flavius's sketches came from?"

"Yes. I'm not surprised that the conceptual nature of this undertaking seems new to you, given the limitations of both Flavius and his renderings." Nero downed his glass and filled another. The warden poured a second glass and handed it to Citius; the slave was grateful for the drink.

"I told the guards to show you we meant business." Nero was assessing his prisoner's beaten face. "It seems they got a little carried away. I apologize."

"I'm fine, sir." For the moment the only thing on his mind was the wine. He had already identified Nero as the man who personally ordered his flogging. The fact that the warden felt the need to lie about what happened in the tower did not affect him.

"Very well. My sources tell me that you are solely responsible for *any and all* progress thus far," Nero offered, still unconvinced. He was searching the slave's eyes for any evidence of deception. He found none.

"Don't worry, I am not going to test your knowledge. The truth is, you hold in those scrolls the only assistance I can give you. I judge results. I don't care how you do it. Just rest assured, your life depends on the swift and successful completion of this project."

"That seems fair enough," the slave responded. His glass was empty. The warden took the jug over to his captive and filled the young man's glass to the brim. Citius was shocked by the dreaded warden's hospitality.

"Good man," Nero said. He could not stop a subtle grin from forming on his chiseled face. The smile must have felt uncomfortable because the Roman grimaced. His cold stare fixed on his prey, analyzing the barbarian. His trust was hard to come by.

"My friend, you have the look of a Roman's bastard," the lord jabbed. "No doubt after centuries of occupation there are thousands with your features running around this land. Abandoned by your whoring mothers to be shunned by your countrymen. Of course, it is just as possible that you are the product of two illegitimates with similarly blended features."

"I would not know, sir."

"You see, I breed dogs and horses. As such, I have a unique understanding of such things. You seem to have been fortunate enough to inherit the Roman's keen mind. This is likely why you learned Latin with such ease. The point being, we share some amount of ancestry—"

"I would not know, sir," the barbarian interrupted.

"Unfortunately, you are noticeably tainted. You stand out like the mutt you are."

"Yes, I am grateful for my *Roman mind*."

"As you should be. Know this, young man—the task at hand is unforgiving. If I do not see results, your crew will not eat. I do not barter, and I never negotiate. Your crew will succeed or starve," the noble declared. There was no anger in his tone. He was calm. Even still, the threat was sincere.

"Get me quality timber and some decent tools. Do this, and I will get you your salt. There's more in that water than there would be in a decade's worth of rock. Although I am not sure how you plan to get it out of solution."

"Leave that part to me, boy. I don't have time to waste explaining my processes to a slave. Winter is fast approaching. Soon, a great wall of snow will isolate us from the outside world. We always wait until spring to send our first shipment. No one will ever know that the salt is out of reach. I can claim that the spring shipment has been stolen by barbarians to buy time. I will bring a war down on the local nomads to cover my trail, if need be."

Citius had already finished skimming through the scrolls. The slave's unwavering eyes met Nero's. The warden was taken aback by the intensity he found. The barbarian spoke, "This design is not transferable to your mine; I will need to improvise. Rest assured, you will get your salt."

Nero was very pleased with the man's confidence. "I dispatched for a forest's worth of timber and enough tar to fill the Main Cavern. In my eyes, everyone in barbarian country is a slave. *Human tools* will not be an issue. Everything has been ordered. I reported a collapse, not a flood. We have precious little time. Know this, slave—if you fail me, it will cost you dearly."

The towering Roman set his glass aside. His long arm reached down to open a sizable wooden chest situated out of sight behind the table. Citius could only guess at its contents. Nero tossed something up over the table. It landed with a thud and did not roll. The warden slammed the chest shut and stared at his captive with an unsettling smugness. The object was a man's severed arm. The hounds that had been resting beneath the table at their master's feet began feasting on the flesh. The snarling beasts fought over the scraps.

The slave finished his wine before locking eyes with the Roman. "They are beautiful animals, sir. I do not doubt your skill as a breeder." Archer's pupil was no stranger to brutal intimidation tactics.

Only the sound of the feasting animals could be heard as Nero decided how to proceed. He was somewhat bothered by his prisoner's calmness in the face of inhumanity. "You are young and arrogant; that's exactly what I need."

Nero snapped his bony fingers; the hounds stopped eating immediately. "Look, boy, you may have led a *somewhat* difficult existence until now. Your hard life may have even made you brave, in the foolish sort of way that the young are. Understand this, *slave*—as long as I own the air you breathe, I can always make you suffer."

"Is that all, sir?"

"*Indifference*," Nero hissed. "Pawns like you are not worthy of the tool."

"I apologize if I have offended you, sir. I am grateful for your hospitality, but I really should get going. There is much to do," Citius responded. The barbarian's piercing black eyes did not leave Nero's as he spoke.

A great sinister grin fanned out across the spider's gaunt face. Feigning amusement he continued, "Boy, you will leave when I deem it so. Your arrogance is remarkable. I take it you were not born destitute. Yet here you sit—at my disposal. What a beautiful world this is. *The gods are good, aren't they?*"

The towering Roman sipped his glass, taking his guest in. "Don't think for a minute that I can't see through you. You do well to hide what is dear to you, boy; eventually, I will seek it out. When I do, you will fall in line like all the others before you." Nero paused to look deeply into the barbarian's determined glare.

The warden continued, "If I had to guess, I'd say you are enchained by the overwhelming lie you tell yourself. You believe in your heart that you are a great man. I pity you. Great men aren't kept in caves. They aren't buried away beneath the earth. You may have talent, but the outside world will never witness your abilities. They will die with you, and like you, *nameless in the darkness.*"

"It would be enough for me, sir, if you died knowing I was great."

In an instant, Nero's eyes went black; his buckling grin did not pair well with their fury. Turning away, the warden downed his wine. Circling his prey, he continued, "You are a pawn—a lowly, rotten prisoner. You loathe your tomb, but you should consider yourself lucky. There was a rebellion; all the others like you are dead. If you had brothers, they're dead. If you had sisters, they've been ravaged. You have been tucked away in this mountain while all your countrymen died in the mud, begging for mercy. All of them were rebellious little shits like you. If not for this salt, you too would have shared their fate. You should be *grateful* to be my prisoner." Nero hovered just inches from the savage's face.

"What will you do with all the salt?" Citius asked, with a forced calmness.

"Ah, that is an excellent question, boy. A man from your strata would not know what to do with such fortune, would he?" The warden wandered back to the table for more wine. This time, he did not refill his guest's glass.

The Roman turned to face the slave. "What came first, the king or the kingdom?"

"The king."

"Precisely—the king forges the kingdom. Before there was ever a kingdom, or an empire, there had to be a king to make it so. *A man of steel*—I am king because I deem it so."

"What of Alexander? This mountain lies in his domain."

"Alexander—*what of Alexander?* Believe me, boy, if you had ever met the man you would know there is nothing to fear. Alexander is old, fat, and gray. Soon he will be dead. *That* is when the man best positioned to do so will assume control of the North. I aim to be that man. Understand, there are many others waiting for that wobbling tyrant to die. Now it is a race to build power without being detected. No man is as well positioned or as equipped to conquer the North as I am. That salt water will be the lifeblood of my force. When Alexander dies, I will take what is mine. They shall call me *Caesar.*"

The barbarian looked hard at the warden. Holding his chains up for emphasis, he spoke, "It seems, then, that we are both prisoners chained to this great block of salt. Tread lightly, sir, for you demand a great deal of this mountain. In the end, your golden chains may prove stronger than this steel."

"Such insolence." Nero chuckled. "Only one man wears chains in this room, boy." Behind his confident façade, there lingered a hateful fear. The young man could tell how dependent the warden was on his genius. All of Nero's dreams hinged on this slave's shoulders.

The barbarian's demeanor changed; Petrarch's teachings filled his mind with astonishing clarity. He felt propelled to speak the Savior's words. "Do not fear me, Nero. For I shall give unto Caesar that which is Caesar's—*and I will give unto God that which is God's.*"

The warden recognized the unruly prisoner's obnoxious

dictum immediately. Overwhelmed with bloodthirsty rage, Nero snatched Citius's throat. Given his meager form, the gangly Roman's immense strength did not seem plausible. Citius was on the edge of consciousness when the animal reluctantly released his grip. His victim gasped and choked for air. The warden flipped his prisoner's chair forward, allowing him to spill out onto the cold floor. The Roman's hounds were snarling and drooling inches from Citius's face, begging for their master's fatal command.

"Know this—on this mountain I am god!" Nero roared, while using his foot to grind the young man's face into the splintered pine floor. "Your god is just. His demands: *salt and sacrifice!*"

— XVIII —

TWO WEEKS AFTER LEAVING DARIUS SOBBING into his chop block, Pallas arrived back at Alexander's estate. Lucinda had insisted that he leave her behind. She could see how eager he was to discover the truth. She knew that having to ride back to the compound at a snail's pace with her belly in tow would drive the warrior mad. Winter had arrived and she was much too far along to continue at a steady pace. The engineer had faith that his woman would be looked after well by her countrymen. He figured word of his arrival at Darius's shop had already beaten him back to Alexander. No doubt, the lord already knew Pallas had discovered his instrumental role in Citius's exile.

The Greek burst into Alexander's study. The Roman was ready. "Pallas, there was a collapse at the mines the winter before your arrival. The mine flooded. I sent for the young man," he paused, watching his listener's reaction. "Pallas—Citius is dead."

"You wasted so much time. Where is this mine?"

"Pallas, the boy is dead," Nicodemus insisted.

"Stay out of this," the wolf roared.

"Pallas—," Alexander warned.

"How could you send that kind of talent to the mines? Over a damn servant girl!"

"It was not my finest hour," Alexander shouted. Shame weakened his glare.

"You are sick with pride. By gods, look at yourself. Did you really think you could compete with a younger man? Damn you to hell, you whoring pig."

"Pallas, I—"

"Damn you! Where is she now? Did you have your way with her then ship her off like all the others? Brilliance *extinguished*." Pallas berated the stammering tyrant with roars that filled the lofted ceilings. "For what?"

"Pallas, you do realize—," Alexander protested, putting on an indignant air as a last line of defense. He was at a loss for words; it had been decades since the baron had been confronted by anyone. Amidst the uncertainty, Nicodemus's hand cautiously shifted toward the hilt of his dagger.

"Long ago, I should have cut you down," the Greek snarled with a terrifying calm. "I should have let your *entitled blood* pool at my feet."

"Pallas, I understand your anger. I do—," Alexander said, not breaking eye contact with his friend. "There was no honor in what I did," he confessed. Regaining his usual unwavering confidence, the lord stood and continued, "If not for you sparing my life, none of this would have been possible. Do not tempt fate by being ungrateful. You never would have come across Citius, if not for my sprawling estate. It's unwise to make wishes against past decisions, old man."

"How do you know he is dead?" Pallas demanded after regaining a fragment of composure.

"I sent for him as soon as you asked. I swear it," Alexander replied.

"Who said the boy was dead?" Pallas shouted.

"The mining warden, Nero. His correspondence arrived yesterday," Nicodemus replied.

"Where is the courier?" Pallas responded. In their moment of indecision, the Romans exchanged accusing glances.

"Probably still on the grounds," Alexander replied, looking to his cousin to confirm his response.

"Yes," Nicodemus sneered, "the peasant is still here." Pallas's stony eyes flashed.

"Send for him," the Greek commanded.

The reality was that it took two weeks to locate Nero's courier. The man had left the compound in a hurry. When they found him, he was brought into the main hall of Alexander's estate by force. Pallas ensured that a good meal was provided for the man. He was well-aware that being dragged back had likely shaken up the courier. In time, the engineer found himself across the table from a jovial little man. Both had full wine glasses.

The entire left side of the peasant's face was bruised, his nose was crooked, and his lip was cut. The man had been given new clothes, which clashed with his grubby calloused hands. The courier had clearly sustained quite a beating, but he was gnawing gleefully on a duck leg and gulping wine between breaths.

"How's the meal, sir?" Pallas finally asked his guest.

"Ah, it's excellent. Haven't had duck in ages. The wine is good—but the duck," the plump Northerner blabbered.

"So, did you carry Nero's letter all the way from the mines?" Pallas inquired. He was tactful in his approach, not wanting to seem too eager.

"Well—not quite. Not that I couldn't have. The mine is only . . . twenty miles . . . from my village," the man replied in broken breaths, barely able to stop stuffing his face.

"How long a journey is it, my friend?" he asked, topping off the courier's glass.

"Good man. Thank you, sir. You certainly know how to entertain," the commoner said, then belched. "It took me two and a half months to get here. Now, I wasn't just carrying this letter. We were hauling furs and goats as well as trading along the way—slows you down. I have heard the trek can be done in a few weeks on horseback—weather permitting, of course."

"I see. Now how is it that you came to hold the letter?"

Smacking his lips, the peasant thought it over for a few chews. "Ah, well now. I was in an upstart village just south of the mountain—on business, of course. Anyway, I stopped at the tavern. There was a fellow in there, much too well-dressed to be from these parts. Dimitri was his name. The whores were falling all over him; the man had more gold than he knew what to do with, see."

"Naturally," Pallas beckoned.

"Anyway, the man was complaining to the ladies about having to leave them to carry the letter. So I told him I was coming through these parts, and that I'd be happy to carry it, for a price of course. Dimitri took one look at the whore at his side, and now here I am." The courier chuckled.

"Fair enough," his host said, offering him another piece of bread.

"Lord Alexander has it all, doesn't he?" The raggedy courier was looking around at all the adornments in the dining hall. "Makes you realize just how little you really have."

"Has the cave-in hurt your village?"

"What—the cave-in at Saltz Mountain?"

"Yes, the collapse at the mines. I imagine it has caused problems for all involved."

"Aw, you wouldn't believe. I'm Amond, by the way. Sorry, so busy gobbling up that duck, didn't even introduce myself. You introduced yourself and I just sat there like an idiot, stuffing my face," the Northerner quipped, before bursting into hysterical laughter.

Pallas patiently let his guest laugh himself out. "How many died?" he finally asked.

"Hard to say, my lord," Amond replied, finishing his glass. His host was quick to refill it. "There he is—thank you." The scruffy man chuckled nervously.

"Yeah, I can't tell you how many died, but I can speculate. We used to send three hundred pigs and nine hundred carts of grain to the mountain annually. This year, we supplied just five hundred of each; what's that tell you? Way I see it, more pigs— that means more guards. And less grain? Fewer slaves," Amond offered, impressed with himself.

"I see." With a change in tone, Pallas pressed on. "Now, where did you get the money for the oxen?" Amond glanced over his shoulder at the heavily armed legionaries standing by and fidgeted in his chair.

Unnerved, he answered, "Well, we have been selling a lot of timber. You see, they have to repair the mine. We are north of most of the trading centers; the mountains keep us isolated. We do what we have to."

"Right, but they would have purchased many more slaves to repair the mine. Why are the villages selling so little grain and livestock if they are repairing the collapse?"

"Look, the whole valley has been asking the same questions you are, my friend," the man replied with a mirthless grin.

"I'm sure," Pallas said, with a convincing smile.

"Believe me," the little man insisted, "when we heard that the mine had collapsed, a lot of people fled. We were worried they'd be snatching up anyone they could find to help repair the mess. They've done it before."

"There were none captured?"

"Not one. Not only that, no one has been allowed on the mountain since. Not even the whores. Now the damn guards come down to our village for that crap." The man was getting fired up.

Pallas quickly refilled his guest's glass, nodding sympathetically. "How much wood is being sent to the mines?"

"Tons. What do you think the oxen are for?" Amond chuckled.

"Right."

"The damn trail up the mountain has turned into knee-deep mud from all the loads of timber. There isn't a tree left on the southern face," the peasant shouted. "Not only that—thousands of drums of tar have been coming from wherever. Ropes too. You should see the ropes."

Entrenched in thought, Pallas did not respond. The wine had eased his guest's vocal cords considerably; the rag-tag trader kept on yapping. "Usually we send a good bit of timber up the mountain. Thing is, it's usually the lowest grade waste wood available. It's amazing those sorry bastards use that garbage for reinforcement. No wonder there was a cave-in." The courier drank deeply from his glass. "Not this time, though. No, sir. *Now* they want only the best lumber available—the very best."

Pallas's thoughts swirled.

"No one is profiting like the blacksmiths. Hell, every smith within a hundred miles of the mountain is steadily making tools and pins for that damn mine."

"Pins?"

"Aye, sir, iron bars, one- and two-foot long. Rumor has it they have their own smiths at the mines. They need stock." Amond dared another large gulp of wine. "I should have been a smith. Always told myself, 'Amond, you should have been a smith.' What did I do? Became a damn goat herder. Well, now I'm in the oxen trade. Things are finally coming together."

"How is all of this being paid for?" Pallas inquired, topping off his guest's glass. Amond fidgeted in his chair again, looking over his shoulder.

The anxious courier answered in a low voice, "Salt."

"*Salt?*"

"Salt," Amond repeated, now noticeably intoxicated. "At first that bastard Nero ran up quite a bill on credit. Then, about seven months back, we all started getting paid in the salt."

"How is it that the entire local economy is thriving on salt when the mine is collapsed?"

"Hell if I know. It's salt, though—high-quality stuff too. It's not the crumbled rock we're familiar with. No—this stuff is like white sand. That's right—just as you'd find on a king's table." The peasant chuckled.

"Refined brine," a stony-eyed Pallas muttered.

"You should see the great plumes of smoke rising from the mountain. She looks more like a wretched, barren volcano these days. Barely a tree on her and always smoking. It's really a sight to behold."

Pallas stood abruptly. The old man slid the rest of the jug across the table. "Thank you, Amond. You have been more helpful than you'll ever know."

Soon after the interrogation, Pallas found Alexander brooding in a distant corridor of his estate. The lord was drunkenly pacing the halls. Many memories and years of regrets accompanied him in these otherwise empty corridors. The ruler was not well.

"Nero has been purchasing timber, iron, and tar by the ton," Pallas shouted as he approached. He was not at all worried about interrupting the baron in his fragile state.

"Right, well there was a cave-in, Pallas," Alexander huffed. "I sent several chests of coins to the mountain to pay for the repairs. Must you remind me of my hardships?"

"*Hardships?*"

"Pallas, leave me be. The boy is dead," the lord snapped. The engineer witnessed shame in his friend's eyes; it seemed the baron was capable of guilt.

"If you sent gold, why is Nero purchasing all the building materials with salt?"

"*Salt*—I sent coins."

"That's right—*salt*. The courier told me everyone is being paid in salt. White sand—not rock."

"Nero, that snake," Alexander roared.

There was little force behind the lord's deep voice. Pallas noticed how physically weak his friend truly was. "Your man has been withholding information," he volleyed on, undeterred.

"Little shit pocketed my gold."

"There are great plumes of smoke rising from the mountain. The fires burn day and night," Pallas fired away.

"Sounds like that thieving rat has built himself a refinery on my mountain. I can't imagine where he is getting the water to make his brine; there isn't a river for miles," Alexander seethed. The exasperated lord began coughing violently.

"Nero is a liar. Citius is alive," Pallas declared, the words hung in the drafty corridor.

"It's possible," Alexander replied. The tired old man guzzled the jug in his hand and then shattered the empty vessel against a wall. "Well, winter is taking hold. Probably already two feet of snow on Saltz Mountain. No sense rushing off to the mines now. I'll just have to wait until spring to chop off that snake's thieving head."

"There is precious little time and we are both much too old for patience. An attack on the mountain is our only option."

"You're mad! You should have left for Rome weeks ago if you wanted to get home in time to meet your first grandchild. Think of your daughter. Think of Adriana. Hell, you stashed your pregnant lover in a damn fishing village, by gods, man. You need to get ahold of yourself."

"What if you or I were to die before spring—what then? What havoc could a man like Nero wreak with a great fortune at his disposal? The courier told me that he's rumored to have smiths at the mines. He's importing iron stock—possibly fashioning weaponry. No—the time has come to strike. I need your fastest horses. Whatever men you can spare from your personal guard will do. I leave at dawn."

"You and Lucinda are leaving for *Rome!* What has gotten into you? You are like a raving lunatic over this. It has become an obsession. I will not let a man of your age walk into a war with a man like Nero. It's not happening. I will send Nicodemus."

"I am going to that mountain with or without your blessing. This has become bigger than any of us." Unmistakable envy swelled in the Roman's eyes. His friend had lost none of his fight. It pained him to think of how weak he himself had become. The white wolf would march toward the mountain alone if it came to it.

"The die is cast. I will dispatch the whole of my army on the mountain. I am not well, Pallas. I fear death has finally come to my doorstep. If I were not so weak, no man would have ever dreamed to betray me like Nero has. *Blacksmiths on Saltz Mountain?* Damn my frailty—it has allowed for this deceit. With my last breath I will show the world what happens to those who defy me. My family's reputation is all I have left now."

Pallas could see Alexander giving in. His friend was weak and dying. "The army will move too slowly. I need whatever horses and men you can spare, and I need them now."

The Roman's eyes went black.

"Consider it done. Nicodemus will meet up with you later

in the week. My nurses are bringing Lucinda back to the compound. I assure you that she will be looked after."

Pallas clasped his old friend's hand and spoke with the highest respect, "You are a man of honor."

As they approached the torchlight, Alexander noticed the blade sheathed at the white wolf's side. "Do you still remember how that thing works, old man?" the Roman asked with a wrinkled smile.

— XIX —

"CITIUS, CAN I HAVE A WORD?"

"Good or bad?"

"We are enslaved in a salt mine, sir."

"Right, Thaden. Well—get on with it then."

The slaves were standing on a towering scaffolding at the top of what had been the underground lake. Several work crews were clamoring beneath them, toiling to operate screw pumps as long as trees that ascended in a multi-tiered zigzag formation from the depths. The entire cavern had already been drained and the lake had been pumped down considerably. What remained was a perilous crater that dropped steeply for nearly a hundred feet to a dark pool at its base.

"There have been whispers, sir."

"Drop the formalities. What is it this time?"

"Many of the men blame you for what happened to Anthony."

"That boy was a damn fool. I warned him not to trust these people."

"Easy now—keep it down, or they'll be after me next," Thaden pleaded.

"I must have told him a dozen times not to talk openly about rebellion. I warned him that we have had a steady trickle of newcomers since this project started."

"I know, sir."

"I told him as plain as day, '*Nero has spies.*' Hell, at first I wondered if Nero sent Anthony down here to stir the pot—flush out any potential rabble-rousers."

"I know—but that's the rest of it. Some of the others have gotten it in their heads that *you* are Nero's spy. They believe that you were involved in Anthony's assassination, and they want—"

"By gods, to hell with these flea-bitten scavengers. Let them come! I'd like to see any one of the bastards outperform my standard. Cursed whores—none of them rushed to help the man when that newcomer stuck a dagger in his chest. All of them stood by."

"I know, sir—Anthony's murder was a low point for us all." Thaden was unable to help glancing over his shoulder. The young man wanted Citius to lower his voice. He continued in a hoarse whisper that he hoped his commander would also acquire, "To hell with these people. We are North men; we need to stick together. Don't worry, most of the others from these parts are with you. Maybe it's time we set up a united front against these entitled foreigners."

"No, we can't afford to divide ourselves any further. These men are bound by more than blood."

"Alright, just don't let those be your last words. I have to say, though, it didn't really help your case when you spoke Latin to the assassin before you killed him."

"The son of a bitch spoke Latin, Thaden. What language would you have spoken?"

"Look, I've known you for two years. I know you. These newcomers—they don't. When they see you speaking, reading, and writing in Latin, it raises doubts. As always, it would go a long way if you stopped favoring the Christians."

"Don't worry, Thaden. I'll handle this."

The servant locked eyes with his leader. "Sir, one more thing—it's not mutiny. Rumor has it they are going to kill you."

"Love your neighbor as yourself," Citius grumbled in Latin.

"See that—that bit right there—that's exactly the kind of shit you need to stop if you want to make it out of here alive. None of us know what the hell you're saying," Thaden scolded in a hushed voice.

"Who do you think is getting out alive?"

"The newcomers have insisted that the warden assured them everyone would be released upon project completion," Thaden declared. Citius could not help but smile; he had underestimated his advisor's gullibility.

"Listen to you—you are far worse than the Christians. At least they have enough sense to focus on existence after this life, if we are calling it that. Released? We are talking about Nero, right? A man who has an untold number of spies amongst us. His eyes and ears have always been on us, and they will be until he kills us."

"Yes, but—"

"Don't trust anyone."

"Understood, but listen—most of us are still with you. Just watch your back."

Thaden slung his pick over his shoulder and descended the scaffolding en route to his workstation. Citius's eyes were fixed on the sprawling network; he feared the project was nearly complete.

It had been almost three years since the Great Flood. The network of Archimedean screws the slaves had constructed in that time was astounding. Thousands of gallons were being lifted out of the mine each day. The largest of these titanic man-powered straws contained a tar-smeared corkscrew large enough for a man to climb through to apply the black slurry as needed when leaks occurred. This was the pump that conveyed water across the Main Cavern, from what was the original surface of the underground lake to the largest stone basin. An expansive scaffolding was in place to support the pump. U-shaped cradles with well-oiled iron rollers dispersed the barrel's weight across the bedrock while allowing it to rotate freely on its fixed axis.

Hundreds of slaves walked on top of the tar-smeared cylinders to rotate the watertight helixes encased within. The men treaded on the barrels for hours on end. With continuous motion, the pumps sloshed the water up into each successive wing of their integral spirals. In defiance of gravity, the brine climbed from the depths. The water passed from one screw pump to the next until it was deposited into the largest basin—a fail-proof pond carved into the cavern's floor. From here a towering water pulley, powered from above, hoisted the brine in barrels up to the storehouse. At its peak, the lucrative liquid was poured into a channel that flowed through a carved tunnel into Nero's refinery. The crank never stopped lowering barrels into the storage pond. The slaves could not sleep unless there was enough brine on hand for the night. Fortunately, the screws were so effective that the storage pond was nearly overflowing at the end of each workday. The refinery could hardly keep up with production.

The material hoist was constantly cranking up scrap wood or lowering supplies into the shaft; it could not be expected to haul the brine up through the tower. The water pulley was Citius's answer. It was a very well-guarded weak point in Nero's defenses. The gear assembly was located at the back of the storehouse, roughly forty feet from the entry tower. Nearly a dozen guards manned the elevated crank, which hoisted barrels of brine into the refinery. If these men ever felt threatened, they would cut the ropes. Only a handful of prisoners had tried to climb the enchained barrels; the archers used them for sport.

As intended, the chain of screw pumps lifted the great lake of salt water from the mine's depths with minimal use of human labor. This network branched off deep into the largest shafts until all of the easily accessible water had been removed. Citius did not toil with the smaller caverns where efficiency would be lost to cramped conditions. He was quick to notice that most of the water eventually seeped down into more accessible locations. Nero's goal was to pump down as much brine as he could, as quickly as possible, to maximize his gain while the price of salt remained high.

Citius pushed the slaves to build and work—not for Nero, but for themselves. For him, it was important to build great things regardless of the circumstances. He built because he loved construction; Nero's spears did not drive him. The threat of death was not necessary to bring the best out of him. The others were inspired by his abilities and determination. This great construction would be proof of their existence to the world. This vision was what the builder used to turn a battered mob of slaves into a fine-tuned machine. Of course, whips were kept on hand to aid those who lacked self-motivation.

The barbarian understood that once all the water had been pumped from the mine, Nero was going to kill them all. His crew would be the only living proof of the great thievery. Citius was not fooled by the warden's empty promises of freedom; he knew the truth. As they successfully drained the shafts, the crew's pace slowed. Many feared the project's completion. The mine had already been pumped down enough to resume regular mining operations, but Nero's greed had spared them all for the time being. With the infrastructure and materials in place, the warden demanded that they pump down the underground lake.

The lake had rested for centuries toward the back of the Main Cavern. This reservoir of salt water predated both Nero and Archer's arrival at the mines by several generations. It had occupied the far corner of the cavern for as long as anyone could remember. The inconsumable salted pool had tormented droves of thirsty miners for long enough.

The crew worked double shifts. The conditions were worse than ever. With the end in sight, Nero began cutting rations. They had already pumped the underground lake down well over one hundred feet. No one could have ever dreamed it would be so deep. The farther they went, the narrower the crater became. The tighter the quarters, the more dangerous the operation became. Good footings were hard to come by. The slaves were forced to transport massive beams down the treacherous slippery slopes. The jagged salt formations and delirious half-starved workers did not mix well.

On several occasions, men fell or their legs gave out from exhaustion. Death began to plague the workforce. Some were crushed by beams, while others drowned. The worst off were those who mishandled the boiling tar. The quarters were so tight that the hot tar was now being rushed down the slopes in small five-gallon batches. Men had to crawl through the giant timber cylinders slathering tar over the corkscrew flaps. This way the screws would hold water as they turned. Slowly but surely, the brine spiraled upward from one storage pond to the next as the men below toiled to construct subsequent basins, which strained to hold back the water between lift stations. For efficiency's sake, the pumps had to be angled upward on the hypotenuse of an imaginary right triangle. As a result, sizable amounts of rock had to be removed on several occasions to unearth reliable pivot points for the screws.

A couple of storage basins had burst over the past year, due mostly to the fact that Nero had begun grudgingly withholding nails, iron bands, and all other metal materials. The warden's smiths needed stock; his true ambition had begun to unfold. Whenever a basin failed, torrents of water cascaded down on the workers at the base of the operation. The massive splinters of wood laced in the rushing water were lethal. Fatalities were kept to a minimum as the weaker, less-skilled workers died off. Those who could not swim often refused to work at the base of the network. The working area had become far too narrow. If an elevated storage basin failed, they would likely drown trying to swim to the surface. To bolster morale, Citius manned the base with those brave enough to join him. All respected his knowledge and unshakeable faith in his own abilities. Self-reliance had always been his salvation.

Up above, Nero rejoiced at the long-standing lake's inconceivable depth, for he was amassing an unimaginable fortune. The Roman had not seen the slave called Citius in nearly two years. His spies had not given him any reason to do away with the network's designer. Given the young man had produced so well, the tyrant never bothered to reconvene with him. After all, the warden could not be happier with his self-motivated slave—a genius, abandoned by the outside world. As the salt poured in, the wise barbarian's existence faded into the shadows of the Roman's staggering fortune.

The day after his conversation with Thaden, Citius was hard at work at the base of the network. He had been brooding over dissension in the ranks, and debating whether or not it was time to construct a second water pulley. Another pulley would be costly; the ropes had to be imported. The screw pumps were becoming inefficient given how cramped the bottomless crater was becoming. He climbed up onto a ledge that until recently had been under water. The point where he stood was roughly one hundred feet below the original surface of the underground lake. The famished builder was struggling to locate a decent footing for their next beam.

There Citius was, covered in tar and soaked to the bone, standing where no man had stood for centuries. When he pulled himself up onto that ledge, he felt it—*a draft*. He watched as the smoke from their fires was drawn into a small cave, accessible from the ledge. He had wondered why it had taken so long to pump down the lake. By its visible cross-section, the lake was not large enough to warrant the great mass of water that the pumps strained to pull from its depths. Surprisingly, it had taken them months to get the lake pumped down to this point. It was now apparent that a much larger portion of the lake had been concealed by the rocks, hidden out of sight. The clever miner realized he was now standing at the point where the two adjoining lakes met. More likely than not, the Great Flood two years before had been caused by the miners undercutting another underground lake, like this. This made sense, but the draft was perplexing.

Citius looked over his shoulder; no one had noticed his absence. His men were busy repairing a scaffolding that had been torn apart when a basin above failed the day before. Great fires provided light and warmth for the emaciated crew; the men brave enough to work the base never needed to be lashed.

The barbarian's heart raced as he inhaled the smoke, which swirled through the faint torchlight into the dark tunnel. He remembered all of the tales about there being a way to escape the mine by finding the entrance to the long abandoned Northern Shaft. These fables had persisted through generations of miners, despite there being no proof of any link whatsoever. All had heard the myth that there was a place where the two shafts met. The young man had even spent his early days searching for this long-lost path to freedom. No wonder no one had ever found the escape route. It was locked away, below over a hundred feet of frigid brine.

The slave's sharp mind played with the idea. He could not be certain; it was just as likely that this tunnel led to nowhere. It could snake upward and exit back into the same cavern. The builder was aware that this configuration could also cause a draft, but that would not explain the great excess of water they had removed. Desperate to avoid suspicion, he kept on working as usual and showed no sign of his inward struggle. The builder found a suitable footing for the beam away from the ledge that hid the drafty tunnel; the rest of the shift was business as usual. The others noticed no change in his mood. Citius dared not tell a soul; anyone could be one of Nero's spies. The barbarian knew that if they all attempted to escape, none would make it. If the salt water ever stopped flowing into the refinery, the guards would seize control of the network and Nero's spies would point his forces toward the escape route.

That night, after a brief internal debate, Citius made his decision. The young man did not take much convincing; after all, it was die tomorrow or die when the job was done. He had already been warned that some of the others were after his head; there had never been a better time than now. The wise slave knew he could not just run off. The warden's eyes and ears were amongst them. The cave would eventually be discovered, and Nero would send his guards after him. This could end in a fate worse than death. No, it would have to be an all-or-nothing break. Even if the tunnel led to nowhere, he would rather die trying to escape than be turned over in chains to Nero. His plan was to simultaneously blow several of the elevated basins. The escape route was just above the new water level, so the floodwater would cover his trail. His hope was that after the disaster, the entire crew working at the base of the network would be presumed drowned.

As the designer, Citius knew full well that if a basin failed, the one below it could usually handle most of the floodwater. Even two failing was possibly survivable; so long as the men kept walking on the corkscrews, the water could be controlled. The overflows would slowly bleed off the excess pressure until conditions leveled off. However, if more than three failed at once, the weight of the floodwater would be tremendous. Many of the men walking on the massive cylindrical screw pumps would likely be blown off their stations by the raging water. Gravity would soon take its toll; the pumps would spin freely, letting their water rush out into their basins. In time, all of the reservoirs would swell. Under this pressure, they would begin to blow in succession, until the drafty cave was covered by what Citius calculated would be roughly twenty feet of icy brine. This would be more than enough to cover his trail.

No one would be able to locate the cave in the pitch-black water. Even if they could swim down and find it, they would never be able to hold their breath long enough to work their way back up twenty more feet, after who knows how long of a horizontal leg, to reach the air on the other side. After flooding his trail, Citius would be presumed dead. Of course, if anything went wrong he would drown; this was a risk he was willing to take.

The young man woke the next morning in a cold sweat. Uncertainty was churning his empty stomach. He was not sure how long he would have to run through the cave before he could start climbing upward to escape the floodwater. He prayed that the time delay on the basin failures would allow him a large enough window to escape a watery grave. Even worse, if the cave led to nowhere, Citius would either drown or starve. There was no time to explore the tunnel. The longer he waited, the less water there would be to cover his tracks. Now that they had pumped the brine down below this hidden link to the larger portion of the lake, their job would progress much faster. Death upon completion was imminent. If this mission failed, he would die, but at least it would be on his own terms. If he delayed, his crew could reach the bottom of the lake sooner than expected; then Nero would dispose of them all.

The builder figured that without his help, it would take his crew several weeks to repair the damaged network. Then it would be a couple of days at least before they pumped the water down low enough to expose the tunnel. This left Citius at best about a month to either slowly starve, escape, or drown in the process. That said, he knew he would only be able to carry enough fresh water to last him a week, two at the most. In the end, all options were preferable to being disposed of by Nero.

The designer spent most of the shift directing his crew away from the drafty tunnel, ensuring it remained undiscovered. Guilt had already begun to set in. Many men who trusted him would die to cover his trail. Lost souls who had looked to him to lead them for nearly three years would drown as he escaped. The leader reasoned that they would all be eliminated once the project was complete. They were dead men, be it by his doing or Nero's.

At serving time, Citius looted the storage cavern. This was fairly easy considering he held the only keys to the barrels of fresh water and chests of preserves. After they ate, the rest of the miners departed to get some much-needed sleep in what was once

Archer's cavern. The wise slave slipped back to the work area to sabotage his network. He climbed the scaffolding with purpose, for he knew every critical joint within his design by heart. Using the many dangling ropes, he swung from platform to platform with a great sense of urgency. The builder went to work on his masterpiece, plugging overflows from top to bottom; now the basins would not shed excess weight quickly enough to prevent rupture. Within hours almost every weak point was set to fail. Afterwards, he climbed down to the base of the network to hide his bundle of stolen supplies at the entrance to the tunnel. The bandit had garnered several torches, hand tools, two jugs of fresh water, and rations for his journey.

The time had come for Citius to loosen the anchoring pin on the largest vertical screw. The barbarian had saved the worst for last; if he was not careful, the entire multi-ton pump could come crashing down on top of him. The others would be awake before long, so there was no time to worry.

Citius knew how well he had trained his men; sabotaging the exposed pivot point at the cylinder's peak would not go unnoticed. Therefore, he had to dismantle the pivot point at the pump's base. The last five-foot portion of the fifty-foot-long pump barrel was submerged in the water. Its central support beam continued an additional ten feet down to the solid rock that made up the basin's floor. It was here that the pivoting assembly was located, fifteen feet underwater at the bottom of the largest manmade pond. The assembly was fixed into the rock. The mechanism was dependent on an iron bar, which was three feet long and three inches around. This critical member was usually rusted in place within a matter of weeks.

The brine was not kind to iron. Even with many coats of hot pitch, the salt would eventually gnaw away at the metal. Citius had already replaced the assembly's pivot bar twice since the initial installation. The workers had watched the salt ruin their tools and metal stock in the months preceding the largest pump's construction. Because of this, the builder had designed a geared mechanism that would pull back on the pump barrel to take the weight off the fixed axis. He realized that, at the very least, the iron would need to be replaced annually; regardless of how well they coated it in tar, the salt would eat away at the metal. Of course, when doing routine maintenance he had the luxury of being able to drain the reservoir of water in order to service the pivot assembly. There was no time for that now; not to mention, if the workers returned to see the basin empty they would immediately suspect foul play. Fortunately, it had only been two months since Citius had last replaced this heavy iron bar. He hoped that rust had not completely locked it in yet.

The young man would be blind beneath the black water, so he would have to undo the mechanism by memory and feel. Citius worked the service crank to pull back on the fifty-foot barrel. The ropes screamed against the massive weight of the screw. Several trees' worth of lumber had been used in its construction. The geared mechanism was designed to be operated by two men.

The slave's muscles burned as he struggled to hoist the pump up out of the water. Once he had raised it about four feet, he locked the pulley and shimmied down the ledge to the water's edge. His plan was to replace the iron axis point with a bar a third of its size and at least a half-inch less thick around. This size bar was exactly what they used at the base of some of the smaller screw pumps. He would have to shim the smaller replacement in place. He wanted to wedge the faulty bar well enough that it would hold just long enough for all of the workers to man their stations and begin pumping brine from the depths. This would ensure a maximum flow of water to cover his trail and give him time to get to the bottom of the network.

The shorter bar would not be supported by the bedrock at its base. As dozens of workers walked on the pump's barrel to spin it, the integral helix would slowly fill with water. As it scooped up the brine, the weight of the fifty-foot-long tube would increase tremendously. This would eventually exert enough force on the poorly sized bar to dislodge the metal shims that held it in place. When the warped shims sprung loose, the thinner, shorter bar would slip out of the bored hole located at the bottom of the central beam. Then the faulty anchor would fall down into the crack in the rocks. Without a fixed axis, the pump would begin to skid down its supporting rollers. The axis point at the top of the barrel was not designed to support the entire screw. Especially not when it was filled with water; it would fail under the weight of the spinning barrel. The titanic screw would crash down into its massive manmade basin's tar-covered, wood plank barrier. The retaining wall would rupture on impact, flooding all the subsequent basins beneath it. With their overflows plugged, the basins would begin to fail in series—this was the plan. That said, if shimmed too tightly, the faulty bar could remain wedged in place. It could possibly hold for days, which would ruin the miner's plans entirely.

There was little room for error in the task at hand. Citius's heart was beating eagerly; he felt freedom. Taking a deep breath, he dove into the dark water. The iron axis was set in place by several months of pressure that the towering screw had exerted on it. It had taken Citius nearly an hour to beat the rusted bar out of the rock the last time he had replaced it. It was not long before a thick layer of rust locked the iron into the rock. Now he would be forced to perform this task submerged beneath fifteen feet of brine. He swam down to the bottom of the basin and felt around blindly for the protruding bar. When he found it he quickly secured a rope to it with a slipknot, then pushed off for the water's surface. He burst from the reservoir, gulping at the air above. Clinging to the rope, he swam across the pond, climbed onto the pump, and secured the rope's other end to the pump barrel's lowest iron fastening band.

With the tether secured, he scurried back up the ledge to crank the service pulley, tentatively raising the massive pump a couple more inches out of the water. In doing so, the rope linking the submerged axis point and the pump's barrel was drawn taut. Citius was not sure how much tension the iron fastening band could stand; it had certainly not been designed for this application. Watching the rope line pull to maximum tension, he gulped. He did not want to push his luck. There was no time for the band to spring loose or the rope to snap.

Now there was adequate tension pulling up on the iron bar. An added bonus was that Citius would not have to search for the axis in the dark water anymore. He could pull himself down the rope to reach the assembly much quicker. The job was moving along, but the work had just begun. The builder tethered his hammer to his waist before diving back into the frigid brine. He pulled himself down the rope to the anchoring pin. Immediately, he began wailing on the fixed bar with his heavy hammer. He was blind so he missed several times, managing to bloody up his knuckles in the process. Fighting through the pain, he was well aware that the water was necessary. It silenced his pounding hammer; if not for the deep water, the clanging would wake the entire mine. The surface above was calm; there was no evidence of the man who struggled below. His lungs screamed for air. He scrambled for the surface again. Twice more he ventured down to beat on the pivot point, but it would not budge. The cold began to take its toll; the shivering mastermind was becoming disoriented.

Chancing disaster, Citius scrambled back up the ledge to the top of the pump. He labored to turn the gears on the service pulley a few more times. The builder was worried that the barrel's iron band would break free under the tension of the rope. Even still, he dared to crank the pulley a few clicks more. The thought of the cold water made him gamble. He exhaled a great sigh of relief; the band had held. The rope was now as tight as he thought it could get without snapping. There was no flex in it, as it extended down from the base of the barrel to the anchor below. The rope was exerting an uncontrollable amount of upward force on the bar. The builder had to be extremely cautious because when the connection finally decided to give, the taut rope would yank the iron in a powerful jolt. The bar would be ripped out like a missile from the rocks. If the prisoner happened to be in harm's way, the blow could be fatal.

Again and again, Citius dove into the water to pound on the bar. He swung his hammer until his muscles burned. Working against the water on limited oxygen was exhausting. The young man began to fear that the anchor was set too firmly for him to beat it free with the water slowing his swing. The delirious miner was not sure how much longer he could stand the cold. He began to chisel away at the rust that had built up where the iron rose out of the rocks. When he could not stand the cold any longer, he pulled himself up out of the water and stood on the pump's barrel.

The slave's eyes moved up from the black pool to look down at everything he had created. The many torches that speckled his sprawling network illuminated its edges. The towers of scaffolding that ascended from the depths, the catwalks, the pulleys—all of it—where it had come from, he did not know. Where his mind drew its wisdom from, he could not explain this either. In the end it was just iron and timber; it meant nothing now.

As hard as it was for the prideful man to kneel, he did. The designer set self-reliance aside and thanked God for giving him the opportunity to free himself. He was grateful that the Lord had finally put his life in his own hands. Then the truth rushed forth; the Holy Spirit's wisdom allowed him to realize that he had never been bound to this mine. He had been beaten by fear time and again, for he had been given a mind capable of escape. He had been given a will to fight, but instead he clung to his gifts for fear that they would be lost. The great man had believed himself too important to risk. He had cherished himself. Nothing was his if he lived in fear. A man could not believe in God and fear death.

With a renewed zeal for freedom, the young man dove off the screw. He surged through the black water. Blocking out the cold, he beat the bar until he thought he would lose consciousness. The believer fought for nearly an hour, alternating between chiseling the rust and pummeling the iron. Without warning, the metal burst from the rock in a violent shot; the straining rope snapped like a whip as the tension released. Citius narrowly avoided the rocketing missile. Desperate for air, the warrior erupted from the surface of the calm, dark water.

Joy filled his heart as he swam toward the basin's edge. He took hold of the faulty support, then leapt back into the frigid brine for what he hoped would be the last time. He could not ignore the cold now. In the blackness, he managed to find the gap in the rocks where the original bar had been fixed in place. He frantically began wedging the shorter, thinner replacement into position. As the builder worked, he was careful not to let the iron slip into the hole. There was no time for mistakes. After several attempts, he finally got it to hold at what he prayed was the correct angle.

Citius labored to reverse the service pulley. The architect watched the multi-ton screw pump slowly submerge into the still pool of brine until the watermark at the barrel's base met the dark water's surface. This was the moment of truth—it would have been easy to make a mistake in the blackness. There was only one way to be sure: Citius would have to rotate the screw; if the monumental barrel were able to spin freely, then its axis had been set perfectly.

Instinctively, the builder anchored his rope to a point roughly ten feet down the pump's barrel. Then climbing through the scaffolding, he wrapped it several times around the wood-planked cylinder. He took the free end of the rope up over the elevated beam that supported the pump from above. From here, he slip-knotted the rope to a hook, then attached it to one of several pulley mechanisms the miners used to safely lower heavy loads down the crater's steep slopes.

The delirious slave began to work the crank.

The rope choked tightly around the barrel, which in turn began to rotate the pump. Ingenuity—this was how Citius could test the pump without the help of the others. Slowly but surely, the empty screw revolved on its fixed axis. The miner winced every time the barrel rotated on its faulty pivot. Once the rope had unwound, the pump's momentum allowed it to undulate freely. The designer's anxiety was warranted, for the pump's main support was now only temporarily shimmed in place. Satisfied that the axis-anchor was properly set, Citius removed all the evidence of his night's work from the surrounding area then raced off to the sleeping cavern for warm clothes and some much-needed rest. He could not sleep; excitement pulsed through his veins as he lay in wait.

The following morning, the builder begged forgiveness for what he was about to do. He knelt, but he kept his back straight and his head high because the Almighty has no time for a trembling man.

Citius made his way down to his workstation at the base of the network without any hint of the disaster he had set in motion. He knew the food stores he had robbed the night before would go unnoticed until the following evening. More likely than not, his thievery would never be discovered. Following the impending catastrophe, most all would assume the remaining survivors had stolen the goods amidst the chaos. When given the opportunity, the men would always bash off the locks and raid the storerooms. Citius knew he could depend on the looters. In a fog of exhaustion, he made his way with the others down the enchained ladders, ropes, and platforms.

The crew climbed down the rickety scaffolding into the massive crater in the earth as they had for months, always unsure of whether they would be fortunate enough to climb out again at the day's end. When they arrived at the base of the network one hundred feet beneath the sabotaged pump, spirits were high. The builder had not been the only one up to no good the night before. One of the men had bartered with a guard for a jug of liquor; the grunts passed it around enjoying the fiery contents. Pure salt would accumulate when shallow puddles evaporated in the shaft. The guards manning the material hoist were always more than willing to trade for it.

A slave handed the jug to his leader; Citius drank deeply. He was not sure how long it would take for the vertical screw to come unhinged, he just knew that it eventually would. The stress of anticipation was more than he was prepared for. The entire morning was unbearable. He gave orders to his men as usual, knowing many would soon be dead. The slaves joked with him, and the shift progressed like all the others before it. All the while, Citius did nothing to warrant any suspicion.

The builder took pride as he watched his crew, for he had invested a lot of time in teaching his workers. Aside from the dark circles under his eyes, their leader seemed no different. His bloody knuckles also went unnoticed; these sorts of injuries were commonplace for salt miners. Two dreadful hours passed in which the vertical screw churned on without fail. The men were a little more rowdy than usual, thanks to the liquor. The morning went smoothly. Citius even began to fear that the pivot point would not give at all. The young man choked down his guilt and waited.

They were in the process of hoisting a massive crossbeam into position when chaos erupted above. The faulty axis-anchor had failed. There were only three men with Citius at the base of the network when the vertical screw crashed into the massive reservoir at its base. They all heard the rushing water long before it came. The torrents roared down on them. Cascading jets knocked the slaves from their feet as they scrambled for the ladders. The dangling beam swung away, nearly killing two of the workers. The miners scrambled and fought against the rushing water. Citius grabbed hold of the ladder and pulled each of the others up onto it. The men scurried up the ladders with rushing water raging past them.

There was a great crash as the weight of the water caused another elevated basin to fail. Another explosion rang out; the chain reaction was unfolding much faster than the architect had planned. Powering on against the rushing water, the wise slave followed the others up the first ladder.

Then, amidst the confusion, Citius vanished.

— XX —

IN TIME, NERO'S SPIES POINTED HIM TO THADEN.
Bodies were still being pulled from the rubble and floodwater.
All knew that the designer had always worked at the base of the
network. Thaden was brought to the surface and taken to Nero's
quarters for questioning. The master was feasting at his table
when the barbarian arrived in chains.

"So, can you tell me where he is?"

"Citius is dead, sir." This was the only logical response
Thaden could give. Nero could see it pained him to admit it. Even
with a spear tip at his throat, the slave's answers remained consistent.

"What caused all of this?"

"We are still trying to figure out what went wrong, sir. Many
of the network's moving parts are dependent on iron assemblies.
The salt eats away at the metal. We service them often, but the
brine is becoming increasingly concentrated. Citius always com-
plained that we were not being given enough iron stock."

A grin crept across the warden's gaunt face. The thought
of the salt water's increasing potency pleased the lord. "Very well.
I shall see to it that more metal is sent down to complete the re-

pairs."

"That would go a long way, sir."

The warden paused to groom his hounds. "My other agents tell me that you managed to get close to the man. I wonder—what was it that drove the scrawny bastard?"

"I believe he enjoyed the challenge, sir. He taught us that without struggle there cannot be progress."

"Right—just another shit simple barbarian mule."

"Yes, sir."

"Well, what had we agreed upon again?" Nero asked, unlocking the slave's shackles.

"Five coins for each year served, sir."

"Ah, was it five—you know, I'm only offering three to the others now. Very well, so that would make it ten total then."

"Yes."

The warden pulled a sack from his chest and counted out the money. The hounds at the warden's feet growled as Thaden's eyes danced across the glimmering silver. The warden handed the slave his money with an all-encompassing smile. "Dimitri tells me that you were the best of them all, young man. Your correspondence was instrumental in this project's success. I just want you to know that, my friend."

"Thank you, sir."

Thaden took his silver from the lord. The Roman smiled at the young man. The slave hesitated. Nero bade him on, "You are free to go, my friend."

With that, Thaden made for the door. He exited Nero's lodging and stepped out into the blustery winter wind. The guards stepped aside, making way for the slave. He trudged through the storm, taking in the majestic valley that spanned out before him. He had survived. It would all just be a bad dream now. The young man had not made it twenty yards when nearly a dozen arrows found their mark. The sack of coins fell from his hand and Thaden collapsed lifelessly into the cold, wet snow. Nero's hound crept up through the white blur. The beast ignored his master's victim. The man lay slowly dying in the harsh wind. The animal took the sack of silver in its mouth and trotted through the storm back to its master.

Several days had passed since the collapse with no results. The slaves finally stopped finding bodies, but Citius was still nowhere to be found. The remains of most all of the other men working at the base of the network had been exhumed. The buoyant corpses tended to surface quickly in the salt water. The men assumed their leader's body must have been pinned down beneath the collapsed structure. In time, Nero reluctantly accepted this explanation; the warden gave the order to stop the search and begin repairs immediately.

Luckily for Nero, Citius had explained his adaptation of the Archimedean screw network very well to the other workers. He had informed his men that he did this in case he died. Knowing they would now be forced to complete the project without him, they were very grateful for his instructions. All knew how difficult this project was; even though they were enslaved, the men appreciated their accomplishment. The slaves relished in the way the occupying force stood in awe of their great construction.

The crew had come to mirror Citius's intensity. The builder's pupils went back to work as they thought their leader would have wanted them to. As they toiled to get the network operational, all those who had conspired against him regretted their poor judgment. After all, the towering conglomeration of pumps was the only evidence of their true worth; Citius had put their real value on display. The accomplishment commanded respect, and they owed it all to him.

As the week progressed, some of the more skilled workers began noticing the remnants of Citius's sabotage. Most of the evidence had been washed away or crushed, yet by the end of that first week one indisputable truth remained: this was no accident. Plugged overflows continued to be uncovered; moreover, ropes thought to have snapped appeared to have been cut, and several critical load-bearing timbers had undoubtedly been notched. Unbeknownst to the crew, Dimitri was keeping a close eye on the renovations. He rushed off to bring the word to Nero.

The warden had personally come down to the mine that morning to inspect the situation with his own eyes. He witnessed the extent of the damage caused by the partial collapse in what was once the underground lake. There were piles of bodies waiting to be burned. Most of the network had been unaffected by the disaster a few days before. The Roman stood in awe of the engineering before him. As he looked down at the massive construction, he remembered the barbarian's words: *It would be enough for me, sir, if you died knowing I was great.* The warden had been building an army. As such, he had ample manpower to seize control of the mine. His men had a firm grip on the slaves below; Nero did not fear rebellion. Dimitri was beyond surprised to see his master when he rushed toward the hoist, for his commander had never set foot in the cavern until now.

"Sir, it appears the network was sabotaged. The slaves' doing, no doubt," Dimitri blurted out.

The servant was shocked by how calm his master remained upon receiving this news. Nero stood by the massive stone basin, marveling at the monumental network the young slave had built. The gears, the pulleys, the lifts—everything was woven together seamlessly. The machine pumped the sea of brine hundreds of yards up to the reservoir behind him. From there a towering water pulley lifted the lucrative solution in barrels into the cave above. Finally, it flowed into the storehouse's newly constructed refinery. Even now, dozens of archers remained in place to defend this weak point.

Nero spoke, "This was a truly awe-inspiring undertaking." The plump guard was perplexed; he had expected the Roman to go mad with unbridled rage.

"Yes, sir. I have to admit I have never witnessed anything quite like it. Your plan was flawless, sir."

"You know, it's a shame the gods dealt that young man to me." Nero's mood was far beyond unusual; his servant had only ever heard the lord mock the gods.

Dimitri spoke freely, "Not many others would have been willing to give a slave the opportunity, my lord."

"In the end, it's our inferiors who define us." The warden's eyes moved away from the network. "So then—it was a final act of defiance. I've met Citius's type before. Some men are willing to die to prove a point." As it was, Nero could not help but commend the young man's fury.

"It appears that way, sir," Dimitri replied. The thought of Citius destroying the network himself had not occurred to the warden's agent. He had thought it was the work of a rebel faction amongst the crew, not one man's doing.

The Roman's cold stare fixed on the expansive scaffolding—the wood, tar, and iron. He spoke over Dimitri, "The mutt knew I'd kill him in the end. I should have kept him under lock and key once the others had realized his vision. No matter—the bastard wanted to die on his own terms. If he was willing to sacrifice his followers to spite me, *so be it*. Let him burn in his Christian hellfire." The warden allowed himself to grin; the barbarian had made him richer than he ever could have imagined.

"Precisely, sir. I did not see it coming either," Dimitri huffed. "One more thing: the men need their rations, sir. I—"

"What?"

"The men—I mean the slaves—they are out of food," the

agent stammered.

"It has not been two weeks. What did they think? That their failure would be rewarded?"

"Their stores are out, sir. They didn't even eat yesterday."

"I take it food was stolen," Nero snarled. Rage swelled in his beady dark eyes as he chewed on his words. The Roman's mind was assessing what the slave had accomplished—what the barbarian was capable of. The entire project was teaming with defiance. Every gear, pulley, and timber voiced the builder's name.

"It was chaos. I'm not surprised." Dimitri chuckled, not realizing the gravity of the situation. The loyal subject watched Nero's eyes go black; the warden did not believe in coincidences.

"Sound the alarm," Nero seethed.

"The alarm?"

The Roman charged at his bewildered associate. In a blind rage, he snatched his trusted servant up by the neck. His long, cold fingers tightened around the man's throat. The subject witnessed a never-before-seen fear in his master's eyes. Nero was scared. As the warden's grip tightened, his victim's eyes bulged. If Citius were to escape, he would talk. This could not happen. If word of his thievery ever made it back to Rome, the lord would be finished.

"You—you—you let that Christian mutt escape," Nero roared. By the time he had loosened his grip, the man was dead. The other guards standing by were shocked by the warden's insanity. Only Dimitri had ever been able to influence their master.

All among them already feared the warden's wrath. Now they distrusted him even more. If he were willing to kill Dimitri, he would kill any of them. Unflinchingly, Nero let his subject's body fall past him to the cold stone slab.

The warden called to the guards, "Sound the alarm. Send ten men around the mountain at once to reinforce the exit to the Northern Shaft; *Citius has escaped!*"

"At once, sir."

"Guard—I did not dismiss you," Nero shouted. The man stopped in his tracks and turned to face his master.

"Yes, sir," he belted out.

Nero was so enraged that he was barely able to speak. The teary-eyed tyrant choked his words out painfully, "I want . . . *that coward . . .* brought back to me . . . *in pieces.*"

A slave laborer was walking by Nero with a heavy load in hand. The Roman slammed the broken-down man hard into the cave wall. The guards watched in horror as he ruthlessly beat and ripped at the old man. The animal tore off the unconscious prisoner's cloak then tossed the bloodied rag to his guard. The subject caught the tattered garment but held it away from himself disgustedly.

"Take my hounds with you. Give them that stench."

"Absolutely, sir," the guard responded. All knew how the warden felt about his prized war hounds. The fact that he intended to unleash them on Citius spoke volumes.

"Once the boy is in sight, release the hounds. Then bring

whatever is left of him back to me. That is all."

"Yes, sir—Lord Nero, sir." The guard took off up the shaft more eager to get away from his commander than the mob of starving workers.

A young slave had been hiding on the ledge above them the entire time. The child had heard of Citius's sabotage and supposed escape. Once the warden ascended out of the shaft, the boy sprinted off. Citius's secret was safe with this scrawny eavesdropper; he did not tell the others. After all, there was no real proof. Nero just had a hunch. It was just as likely that the designer brought down the network and killed himself to spite the Roman, which was what the other slaves already believed to be true. They all thought their leader had fought back against Nero the only way he knew how. The starving mob was inspired by Citius's final defiant act.

Rebellion was in the air.

Around the mountain, at the exit to the long-abandoned Northern Shaft, Thadius stood guard. He had spent another peaceful morning hunting small game from his sentry tower. The old man sipped his jug and took in the view. It was just before noon, the awful blizzard that had rattled the walls of the outpost the night before was finally losing momentum. Snow still fell, but with much less intensity. There was now a deep layer of fresh powder on the frozen ground. The soldier was busy whistling a long-forgotten tune when he heard the alarm: three consecutive blares from the ancient horn at the southern face. The horn was accompanied by a quaking drum. He waited. It was probably just a drill. Then the horn and drum sounded again; three consecutive booms quaked across the mountainside. Thadius stood in disbelief.

"That's the *escape signal*," he growled.

The young men under his command exited the warmth of the outpost to investigate.

"Was that the escape horn?"

"Aye—that it was, boy."

"Is this a drill?" another asked, bracing against the freezing wind.

"I fear not. Get geared up," Thadius called to his men.

Pecius made his way out of the barracks into the fading flurries, already dressed for battle. He shouted up to Thadius, "Is this some kind of a joke? Did some drunken mercenary get ahold of the warden's horn?"

"You tell me, boy—is Nero one for practical jokes?" Thadius boomed back with a whiskered grin.

Pecius slammed his decorative war helmet onto his head. "No—not in the slightest."

"Gear up," Thadius commanded. "They're probably sending reinforcements to relieve our watch. In this snow, it could be hours before they get here."

"At least," Pecius huffed. The cold was already getting to him.

"No worries, men. We have drilled for this," Thadius shouted. "Mind your training. We will handle these runaways. I want two men outside the shaft, one at the entrance to the barracks, and two at rest, staying warm. We will work in shifts, so you all don't freeze."

"You don't seriously think anybody is going to walk out of that mine—*do you?*" Pecius questioned.

"That's the only reason they'd sound the horn, boy," Thadius barked.

Pecius obnoxiously threw his arms up in jest then he trudged over to the abandoned shaft's entrance to take first watch while there was still daylight. Thadius was annoyed by how the noble smugly leaned against the post. More than anything, though, he got a kick out of how ridiculous the young man looked in his fancy plumed war helmet. The veteran smiled because he knew the centurion helmet had to be freezing; it was not winter issue.

"Bring me extra furs," Thadius commanded. "Start warming some others by the fire. I am going to need new warmed furs every shift change, so I don't freeze."

"You aren't seriously going to stay up there all day?" Pecius protested.

"You better get serious, Pecius. This is not a drill," Thadius barked.

The disenchanted noble shrugged and shook his head. Thadius enjoyed watching the pompous little schmuck shiver at the post in his ridiculous formal gear. Once again, he could not help noticing all of the overgrowth outside the shaft. Around where Pecius stood, several bushes and saplings obscured his view of the abandoned mine's exit.

"You lazy dogs! How many times did I tell you to clear that brush?" he shouted at his men. Pecius waved him off, dreading the fading sun.

"Damn ingrates," the bowman grumbled.

— XXI —

CITIUS HAD LOST TRACK OF TIME IN THE UN-
ending darkness. Loose stones spilled as he climbed; the
only sounds were of his own breath and the occasional drop of
water that fell from the ceiling above.

There was no chance of returning to the mine; black water
had filled the tunnel behind him. Doubts remained as to whether
or not he had found the abandoned shaft. The cavern was just as
likely a forgotten flooded arm of the mine he knew well. If this
was the case, he may have sealed himself off in what would become his tomb. Above all, he knew he had to snuff out negative
thoughts before they overwhelmed him. He was convinced that
he had begun wandering in circles.

There was no time for uncertainty, and his resources did
not allow for foolishness. To get his bearings, the young man
stopped looking for an exit. Instead, he retraced his steps to
round up all the waste wood he had come across. He piled the
ancient debris into a great heap at a highpoint in the cavern floor.
Once he was satisfied with the size of the mound, he lit it. The
flames gnawed at the timber until a great fire burned; he needed
a beacon to guide him. With a sizable fire burning in the distance,

his search for an exit intensified. Now, instead of passing by any wood he stumbled across, he hoarded it. Whenever an opportunity presented itself, he would light an additional beacon fire. With multiple guides in place, he began mentally mapping out the cavern. He would not retrace his steps again.

With his supplies dwindling, Citius increased his pace and slept less. He was desperately waiting to feel a draft, the sign of his route to freedom. In time, hunger and thirst began to take a toll on his self-confidence. The fugitive had stolen more than enough supplies to last him a week. Unfortunately, the holding basins had blown faster than anticipated; nearly all of his stash had been washed away. Guilt over the men he had killed weighed heavily on his soul. Self-reliance was giving way to doubt and fear as he followed the trickling smoke deeper into the unknown.

In a fog of exhaustion, the staggering runaway remembered the last time he had felt such uncertainty. It had been during his first year trapped in the mine when Mule, Archer's giant, hunted him. *Given his fragile state, the memory took hold. . . .*

The giant had never forgotten his young assailant's face. Citius did well to avoid the brute for months following their initial altercation. The mine was large enough that a man could avoid anyone for a time. Food and water were given out once daily in the Main Cavern—this was where Mule kept his watch. The oaf was eager to strangle the life out of the scrawny newcomer who had split his nose.

For months, Citius was forced to barter with others. He would let them turn in his day's salt harvest, and they would then give him his rations after taking their cut. The slave knew the arrangement was not sustainable. His hands were numb every morning and every night from beating a living from the rocks. With his hair getting longer and whiskers growing in, he was becoming less recognizable with each passing month. After a year's time, he was finally able to approach the rationing tables on his own. The barbarian had grown strong from working the salt deposits. After all, he had to earn enough for several men to eat in order to survive. For a few weeks, he enjoyed the extra rations that his hard work demanded.

Those who had profited from his fear were less than pleased. These freeloaders had grown accustomed to taking their cut of the newcomer's earnings. The former bandits decided to blackmail the hardworking miner. For a time, Citius was forced to work even harder to maintain the increased food allowance that he had grown accustomed to. It was not long before the demands of his former guardians became unmanageable. The powerful slave lashed out, beating his oppressors down into the salted gravel. The victory was short-lived, one of the men died from his injuries and Archer became involved.

After Citius stood up to the freeloaders, Mule was reminded of his existence. With the giant hunting for him, he returned to hiding. The miner was well aware that he would soon find himself toe-to-toe with Mule. Every day, the unruly brute petitioned his master to order the disrespectful slave to come out of hiding to face judgment for murdering a producer. Justice was not his concern. Many of his colleagues had been heckling him for months over his crooked nose. All knew a scrawny scrap had wounded the giant; they did not let him forget. Once the Lord of the Mine had blessed it, a challenge could not be avoided. A producer was dead regardless of the circumstances. Trial by combat was ordered.

The slave was given three days to meet Mule at serving time. Despite his miserable existence, he was not ready to be slaughtered before a crowd of howling spectators. He had to find a way to level the playing field. While in hiding, the miner remembered how helpless Mule had been when he swung his chains across the giant's brow. The fool had rubbed his eyes like a scared child. Citius had one more day to stand against Mule before Archer put a bounty on his head.

That night, the young man went to work. He had stockpiled a good bit of rock salt to pay others to bring him his food and water. After gathering his tools, Citius went to a place where he had stumbled across bits of black volcanic glass. The shards of obsidian were remnants of archaic shanks and tools used to work the deposits centuries earlier. He spent most of the night grinding and breaking the glass into a coarse sand. Afterward, he laced the shards with finely ground rock salt. The miner designed a pouch and tether mechanism for the lethal powder. Unfortunately, the design required him to be within arm's reach of the giant to blind him. The leather string was only three feet long; even if he could have found a longer tether, he doubted the effectiveness of the powder at a longer range.

The slave filled the pouch with loose gravel to give it a working weight similar to the salted glass. Over and over again, he threw the leather ball at a target close to the height of Mule's head. The miner was every bit as good with his left hand as his right; his ambidexterity would be a great advantage in battle. He would keep the sling at the center of his back; so long as he had one free hand, he would be able to wield the weapon with confidence. The goal was to throw the ball of gravel, then snap it back just before impact. In doing so, a sharpened stone inside the bundle would recoil and the pouch would rip open, releasing the lethal concoction into an oncoming attacker's unsuspecting face. Stopping the projectile a split second before impact gave the victim enough time to blink. When his eyes opened, they would be engulfed in an unforgiving cloud of salted glass.

The following evening the slave emerged from the darkness to accept his fate; he wore a baggy tunic and slouched to mask his athleticism. Even still, Mule quickly noted the increased size of his opponent. This was not the scrapper he remembered. Citius pretended to be afraid of climbing down the ledge into the arena. He purposefully erred several times, nearly falling, as he descended into the pit.

While watching the uncoordinated combatant struggle, Mule's confidence soared. The rest of the miners laughed at the bumbling fool who had been forced to stand before the giant. The prisoners began betting against the feeble newcomer. Miners even dared to place bets on credit. Some put a week's harvest on the line. Roars of anticipation filled the cavern; no one had ever dared to face the giant in combat. The women danced and Archer dispensed liquor to the starving mob. All were ready for a good show.

Grunting and flexing before the crowd, Mule was supremely confident that he would crush the young fool. He planned to make the event memorable for his spectators. Eager to strike fear into the hearts of his enemies, the brute was desperate to put the fullness of his power on display. The heckling about his crooked nose would end. Armed with a spear and a length of chain, Citius wanted only to last long enough to deploy the mechanism. The henchmen monitoring the crowd threw flaming spears into a bonfire in the center of the arena to provide additional light for the rowdy spectators.

Archer stood; the crowd went silent.

The tyrant roared, "I am the wrath of God. If you had not committed great sins, God would not have sent a punishment like me upon you. Amen, I say to you—whoso sheds the blood of man, by man shall his blood be shed!"

The mob erupted.

The young miner surprised them all by charging at the mountainous enforcer. Roars of anticipation filled the cavern. There was no place for fear in the pit; Mule was pleased. Citius swung his long length of chain at the giant, striking with deathly accuracy. The brute struggled to get close enough to obliterate his fast-moving attacker. The fighter leapt and ran, dodging crushing blows from the giant's battle-axe. At every opportunity, the unknown warrior pelted stones at his attacker's face, conditioning him to swat and blink quickly without reservation. Mule was beginning to move slower; he struggled to remain balanced against his ambidextrous opponent. Archer's men dropped extra spears down to their colleague as needed. The pillars of rock did little to keep the young man out of harm's way as the giant hurled a steady succession of spears at his evasive shadow.

Hearing his opponent's heaving breaths, the slave shrugged off his encumbering tunic. The giant was exhausted; the time was now. He bolted into Mule's kill zone. Narrowly avoiding the giant's spear, Citius swung his chain recklessly, baiting the wretched fool. When Mule finally snatched the whip from the air, he dug his heels into the gravel floor. Taking hold of the steel with both hands, the giant began to reel in his attacker.

Keeping his grip on the chain, Citius launched his javelin. The short spear plunged into the giant's right shoulder. The unaffected brute barred his teeth and pulled his ensnared victim closer. With death close at hand, the barbarian waited until he was just out of range of Mule's battle-axe before reaching behind his back with his unbound left hand. The fighter hurled the ball of glass, snapping it back at the last possible moment.

When Mule opened his eyes, they were torn by the fast-moving black powder. Shards plunged into the unsuspecting giant's eyes; the salted daggers burned. Citius immediately pulled the pin out of the cuff that secured the chain to his right wrist and rolled out of harm's way. Mule lunged for him, but the fleeting savage was already gone. The incapacitated oaf panicked. Releasing his hold of the rusty chain, he rubbed his face violently, which only forced the glass deeper into his bloodied eyes.

Terrified howling filled the shaft; all above stood in shock. Red tears streamed down the enforcer's face as he stumbled blindly around the arena. Silence fell as everyone looked on in dreadful anticipation. Most all had wagered their day's harvest on the blinded brute. The crowd began to grumble; the end was near.

"You bastard . . . you cheat . . . you coward," Mule screamed out in incoherent agony, knowing full well that he was breathing his last breaths. Citius remained silent; he would not give away his position.

The warrior made quick work of his blinded pursuer. He launched one javelin after another into the stumbling man's chest. The powerful fool fell to his knees with several spears protruding from his massive torso. The giant's arms went limp at his sides as Citius approached his trembling victim. The enforcer had not been prepared to die that day. The blinded behemoth shook with fear. Up above, Archer waved his hand; his grunts began moving through the crowd collecting the earnings. Many gamblers were furious with the newcomer's trickery, but the lord was more than pleased by the day's profits.

Mule choked on the salted air as his fingers released his

battle-axe.

The barbarian could feel the dying man blindly searching the shadows. Citius unsheathed his dagger. Looking down on the bloody scene, Archer recognized the blade and a grin crept across his branded face. This was surely the same knife he had given the boy. With pinpoint accuracy, the young man threw the well-balanced blade into Mule's thick neck. The oaf collapsed into a cloud of dust.

The lost wanderer had been stumbling alone for days on limited rations. Solitude was beginning to affect him as much as hunger and thirst. He was buried alive; doubt had invaded his psyche. The slave had not asked for any of this. He felt he had not done anything to deserve this death. Under the great weight of stress, he broke down. Tears began to roll down his face as he cursed the dismal end to all of his hard work. He felt sorry for himself. He was being forced to realize the limitations of his self-reliance. The builder was haunted by all that he had accomplished. Regret choked the air from his lungs; guilt and pain overwhelmed him. He confessed that he had succumbed to worldly fear and sacrificed his brothers.

Citius turned to his fallen friend's Redeemer, he called out to Jesus for the first time. Praying for Christ's mercy, he found wisdom that made him tremble before the Almighty.

Not only had he done nothing to deserve to be banished to the mines, he had also done nothing to deserve his talent. As grace washed over him he contemplated the abilities that had taken him this far. His mind defied the limitations of the world around it; he had not asked for this either. His speed and strength had also been given without payment or proof of his worthiness. If God was indeed the master of this universe, then he was nothing more than a figment of the Great Being's imagination. Self-reliance, his belief in his own abilities, was then a veiled belief in his Creator. As he accepted this truth, his crippling pride began to fall away. The lost soul had only ever gone as far as his gifts had allowed him. His accomplishments were the least he could have done in exchange for all that he had been given. He fought when he had to, he built because he was made to, and he believed in God because he was born to. In humility, he found strength. Faith became his newfound salvation.

The man acknowledged the Lord's presence. Indeed, Citius realized that he had never accomplished anything alone. He wiped the tears from his eyes. He let go of every accomplishment, every triumph. The abilities he cherished were not his own. The trapped slave found restored hope in humbling himself before the Almighty. In a great wave, the pressure began to fall away and the momentum pulled him through. The fugitive stopped pushing himself; he began instead to pray for the strength to push on. For in realizing all that he had been given, the man knew he owed it to his Creator to die fighting. Gratitude is not weakness; with faith comes boldness.

— XXII —

THE WHITE HORSE EXHALED STEAM INTO THE passing breeze; Pallas had ridden the stallion deep into the Germanic Mountains. Finally, the great Saltz Mountain came into view. It stood majestic, great plumes of smoke were steadily rising from its towering peak into the heavens. That entire week they rode on with the mountain in sight, yet it never seemed to get any closer. As they drew nearer, its true enormity commanded the horizon. Curiously, a few days before they reached the base of the mountain, the great fires at its peak ceased. The smoke stopped rolling. None knew what to make of this.

The forty horsemen arrived at the mountain amidst a terrible storm and were forced to take cover from the fast-moving blizzard before they could begin to climb the southern face. Alexander had spared no expense; he sent the most prized soldiers in his guard to bring Nero to justice. In addition, he conscripted an army of fifteen hundred men to take the mine back by force. Against his friend's wishes, Pallas had refused to wait for this legion to mobilize. Instead, he formed a band of the lord's fiercest warriors. This crew road out ahead of the army on the fastest horses available. They tore through the countryside much faster than expected. Nicodemus did not catch up to them until after they had made camp at the base of the mountain. The violent snowstorm ripped through the valley for days. Had it not been for the blizzard, these reinforcements may have never tracked the old warrior down at all.

The men who rode with Pallas were from the northern province of Gaul. Alexander was a wise ruler. When Germania had rebelled, he brought in conscripted legions from Gaul to aid him in his conquest. The region had a long history of warring with Germania; their hatred ran deep. The mercenary soldiers fought the Northerners willingly. Rome was adept at utilizing the rivalries of antiquity to its every advantage. Eventually, Alexander used more localized divisions between barbarian clans themselves to collapse the rebellion from within. It is amazing what a little gold in the wrong hands can accomplish.

The next morning, with the storm losing strength, Pallas began to witness signs of great construction. Entire forests at the base of the mountain had been cleared. Beneath a fresh layer of powder, the trail that wound up the mountainside was a muddy, torn mess from all the oxen and carts that had lugged materials up the steady incline. At midday, they heard a great horn sound from on high. Three powerful booms erupted from the mountain's peak; the shockwave rumbled down the snow-covered mountainside. There was a mighty drum that accompanied the horn; its thunder quaked and unnerved the horses. A long pause, then again three long booms from above.

"Do you think they've seen us?" one of the men asked.

"Through the storm?" another huffed in disbelief.

"It's possible, but unlikely—especially given the snow cover. Besides, if they'd seen us, why would they let us know?" Pallas replied.

"Agreed," the man growled.

"How in the hell do you think they'd have seen us through the pines and two feet of fresh snow?" another badgered. The soldiers continued grumbling amongst themselves until their leader waved them off.

"What do you make of the horn?" Nicodemus asked the local guides. Pallas had acquired these men from the nearest village.

"I've been living at the base of the mountain my entire life, sir. I've never heard that horn. All I know, I doubt if it's a good thing, sir," the man replied.

"I know that horn," the oldest guide answered from amidst the group. The elder came before Pallas. "I was a boy the last time I heard that great horn blast down the mountain. Even still, I have not forgotten its ring. My father was a guard at the mines. Can't say I'm proud of it, but it put food on the table. Now, I may be mistaken, but I believe it is the alarm for an escape."

"Should we make camp?" another guide asked. The young man's teeth were chattering and his lower half was soaked through from tending to the horses.

Pallas's stone gray eyes drifted up the mountainside. "How long until we reach the mining operation?"

"At this pace?"

"No, on foot. I want to leave the horses behind."

"Trudging through this crap, we wouldn't arrive until around nightfall," the disgruntled young local answered for his elder.

"How many guards does Nero have?" The Greek had asked the guides this question on multiple occasions already, but never with such urgency.

The elder answered, "It varies, sir. Usually it's around one hundred. Could easily be more. No merchants have been allowed to enter the stronghold for two years. I really can't be certain. All I know is we have seen higher quality food and wine being sent to the mountain of late. It is not the sort of fare typically served to slaves; I fear Nero's numbers have grown considerably."

"Very well, you men will stay behind with the horses. Make camp a ways off the trail. I will send for you in the morning. If you don't hear from us by nightfall tomorrow, take the horses and go," Pallas said to the shivering peasants.

"The horses aren't yours to give, Greek," Nicodemus sneered.

"By gods, boy. You'd be dead if we didn't make it back, and you're worried about the damn horses," the engineer rattled off.

"I thought we'd wait here for the rest of the army," Nicodemus offered. The commander ignored this advice entirely; he knew that the snow cover gave them a great advantage.

"No camp will be made," Pallas barked to the rest. "We will

arrive under the cover of darkness. I have seen and heard enough to know these men won't go quietly."

"Aye, sir," the troops replied.

"Keep the horses in the pines, and stay quiet," Nicodemus snapped at the peasants.

With that, the men pushed on; warriors from northern Gaul had a long-standing reputation for brutality and fearlessness. All of these men had served in crushing the Northern Rebellion. If Nero intended to fight, they were more than ready to meet him. There were four master archers among Nicodemus's crew. These assassins crept out ahead of the others to neutralize any sentry towers. Skilled in their craft, they moved through the forest in silence. Pallas and the others passed six towers altogether; the occupants within had already been disposed of. There were only two men guarding each tower; the archers made quick work of these unsuspecting watchmen. Nero's men had nearly frozen to death in the storm the night before. An attack was the last thing on their minds. Nicodemus reveled in the prowess of his brood.

Avoiding the trail, the men trudged through the cold evening air. The sun was fading out behind the mountains, casting long shadows across the valley. The storm had passed, and it was becoming a clear, windblown night. A bright full moon hovered over the range to the east. When the mining camp came into view, the men clutched their spears and crept silently through the deep powder toward the flickering torches. The gateway into the fort was wide open. The archers had scaled the walls and killed the handful of novice hired hands guarding the entrance. Two arrow-riddled guards lay dead in the snow pile just outside of the gates.

To their amazement, they marched into the middle of the mining camp undetected. No one was patrolling the fort; there was not a soul to be found. The guards had taken to drinking during the storm, which had halted operations above ground. Reconstructing the collapsed network had become a top priority. Most of the guards were in the mine overseeing repair operations. That afternoon, the warden had sent nearly a dozen of his best men around the mountain with his hounds to capture Citius. Multiple fronts left him with barely half of his force guarding the mining operation itself.

The temperature plummeted with the sun; plumes of steam accompanied the soldiers' breaths as they assessed the poorly guarded compound. The legionaries found hundreds of barrels stacked in heaps in the courtyard. Pallas inspected them. The larger barrels were empty and lined with tar. The others were smaller and tightly sealed; painted symbols indicated that these were filled with wine. The engineer took a hatchet and drove it into a barrel. No liquid flowed.

"Frozen, maybe," one of the men noted.

Pallas was not satisfied; he took an axe from a nearby chop block. In one powerful blow, he split the barrel wide open. All the men watched the coarse sand spill out into the torchlight. Nicodemus rushed over and tasted the substance—refined salt. The soldiers looked at the great mound of barrels in disbelief. This was the greatest fortune any of them had ever seen: enough salt to pay an army for a decade.

"Kill them all," Nicodemus commanded.

A lone guard wandered out of one of the many stone buildings surrounding the courtyard. They all froze as the fool leaned against a wall to relieve himself. When the drunk looked up to see the band of heavily armed soldiers with weapons drawn, he panicked and attempted to flee. Four well-aimed arrows found their mark. The guard fell lifelessly into a snowdrift outside the building. Nicodemus's archers revealed their positions and made their way toward the rest. There was quite a ruckus coming from within the stone building that the guard had stumbled out of. The warriors surrounded the structure. The thieving guards inside had taken to drinking; they were in for a rude awakening.

The largest man from Gaul led the way. In a single burst of power, he kicked the door off its poorly crafted hinges. The guards' banter ceased. The towering soldier anchored the unit, forming the pinnacle of the Roman wedge formation. The invaders locked shields to advance on the ensnared mercenaries. No mercy was shown to Nero's drunken henchmen. The warden's intoxicated brutes were no contest for these seasoned legionaries. The cowards panicked and scrambled for cover; spears pulverized the disorganized rabble. The fearsome warriors displayed pinpoint accuracy in throwing javelins over their united shields. As the line pushed forward, the archers leapt onto tables and arrows filled the air. All at once, the legionaries unsheathed their gladius swords, which were lethal in close combat. The cornered thieves desperately fought to break through the unflinching shield wall. The slaughter was quick.

Pallas remained outside with Nicodemus as pandemonium broke out within the structure. If at all possible, he would avoid the bloodshed. An unarmed guard fled from the structure. Nicodemus charged at the defenseless man and cut him down skillfully. Alexander's agent then entered the building, gladius in hand, to finish off the leftovers. The woeful cries ceased, and Pallas's men marched out of the guardhouse. A few of them were bloodied, but for the most part they remained unscathed. There was a particularly fat captive among them.

"Found this sniveling piglet hiding under a table," Nicodemus jabbed. He kicked the man in the back. The oaf fell into a pathetic heap at the Greek's feet.

"You are going to tell me everything," Pallas said, pressing the tip of his sword into the captive's gut. The guard squealed and squirmed; the warriors laughed coldly.

Once they brought their captive back into the barracks, the man did just that. Surrounded by his fallen associates, the guard's mouth ran freely. The strike force learned about the mine, the network, the theft, Nero's blacksmiths, and the slave called Citius. The oaf spilled his guts out in a final attempt to save his neck. This conscript was quite the talker; he gave very specific details and answered all questions willingly. Nicodemus pressed the man for details on the total number of salt barrels stolen thus far. The noble was amazed at the enormity of the theft. Pallas soon lost his patience when Nicodemus's interrogation tactics began to take a needlessly violent turn.

"Where is Nero now?" the Greek interjected.

"In the mine, sir. He is overseeing the construction personally, now that—" The man stopped himself.

"Now that *what?*" Nicodemus snapped.

"Now that—now that Citius is dead," the man replied.

"I thought you said he fled."

"The slave is only presumed to have escaped, sir. He flooded the mine in his wake. In all likelihood, the young man is dead. Nero is just paranoid. Look, I really don't know," the man blabbered. His eyes were fixed on the bloodied swords and spear tips in the soldiers' hands.

"Alright then, boy. Take me to this entry tower. It is time for Nero to answer for what he has done," Pallas said.

The portly guard reluctantly left the warmth of the barracks to stagger through the snow toward the largest building at the mining operation. En route to the entrance, they passed the ironworks. Nicodemus was the most startled of all. Dozens of anvils and smith stations lined the path to the refinery. Nearly a thousand freshly made swords and shields were visible on the neatly organized shelves that stood in rows along the path; the true ambition of Lord Nero was on display. When they arrived at the storehouse doors, the fearful guard stopped and turned to face Pallas.

"The entry tower is heavily guarded, sir," the desperate captive warned.

"That's why *you* are leading the way," Nicodemus jabbed, giving him a nudging shove.

The conscript gulped and creaked open the massive doors. The strike force crept into the hall. Nicodemus slaughtered the plump guard before closing the double doors. The men soon realized that the building was actually the entrance to an ancient cave that stretched deep into the mountain. Pallas marveled at the complex refinery hidden within the rock.

"Incredible," Nicodemus muttered, taking in the masterful industry at hand.

"That it is, boy," Pallas added.

This hall was kept uncomfortably warm to allow the water to evaporate and leave the salt behind. When operational, the pump network provided a steady stream of salt water from the mine below. This brine flowed through a channel carved into the bedrock. There were multiple screens in place to catch suspended solids—tar chunks, wood bits, and gravel. The water was then directed into a ceramic pipeline. The piping took the brine into a holding reservoir. A series of barrels attached to a heavy rope rolled through this pond-sized storage basin, lifting the brine up to the top of the refinery. This water pulley was a much smaller version of the one Citius had designed for the shaft. It was actuated by an iron gear-operated pulley at its peak, which worked in tandem with a brass wheel anchored into the rock three feet below the water's surface. A scaffolding staircase led up to the machine's operating platform.

The water pulley scooped up the brine and lifted it into a second ceramic pipeline. This piping carried the precious liquid, by gravity flow, to any number of massive ceramic heating pans. These pans would be filled to the brim. Well-fed fires were kept lit beneath the pans to cook off most of the water. This produced the constant cloud of smoke they had seen being emitted from the mountaintop. Given all the firewood this process demanded, Pallas was not surprised that so much of the mountainside's forest had been cleared. The remaining highly concentrated brine was then poured into several smaller cheap ceramic pots. These were transported by hand to lower-temperature firing ovens. The massive stone ovens greatly accelerated evaporation. Once the water had evaporated, these cheap clay vessels were cooled rapidly in the snow to help prevent the contents from sticking. Workers would then smash the pots and collect the gray salt cakes that remained. The cakes were crushed so that the coarse finished product could be stored more easily in the aforementioned barrels. Given the network's collapse and the recent blizzard, the refinery was not operating.

Nicodemus was taking in the magnitude of Nero's salt refining operation. The extent of the fortune stolen was more than he ever could have imagined. The young man had personally visited Alexander's holdings on Saltz Mountain just three years before. None of this had been built. He could only dream of what had been constructed below the surface to bring forth the amount of water that a refinery this size demanded.

An alarm horn sounded abruptly; they had been spotted. An archer atop the entry tower noticed them after feeling the cool draft from the outside world. Nicodemus's archers rushed for elevated positions on the water pulley's scaffolding. Arrows soared through the massive hall; the legionaries took cover in the maze of barrels. The obstacles provided excellent coverage from enemy fire as they made their way toward the towering stone fortification. Unfortunately, the close quarters between the stockpiles would not allow the soldiers to link shields properly. The invaders were not trained to fight this way, and the opposition knew the refinery well. Nero's guards lay in wait all over the storehouse they exploited the Roman formation's weak points by attacking from the sides. The tower's archers were deathly accurate; nearly a third of Pallas's men were struck down.

The Greek worked his way through the maze of materials behind his men as arrows rained down on them. The old man had long since buried his memories of war, but the warrior from his past was biting at the surface. Thanks to their elevated firing squad, Nero's men had taken the upper hand. The hired thugs were rushing through the refinery, hacking at the invaders. The strike force began to fall back toward the double doors. They were being forced out of the cluttered refinery. Pallas grabbed hold of a torch and flung it onto a heaping pile of empty tar barrels. The other men began to follow suit, setting fire to the stockpiled materials.

"That's all salt, you idiots," Nicodemus spat, as arrows whizzed by.

"To hell with it—burn it. We need the smoke, or these archers will kill us all," Pallas roared. Just then a guard leapt from the mess of crates at his side. When Pallas plunged his sword into the first attacker that slipped past his men, it all came rushing back. He transformed into the fearsome warrior he had forcibly forgotten. The white wolf weaved through the flames, excising judgment.

Great plumes of smoke filled the refinery. The legionaries pelted the enemy with the javelin-like darts they kept attached to the backs of their shields. These proved lethal amidst the maze of salt barrels. The enemy archers were disoriented and struggling to breathe; their arrows lost volume. The steadily rising black clouds were forcing them to flee from their elevated positions. The bowmen could not easily identify their targets through the overwhelming smog. Many panicked and began firing at anything that moved. Friendly fire plagued Nero's foot soldiers. After hurling their armor-piercing pilum at oncoming attackers, the invaders unsheathed their secondary weapons—short swords.

Pallas stormed through the raging bonfires with his men at his heels. Fighting the smoke, Nicodemus's archers had retaken the high ground. From atop the scaffolding, they rained hell down on the opposing side. Across the way, the bowmen guarding the tower scrambled to take cover. Fearing defeat, what was left of the mercenaries charged at the invaders in a desperate attempt to make for the double doors. The wolf zigzagged through the barrels, disposing of the unsuspecting guards. He sprinted through the smoke-filled cave, slashing at arteries, vitals, and tendons, leaving death in his wake. The emboldened warrior climbed the tower's winding stairs, methodically cutting down Nero's cowering archers as he ascended.

The assault on the refinery was successful, although it came at a heavy cost—many brave legionaries littered the cavern floor. Accompanied by those who remained, Pallas marched onto the ancient circular platform. The men had a newfound respect for their commander. It was no longer any wonder to them why this man was so esteemed by Lord Alexander. Nicodemus was more taken aback than anyone by the humble Greek's ferocity.

"Let us down," Pallas ordered from the Main Pulley's platform. The feisty old dog had been injured in battle; he was limping and nursing his right arm.

"Pallas, our numbers are much too thin. We should hold this position and wait for the army to arrive. Then we can starve them out," Nicodemus advised.

"That is wise. You wait here. If you do not hear my voice, do not raise the platform. If I die, you can starve them out. With the rest of the army at your disposal, Nero will not stand a chance."

"Going down there is madness. If Nero doesn't kill you, the starving slaves will," the noble pleaded.

"I have lived long enough both in years and in accomplishments—*lower the damn platform*," Pallas demanded. Nicodemus shook his head but ordered his archers to turn the crank. The ancient lift began to lower into the stone tower.

"Not as fast as you used to be, are you, old man?" a warrior from Gaul jabbed over the cranking gears. The white wolf chuckled as they fell into the shadows.

— XXIII —

THE BELIEVER HAD ASCENDED FROM THE depths with unwavering determination.

At the top of a substantial incline, Citius lost his footing when the loose gravel gave way beneath his feet. He was sent tumbling downward along with this rockslide. He lost his torch in the swirl of debris before slamming into something hard, though much softer than stone. Fumbling in the darkness, the fallen fugitive realized that the object was a long-forgotten ladder. His torch was gone. He felt through his bundle; there he had three remaining. These final torches would provide just a few hours of useful light. Once they were gone, Citius would be forced to navigate in total darkness. If it came to this, he was sure he would never make it out alive.

With little time to investigate, the fugitive took hold of the ladder. The frame was in decent condition. As for its rungs, they were worn out and failing. There was no way the floodwaters could have deposited this ladder upright so far into this cavern. Citius's spirits soared; he was now certain that he had found the long-lost Northern Shaft. He sparked a torch. In the faint light, he saw that the ladder rose to a ledge above. The slave had no choice; he began to climb. The seasoned miner tested each rung before placing his full weight on it, skipping over several that felt weak. A few broke in two when he tugged at them. This was disconcerting, but there was no time to worry. The first ladder took him to a narrow stone ledge, which led to an additional ladder. This was relieving but time-consuming; the fugitive's first torch was already burning low. The slave climbed until he arrived at an ancient wooden work deck. So far he had counted a total of seven platforms and ledges.

Finally, he felt the cool draft he had been waiting for. Tired and hungry all the same, Citius was exuberant. He could taste freedom on that breeze from the outside world. The emaciated runaway wandered around the rickety wooden platform but could not find the last ladder. The steady draft from above whipped around him as he came close to the edge of the ancient elevated work deck. His first torch was gone and his second had burned down halfway. The torchlight did not come close to traveling far enough to reveal the cliff's enormity. Even still, he could sense the long drop down to the rocks.

With his options running thin, the fugitive decided to turn back to retrieve the ladder he had used to climb up to this platform. He struggled to pull the heavy wooden load up onto the ledge. The ladder began to slip. Citius feared the swaying weight would pull him over the edge. He struggled to steady himself in the turbulent draft from above. In doing so, the famished runaway lost his torch; it fell into the darkness, sailing past all the previous ledges.

When the flame finally landed, he could barely hear it impact the cave floor. Huddled toward the back of the ledge, he struggled against the whipping draft to get another torch lit. Finally, he managed to spark a piece of his cloak and ignited the tar-soaked stake. After his first failed attempt, the young man adjusted his grip. Again, he had to lean over the daunting ledge to manage, and he was now well aware of the emptiness beneath him. After a great struggle, he wrestled the ladder up to his elevation.

With his newfound key to freedom in hand, Citius desperately searched for signs of where the missing link had been located. Proper placement of this final ladder was imperative. Precious little time remained; it could break apart if he kept climbing up and down the fragile rungs. He was beyond exhaustion after his near-death experience trying to reel in the ladder, so he decided to eat the remainder of his rations and drink the rest of his water. The runaway reasoned that if the rungs gave out and he fell to his death, at least he would not die on an empty stomach. Running on faith, the slave sat to eat what he prayed would not be his last meal.

After much internal debate, Citius decided that a log fastened near the platform's leading edge had been used to prevent the original ladder from kicking out as the miners of antiquity climbed toward fresh air at the end of their workday. The veteran could see why this shaft had been shut down. He was hard pressed to imagine hundreds of miners climbing up and down this cliff each day to mine the great cavern. The fugitive secured his escape ladder into position against the kicker with confidence.

When Citius pulled himself safely onto the ledge above, he breathed a deep sigh of relief. The draft from the outside world was strong. The slave exulted in the cool air of freedom. He was at the end of a long, dark tunnel; the shaft uncoiled out in front of him. With a great sense of urgency, he pushed on against the steadily flowing air. Still unable to see the light of day, he trekked upward tirelessly, forgetting his bloodied elbows and knees. Traveling through the interlinking passageways, the fugitive stumbled upon several skeletons. Signs of the great excavation surrounded him. As the temperature fell, he came upon several storage rooms filled mostly with wood and archaic excavating equipment. The runaway lit a small fire from the aged scrap wood to warm himself.

The shaft was getting much colder as he ascended from the depths. The miner searched through the artifacts for anything useful—namely, a cloak or blanket to provide much-needed warmth. He entered a storage cave and found bundles of ancient textiles. He draped himself in these dusty rags, which helped considerably. Unfortunately, he found no usable sandals or boots among the dead. No matter, the increasing cold meant he was getting closer to freedom.

When the young man could feel the harsh wind from the outside world, he began to jog. As he leapt and climbed over the rocks, euphoria set in. He could see a stream of light off in the distance. Exuberance filled his soul; he recklessly charged toward the light at the end of the tunnel. Disoriented by thirst, he sprinted foolishly toward the beckoning brightness, dreaming of tasting the wet snow. Quite suddenly, he found himself face down in the gravel. The plume of dust surrounding him was a sharp contrast to the cool snow he had been imagining. Citius skidded to a painful halt on the steadily rising slope. The slave slowly stood to brush himself off. He had stumbled over a skeleton. There in the gravel next to the remains lay a long-forgotten dagger and a pickaxe. It was clear that these bones had belonged to a man who died fighting long ago.

This was a much-needed wake-up call for the tired runaway. He internally scolded himself for his foolishness. Citius picked up the forgotten remnants of past rebellion, gathered his rags, and braced against the uncertain wind from the outside world. If not for the bones, he would have bolted blindly out into the light of day; overwhelming thirst had almost cost him everything. He lifted the skull out of the gravel; his beating heart was thankful for this man. With his wits renewed, the slave snuffed out his torch; he had to assume disaster awaited him on the outside.

Focused on the task at hand, the fugitive crept slowly toward the light. He remained hidden behind the rocks as he peered out into the swirling snow-blown draft. He could see two sentries standing guard by a post outside the exit. Beyond a dense thicket, there was a small barracks with smoke rising from its chimneys. Past the thicket, to the left of the barracks, stood the lone sentry tower. Citius could see only one bowman, bundled in furs, manning the tower. The runaway was grateful for the overgrowth around the mine's exit; it would provide much-needed cover from the archer above. He lay in wait until a pattern unfolded.

There was no way to know for certain how many guards were within the barracks. The men rotated from time to time. Citius studied the rotation and found it fairly simple: two men manned the post and one guarded the entrance to the barracks while two more entered the structure to rest. All the while, the bowman kept watch from his tower. The slave remained undetected within the cave. It was freezing, but he braved the cold to study the rotation pattern. He knew that he was going to have to wait until nightfall to make his move. After several hours of observation, he recognized only five faces among the rotating guards at the post outside the abandoned mine. More importantly, he realized that after every shift, whoever was standing guard in front of the barracks would bring fresh sleeping furs to the archer in the tower. The watchful miner also noted that the lackadaisical guards were drinking. This was fortunate.

There was one guard in particular who took longer than the others to get the furs out of the barracks for the bowman in the tower. This was likely in an attempt to remain warm by the fire longer. Citius decided that he would wait for the cover of darkness to make his move. He would strike when the guard wearing formal gear went in to retrieve warm furs for the bowman. The slow mover wore an elegant plumed helmet, which he could easily identify in the flickering torchlight. As night fell, the young man was grateful that the moon was strong; this helped him continue to spy on his adversaries from a safe distance. The fugitive lay freezing at the Northern Shaft's exit for several hours. All the while, he remained focused, waiting for his window of opportunity.

It was just hours from sunrise when the moment finally came. Citius watched the lazy guard wearing the centurion helmet enter the barracks. He knew that this soldier would take his time gathering furs for the man in the tower. The believer prayed for strength. Just then, the distant howling of ferocious hounds came within earshot.

"Nero," Citius snarled. The time was now.

— XXIV —

DESCENDING FROM THE TOWER, THE SOLDIERS were astonished by the great industry they witnessed. An untold number of centuries had been spent mining salt from this mountain. Even more impressive than the magnitude of the excavation was the recently constructed network, consisting of dozens of tar-laden wooden basins, Archimedean screws, reverse overshot water wheels, channels, and water pulleys. To see all the moving pieces linked seamlessly was breathtaking.

The engineer understood the conceptual mastery necessary to propel a project like this forward. An undertaking of this magnitude typically required an imperial budget, not to mention the greatest minds in the known world. Even then, the entire project could go up in smoke if not managed properly. The genius at hand was like none he had ever witnessed. The fact that a slave, with limited resources, had accomplished all of this in a few years' time was earth-shattering. Men were simply not capable of such things. Pallas's humble awe gave way to rage. To think that this talent had been buried away and possibly lost forever; punishment was long overdue.

The platform struck the stone slab with a resounding thud.

Nero was amongst his guards when the lift unexpectedly boomed to the cavern floor. It was obvious that his men no longer controlled the pulley above, for they would have slowed the crank after the warning tethers began to pass by the gear. The heavily armed warriors pushed forward fearlessly—marching, shields linked, spears pulverizing into throngs of the warden's guards. The captives roared triumphantly.

"Archers to the ledges! Kill them—kill them all," Nero roared.

The strike force was overwhelmingly outnumbered. Pallas called out to the starving captives in every barbarian language at his disposal, "Men, you are free—fight!"

Indecision lingered over the starving workforce.

"Fight if you want to live," Pallas roared for all to hear.

All at once, a great wave of slaves consumed the guards. The archers scrambled to find elevated ground, but at every turn they were pelted with stones. The rebels hurled everything they could find at the warden's terrified henchmen. The workers wielded sledgehammers, picks, and stakes; these ragtag barbarians settled the score. The starving men fought desperately to earn their freedom.

"Burn it—burn everything to the ground," Nero shouted. Wielding a torch, he set fire to dozens of barrels of pitch then rolled them off the ledge at the warring rebels. Liquid fire erupted on impact.

The archers began firing flaming arrows at the tar-slicked

woodwork. Flames engulfed the towering structure's scaffolding. Embers fell from above as massive plumes of smoke poured out into the storehouse. Unhindered by the billowing smog, Nero hacked and brutalized the swarms of savages who charged at him through the raging fires. Guards were being picked off in droves by well-aimed rocks flung by slaves who had successfully taken the high ground. The chanting began, first as a slow rolling rumble, then as a booming drum.

"Citius—Citius—Citius!"

The starving rebels roared in unison as they bashed guards with tools and rained stones from on high. Massive chunks of the network burned above, dropping ash and sparks onto the battleground.

"This is my mountain," Nero roared. "Everything in it belongs to me."

With all of their javelins spent and most of their spears broken, Pallas's band was forced to break formation. Their ranks dissolved into the swarm; they charged into the flaming network at what remained of the guards. The slaves above had scaled the burning scaffolding; they were using axes to chop holes in elevated storage basins. Jets of brine flew from above onto the violent flames. Steam filled the turbulent air as the crashing water knocked the mercenaries from their feet.

The gangly spider fought with a vicious bloodlust. Given his sickly form, Nero's ferocity and strength were incredible. Several of Pallas's men were brutally cut down by his far-reaching spear.

The towering figure forced his way through the starving mob that scattered and trembled in his wake. The warden was fearless; his evil permeated throughout the plumes of smoke around him as he drew down on Pallas. The chanting of Citius's name continued to thunder through the smoke-filled cavern. Steaming fires hissed and spat as brine spilled from the basins.

Fighting through the blur of smoke and rushing water, Nero became locked in battle with the largest of the legionaries. This massive warrior from Gaul rammed the tyrant with his shield. The Roman stumbled backward but managed to hold his ground in the loose gravel. The powerful warrior shoved him back again and raised his sword to deliver a fatal blow. The spider countered; his long, bony arm darted forward undetected. The gangly ghoul's shank plunged into his enemy's throat. Nero wriggled and twisted the weapon mercilessly until the great man fell. The warden cackled wildly, letting the entire cavern fill with his unrelenting rage.

The smoke was fading. Jets of water rained down on the battleground; the fires had become steaming embers. The chanting slowed then halted. Pallas stood before the beast. The blood-spattered madman fumed in the torchlight. The last of his guards were being disposed of by the stone-throwing, tool-wielding mob. Nero was surrounded. The Greek was badly injured when he entered the mine. Now he was just trying to keep his footing in the loose gravel as frigid brine rushed down the incline.

"We have been sent by Lord Alexander. You were not wise

to cross him. You will have to answer for what you've done," Pallas shouted. "Where is Citius?"

Nero cackled madly; he hissed and spat blood onto the cave floor. "Do you really think I am going to leave this hole in chains?" he seethed.

"Where is he?" Pallas demanded. The savages armed with stones were tightening their circle around the warden; he spat and jeered, wildly taunting the nameless mob.

"You all are nothing—*nothing!*" One of the slaves foolishly charged at him. The gangly spider brutally disposed of the poor man with ease. He drooled blood and shouted at the crowd, *"On this mountain, I am god!"*

The stone-wielding mob kept a safe distance; they looked to Pallas for their cue. The bloodthirsty despot scrambled around tirelessly—jeering, hissing, and spitting at the starving slaves, taunting them with his far-reaching spear.

"Damn it, Nero—you're finished, you fool. Where is the builder?" Pallas demanded.

"That sniveling *mutt* is dead. *All those who defy me die!*"

The Greek could see that there would be no reasoning with this lost soul. The chanting slowly resumed.

"Citius!"

"Citius!"

"Citius!"

The rising voices echoed throughout the cavern. The sound of the young man's name booming pushed Nero to his breaking point. The Roman charged.

The two remaining legionaries rushed to the injured old man's aid as Pallas braced for an impact that never came. The mob erupted; a great gust of stones was unleashed on the tyrant. Nero skidded to a lifeless halt. The rebellious crowd heaped several rounds of stones onto the fallen beast. It was no question whether he was dead beneath the mound of rubble. A great silence followed. Emptiness consumed the salty steam as a great evil burst from the shaft. Nero had been vanquished.

Pallas broke the silence. "Can anyone tell me what has become of the man called Citius?" No one answered. He knew that many Northerners distrusted a man who spoke Latin.

The Greek repeated his words again, this time in a well-known dialect of Germanic origin. "Men, as of this moment, you are all free. Now, does anyone know what has become of Citius? We are not here to punish him." The old man hoped a reassuring oath in a language familiar to the captives would gain the mob's trust. The slaves could not believe their good fortune; most had not processed a single word the foreigner said after they heard of their newfound freedom. The men cheered victoriously and pushed toward the platform. Others began climbing the water pulley to gain entry to the refinery.

"Where is Citius?" the staggering warrior shouted again and again, to no avail.

Finally, a small voice fell to him from the ledge above, "He has escaped through the Northern Shaft."

"How do you know this?" the engineer hollered over the elated mob. Several slaves had already scrambled up the water pulley into the storehouse. They now controlled the lift and were hoisting the others from the depths.

"I don't, sir," the young one replied. Gaining courage, the lad shouted over the rest of the laborers, "I just hope it's true. This afternoon, Nero sent a band of guards around the mountain. He sent them there to kill Citius."

The plump guard's story had been corroborated; Pallas hung his head in defeat. His limbs were weighted down with a dreadful sand. The boy disappeared into the crowd as the warrior fell to one knee in the slow flowing brine. Suddenly, he felt a hand on his shoulder. There stood an elderly slave, decrepit and pitiful, but beaming with toothless joy.

The misty-eyed man helped Pallas to his feet, and said, "Fear not, my friend, for where sin abounds, grace abounds all the more."

— XXV —

O N THE OTHER SIDE OF THE MOUNTAIN, A half-frozen Thadius remained alert and ready. As usual, Pecius was taking his time gathering freshly warmed furs from the barracks. Bracing against the wind, the elder heard howling off in the distance.

"Well, they're sending reinforcements after all," Thadius mumbled. "About time." He was shivering horribly. Great plumes of steam were emitted from his bundle of fur with every breath he took.

At the wooden post outside the abandoned mineshaft, the guards heard the hounds as well. Reinforcements meant more time by the fire and less time struggling to keep warm. The two young men turned and began to wave, trying to get Thadius's attention up in the tower. They wanted to turn in and let the new arrivals take first watch. Their leader was looking across the mountainside. Far off in the distance, he counted ten torches bobbing through the snowdrifts toward his encampment. He was surprised that Nero had sent so many guards. He wondered just how many workers had managed to escape. The howling beasts were getting closer.

When the old man finally saw his men trying to get his attention, he leapt out of his bundle. His hands were numb and clumsy, and his many layered furs made it a struggle to get to his bow. His men, noticing his frantic movements, turned to see what he had seen. There was something racing toward them. The panicked soldiers fumbled for their weapons. The dark figure brutally disposed of the first guard with a pickaxe. The second drew his sword frantically, but it was too late. The shadow plunged a dagger into the young soldier's neck. The commander looked on in horror as his men were cut down in rapid succession.

The moon provided ample light, but the brush around the cave obscured his view. Thadius drew his bowstring to the anchor point, fearing he would not have a clean shot. The veteran let several arrows sail from his tower; none made it cleanly through the windblown overgrowth. The figure vanished. The archer scanned the tree line; there was no sign of the fleeting assailant.

"To arms—to arms," Thadius shouted. To his disgust, no one exited the barracks. "*To arms*, you lazy fools!"

A carefree Pecius swung the guardhouse door open without any sense of urgency. He strolled out of the barracks with an armful of sleeping furs for the old man. All the while he looked up smugly at his elder, figuring Thadius was trying to ruffle his feathers for sneaking so much extra time by the fire.

"*Arm yourself!*"

There was a very real panic in his commander's tone and gestures. He saw the bow in his leader's hands. The wide-eyed young man dropped the warm furs into the snow as he registered the sounds of howling dogs drawing near. Pecius saw the torches moving across the mountainside in the distance—*this was no drill.*

A dark figure emerged from the shadows. It stepped out into the faint torchlight surrounding the barracks. Having shed its many layers, the warrior moved even faster now. Thadius fired arrow after arrow at the sprinting shadow; none made it through the dense brush accurately. The silent assassin charged at Pecius. The noble turned toward the apparent disturbance. When he saw the raw hate in the slave's wild, black eyes, he froze. Hesitation cost him dearly. The barbarian leapt into the air wielding a stolen sword. Pecius's lifeless form collapsed into the snow. Thadius was stunned by the runaway's boldness.

The fugitive took cover behind the firewood stacked against the barracks wall. Arrows thudded into the woodpile around him. The ghost did not flinch. The last of the guards rushed out, swords unsheathed. The howling dogs sent a chill through the air. Pecius lay dead and Thadius appeared to be firing arrows at them. The cowards spun around to take refuge within the warm hamlet. They were not prepared for the fast-moving figure that met them. The shadow made quick work of these inexperienced swordsmen then wisely used the last man's body as a shield to absorb the arrows. Thadius was down to his last shot; he waited, keeping his bowstring flexed. The mysterious figure cast the dead soldier aside and darted into the guardhouse. The runaway was not in the outpost for long; he took off after stealing winter gear.

In a flash, the fugitive was bounding down the steep mountainside. The hounds were getting close, but the fumbling torches remained distant. Thadius craned for a clean shot at the sprinting savage. Finally, it came. Thadius took aim at the fleeing man's spine—a kill shot—something made the elder pause. He aimed away from the center of the man's back. Instead, he picked a spot on the fugitive's upper right shoulder. The howling hounds were distracting. It was a distant target in poor lighting; the old man's confidence never waned. Thadius released the bowstring and sent his final arrow sailing through the thin air.

The arrow plunged into the sprinting fugitive's back. The figure lost its footing, collapsing in mid-stride. He tumbled down the incline and lost his ill-fitting boots before skidding to a halt in the deep snow. Judging by the close proximity of the howling, the dogs were only minutes away. Thadius decided he had better go round up the prisoner before the hounds got hold of him. The man had fought bravely; Thadius reasoned he deserved a better death than the beasts would give. Then, to the old man's amazement, the wounded warrior fought back to his feet. The fugitive took off haphazardly, hobbling down the steep mountainside.

"Stay down, you fool," Thadius shouted down the mountain.

The hunter scrambled down his tower's ladder. He got a chill as he ran past the lifeless bodies of his fallen men. After seeing their mangled remains, he jogged back to the barracks to grab a dozen more arrows, his sword, his spear, and his shield. The heavily armed soldier uncorked his prized jug; he drank deeply. The exhausted elder left the warm fire to jog through the deep snow after the stumbling runaway.

The veteran had been at it for nearly a quarter mile, navigating through the unforgiving snowdrifts after the fugitive. At the ravine, he plunged into the knee-high, icy mountain stream. Thadius had never, in his long years on the mountain, crossed the creek during the dead of winter. The thought of the climb back up to his outpost was torturous. The cold, dry air ripped at his lungs; he stopped at a tree to get a grip. The howling was dangerously close; several jet-black hounds stormed past him through the pines. Nero's snarling man-eaters bounded through the deep snow after the fleeing slave. Without warning, one of the wild-eyed animals leapt at the bowman.

Thadius rolled through the snow with the beast chomping relentlessly into his left forearm. The mad dog was starving, confused, and exhausted. It was prepared to rip him to shreds for sustenance. The soldier repeatedly plunged his short sword into the snarling beast until its jaws opened, releasing his badly mangled arm. There was no time to wrap the wound. In spite of his pain, the old man pushed forward relentlessly. He was an accomplished tracker and knew this mountainside better than anyone. Even still, the hunter struggled, losing his balance from time to time on the steep snow-blown inclines. All of the hounds were out in front of him now, howling in pursuit of the renegade miner.

The Roman continued to follow the blood spatter in the

snow. Given the conditions, he was amazed at how far the run-away had made it. Especially with an arrow lodged in his back.

The howling ceased. Thadius sprinted forward, knowing the bloodthirsty animals were close to their prey. He had not come this far to have to lug a dead body back up the mountain. The hunter came to a familiar gap in the gorge. The blood trail told him the runaway had slipped through this narrow opening in the rocks. A great disturbance in the snow indicated that several hounds had followed the wounded man into the gap. Thadius had always thought this crevice impassable; he knew another way. He set off around the ledge so that he would be able to come down on the other side of the gorge.

When Thadius made it to the top, he saw four hounds bob-bing through the snowdrifts toward a lifeless figure. The fugitive lay collapsed in the small valley at the base of the gorge. Without hesitation, the old man snatched an arrow off his back and stead-ied his bow. The animals were sinking and leaping unpredictably through the deep drifts, drawing down on the runaway. Thadius began to unleash a steady succession of arrows at the target out in front. One hit home, but the beast continued to claw its way toward the fallen man. Thadius fired away and successfully took down two of the hounds in the process. The remaining beasts were mere feet from the slave's lifeless form. The man-eaters leapt at him ferociously.

The elder looked on in shock as the motionless figure be-came a thrashing and fighting wild man. He fought viciously in the deep powder. The two hounds that remained tore at the wounded barbarian. Thadius fired his final arrow into the back of the hound that was chomping on the man's leg. The animal went limp. The fugitive was locked in close combat with the last man-eater. The beast whined and both fighters collapsed lifelessly into the snow pile.

— XXVI —

PALLAS FORCED HIS WAY THROUGH THE CROWD
of fleeing slaves. The stumbling wolf found Nicodemus with
his men on horseback in the courtyard. The smoke from the battle
below had forced them out of the cavern. Alexander's agent had
commandeered Nero's prized horses. They had lost much of their
force. Only two other legionaries had survived the battle; these
injured men could not continue onward.

In the snow, the journey around the mountain would be
arduous. Pallas filled the noble in on the suspected whereabouts
of the talented slave. He relayed that they were now dependent on
directions from a dying guard. This was worrisome, but there was
little time for debate. The archers helped the struggling warrior
up onto an ashen horse. None of his wounds were fatal, but their
leader was in a great deal of pain. Starving slaves were swarm-
ing out of the refinery. The lift lowered again and again, hoisting
them from the depths.

The chanting continued as the mob breathed free air.
Citius's name thundered down the mountainside.

Nicodemus addressed the lively peasants, "Men, no one
is to take any salt. Whatever food, wine, or clothing you need

is yours. The salt belongs to Alexander! If my warning is not enough, just know that an army of well over fifteen hundred soldiers is just hours away." Pallas translated a much kinder version of the message for the starving Northerners. The slaves cheered and began feasting on pork and wine.

At midnight, they left for the outpost. Lord Nero's beasts were well rested; they thundered down the mountain. Pallas's determination was tested as he struggled to keep pace with the others. The pale rider fought through his pain and exhaustion. It was a clear, windblown night. The moonlight was strong. The eastward horizon was already beginning to gray; the sun was eager to rise.

The expeditionary force galloped down the mountain to reach the trail that led to the northern face. Given the source of their directions, they could not be sure whether they were taking the correct route. The deep snow that had muffled their initial ascent was working against them now. Finally, they came across fresh tracks in the white powder. The tracks could have been made by anywhere from ten to fifteen men, accompanied by four to eight dogs. The guards had been huddled together, which made accurately estimating their numbers more difficult. The sudden appearance of the tracks told them not only that their suspect directions were indeed accurate, but also that the boy's account of the hunt for Citius was true as well. Nero had undoubtedly forced this search party off into yesterday's blizzard. Clearly, the young builder had given the warden reason to hate him.

The outpost at the abandoned shaft came into view just before dawn. It was a clear winter morning; the rising sun and the fading moon were sharing the sky. Pallas unsheathed his sword; the weary men dismounted cautiously. They crept through the long shadows cast by the tall pines, closing in on the small barracks and lone sentry tower. Steady plumes of smoke rising from the chimneys told them that the fort was occupied. The exhausted men waited in the soft morning light outside the barracks. They saw signs of a great struggle: five young soldiers lay slain and spent arrows were scattered about the battleground.

The archers had their bows ready; they fanned out around Pallas and Nicodemus. The wolf studied the tracks in the snow. He followed them until he stood by the wooden post outside the shaft where two young guards had been felled. From here, he could clearly make out a lone pair of footprints in the snow. The prints were heading out of the mine—moving fast. The old man hobbled back toward the barracks. He locked eyes with his friend's cousin and nodded. Then he staggered toward the entryway. With surprising power, he kicked open the door.

The drunken mercenaries were roused by the sudden commotion; they scrambled for their weapons. As the guards' eyes struggled to adjust to the light of day, the archers let arrows fly. Nicodemus raged into the fort, viciously hacking at the rousted guards. To him, they were all thieves. A vicious skirmish broke out within the small structure. Battle reigned until the last of Nero's men lay dying. Two of the archers sustained injuries in the scuffle; the bowmen were not accustomed to close-quarters combat.

Pallas interrogated an arrow-ridden guard clinging to life on the outpost's floor. "Did you find Citius?"

"Who the hell are you?" the dying man groaned.

"We are Alexander's men. Sent to make an example of Nero and his thieving henchmen," Nicodemus snapped.

"Is Nero dead?" the dying man asked in broken Latin.

"Yes, he was stoned to death by the workers last night," Pallas replied in a well-versed northern dialect. A subtle grin wrinkled the dying man's whiskered face.

"Good," the guard replied.

"Where is Citius?"

"Not sure—the hounds chased something down the mountain last night. It was too cold to follow them. The old man that runs this outpost is missing." The captive groaned. He was clearly much more confident in his native tongue, but his pain was taking its toll.

"This man, what is his name?" Pallas interjected.

"Thadius," the wounded guard replied. The mercenary was bleeding out; the Greek shook him to keep him alert.

"You say the hounds chased something down the mountain—what was it?"

The man was losing consciousness. "I don't know—whatever they chased, they never came back." The dying commoner looked at the fire and began coughing up blood. The wolf delivered a final blow to send the man on his way. In the meantime, the archers had helped themselves to the guards' food and jugs.

"Men, don't get too comfortable by the fire," Pallas warned.

"What did the peasant say?" Nicodemus sneered.

"We are heading down the mountain. Pray the winds have not covered the trail," Pallas said, too exhausted to deal with Nicodemus. The old man grabbed hold of a jug and drank deeply.

"We will go look for Thadius and the slave. You are in no condition to travel down the mountain," Nicodemus said, noticing his elder's declining stagger. It seemed the noble had gotten the gist of what the dying mercenary had said after all.

"Thank you, Nicodemus, but I can't quit now," Pallas answered as he hobbled out of the barracks. The battered archers begrudgingly left the warm fire.

Trudging out into the crisp morning air, the weary warriors followed the fresh rifts that led down the mountainside. They followed the blood-laced channels in the snow out across a frozen creek. A moment later they came upon a hound that had been slain. Blood filled the snow around the fallen beast. The morning sun was blindingly bright as it reflected off the white blanket that stretched out all around them. The men were eager to reach the shadows cast by the tall pines to rest their tired eyes. The trail of blood took them to a narrow gap in the gorge. There was a great disturbance in the snow at this point and a lone rift heading up the ledge. Rather than clamber through the opening between the rocks, the men opted to follow the channel etched in the deep snow that continued up the ledge. This track had much less blood spatter than the other. After climbing up the incline, they came to a high point overlooking the gorge. Pallas winced, straining to look down at the bright snow. There were several more arrow-riddled beasts spread out in the valley.

"No doubt the man fired from here," an archer said, as he noted the great disturbance in the snow to Pallas's left. He drew his bow to aim at one of the fallen hounds. "Not an easy shot," he added.

Another archer drew his bow, then fired. The shot landed with a thud into the furthest carcass. "Maybe for you," he gloated. The men were growing rowdy; they had deposited the jugs' fiery contents into their empty stomachs. They were all reeling from battle. None had slept.

The other bowman's eyes remained fixed down the mountain. When the chuckles subsided, he replied, "I'd like to see you do that at night. When the beasts are charging through the snow." The rowdy hunters laughed and fired arrows at the fallen hounds for sport; liquor had elevated their spirits.

"Gentlemen, conserve your arrows," Nicodemus snapped, realizing most all of the men had spent their firepower.

"Relax, Nicodemus. We are tracking a half-frozen slave who bled all over the mountain and an injured old man. This isn't a damn bear hunt, boy," Pallas joked, even though the trek was taking its toll on his battered bones. A few of the men chuckled half-heartedly at their employer's expense. Nicodemus surprisingly took the heckling in stride. The cold must have been getting to the privileged noble.

"Look there," one of the archers insisted.

Just beyond the clearing was a slowly rising band of smoke. The staggering soldiers pushed through the snow toward the gray pillar. As they traversed the steep decline's deep drifts, Nicodemus missed a step and found himself up to his neck in white powder. Surely, the noble was not accustomed to marching on limited sleep.

Pallas chuckled as the bowmen helped the novice tracker out of his predicament. "Don't worry, boy. Sooner or later, you'll develop a feel for the drifts," he jabbed. Taking the lead, the elder hobbled past the slain hounds with the others in tow. Before long, they crept to the entrance of a cave—weapons drawn—ready for whatever awaited them inside.

"Can I help you?" someone growled in common Latin.

The exhausted trackers spun around to find a kind-looking old man with a bow over his shoulder. He was holding two freshly killed rabbits and nursing his wounded left arm.

"Are you Thadius?" Nicodemus demanded.

"Aye, I'm Thadius. Now who the hell are you?"

"I'm Pallas. We have been sent by Alexander."

"I know who you are," the old man barked. Nicodemus glared at his leader accusingly. Pallas's eyes told him that the Greek did not know this man. "Ah, so the old fool finally realized that Nero's been robbing him blind."

"It does not take Alexander long to seek out *usurpers*," Nicodemus declared.

"Right," the commoner said with a chuckle. "I suppose Nero is dead then?"

"That he is, sir. The slaves stoned him to death last night," Pallas replied.

A huge grin fanned out across the hunter's weathered face. "Excellent," he boomed. Nicodemus's men laughed at the quirky Roman. Pallas gave him a hard look. He was sure he had never met this man.

Thadius took notice of all the unsheathed swords. "Are those for me?"

Pallas answered, "That depends. It seems you may be the only one who did his duty. We are here for the runaway—a young builder called Citius."

"Have you seized the fugitive?" Nicodemus inquired.

"Can't be sure what the wild bastard's name is. If he ever wakes up, you can ask him." Thadius sipped his jug, then continued in a hoarse voice, "Damn fool kept trying to run off—even half-torn to bits, with an arrow in his back. Can't say I blame him. Nero must have really had it out for the man if he sent his beasts after him. That scheming bitch cared more about those mutts than his men."

"Where is he, old man?" Nicodemus spat.

"Watch the way you talk to me, *boy*. I didn't run around all night up to my knees in this white shit to have to hear your mouth," Thadius snarled. Pallas stared Nicodemus down; the noble eased off.

"Friend, we apologize. We did not sleep last night either. My associates and I, like you, are in need of rest. We have come a long way, and those rabbits you have there look delicious," the Greek said, hoping to subdue the situation.

"Well, come on in. I have a fire; I'll get a stew going," Thadius replied, not wanting any trouble. The elder hobbled past the others toward the cave's entrance. This rambunctious man gave Pallas a knowing look, which unnerved the old wolf. He was not one to forget a face.

"Thank you, sir," Pallas said, with no hint of discomfort.

"Is Citius within?" Nicodemus snapped, inciting another highly annoyed glare from Thadius.

"Honestly, Nicodemus. How many different ways does the man need to tell you? The boy is in there, possibly dead by now, sleeping by the fucking fire," Pallas barked. Thadius struggled to remain professional, but inside he was shaking with laughter. The noble was taken aback by Pallas's nerve.

"Very well, you boys go ahead," Nicodemus jabbed. "My men and I will set a perimeter." The injured archers were noticeably disappointed; they too were eager to take a seat by the fire. Their drunkenness was quickly declining into foggy exhaustion.

The elders entered the cave.

— XXVII —

"LIKE I SAID, HE WAS UNCONSCIOUS BY THE fire when I left to fetch breakfast. The boy is damn lucky I found him—*damn lucky*. The hounds would have finished him off, for sure. Even more fortunate that the splintered arrow came out of his back. The young man is in terrible shape, Pallas." There it was again—the Roman had spoken his name with familiarity.

"I'm just glad to hear he's alive." The battle-weary Greek was staggering through the cave, still trying to find a name to go with this hunter's face.

"That boy made quite a scene at my outpost last night," Thadius huffed. "What a disgrace. Five armed guards slain by a starving slave."

"Many more died in the shafts."

"I had a clean shot at him last night. I could have put him down right there. When I heard the hounds coming, I figured Nero wanted this one alive." Thadius stopped and turned to face the Greek. After getting a little too close to his guest's face, he continued, "But you know, Pallas, Nero wasn't what shifted my bow. I couldn't shoot a warrior like that in the back. I shot the little bastard, but you know what the hell I mean."

The narrow, winding passageway opened into a sizable cavern. Pallas noted the small dwindling fire near the center of the cave. Thadius went over to a stack of logs. He snagged a few and dropped them into the crackling coals.

"Well—that's convenient," Pallas said, pleasantly surprised to see the neatly stacked firewood.

"Aye, this is my retreat. I use this cave when I go hunting during the warmer months," Thadius replied, grinning ear to ear.

"So where is he?" Pallas was barely able to contain his eagerness.

Thadius crept over to the far corner of the cave; he gestured for his guest to follow suit. There Citius was, bound and covered in furs, half-torn to bits just as Thadius had described him. The runaway was not moving; after coming so far, Pallas feared the worst.

"Are the ropes really necessary?" Pallas objected.

"Damn right they are. If you'd seen what I saw last night, then you'd know."

The barbarian woke unexpectedly to Thadius's exclamations. Citius noticed the blade at the Greek's side. Pallas saw the pain of defeat in his dark eyes. The captive struggled against his bindings as he fought to his feet to defend himself.

"Citius, I mean you no harm. Nero is dead, son. Rest." Pallas spoke crisp Germanian. "Your troubles are over. Nero is dead—he's dead." The Greek's fluent language surprised Thadius and the young fugitive. The prisoner's eyes rolled back into his head as he began to fall forward. Thadius caught him before he hit the ground.

"It's him then, isn't it? The one called Citius."

"I cannot be certain until he wakes for questioning, but yes, I believe he is the man I have been looking for," Pallas declared.

"I feared as much," Thadius replied. "Much more suffering awaits this young man—such is the weight of greatness. The fact that someone of your prominence has already sought him out is disconcerting enough. I know who you are."

Pallas looked curiously at the hunter.

Thadius continued, "This world is built to snuff out this young man's kind. His abilities are his chains. I fear he will continue to be used by men like Nero, and yourself."

"I am not Nero."

"No, you are the Master Engineer of Rome," Thadius huffed. "Understand this—I have witnessed this entire valley's resources be absorbed by this mountain. For a hundred miles around this great peak, the economy swelled to meet the demands of the industrious mind at our feet. I have never seen a man so capable of manipulating the world around him. He is much too young to wield such power."

"Your wisdom becomes you, sir. You have provided a valuable service to Lord Alexander; your life will be spared. That said, I'm curious—how is it that you know who I am? Did I serve with you long ago?"

"Well, I didn't know you were planning to kill me—but

thanks," Thadius shot back, more than stunned.

"Alexander's orders were to dispose of Nero and all his men, but none of that matters now. Nero is dead, and some semblance of order has been restored. I apologize for that," Pallas insisted, wishing he had not mentioned anything at all.

"No worries," Thadius grumbled. "That's just like Alexander—has to kill everybody, everywhere he goes. And yes, sir, you did."

The Greek was observing the impressive speed at which the hunter skinned the animals. He waited for the bowman to finish his thought.

"You served with me, except I only knew you in passing. I'm a good bit older than you are, friend, but I never forget a face," Thadius said with pride.

"This young man was truly fortunate that you were there for him."

"You look terrible. Are you sure you don't want to lie down?" Thadius asked, observing his guest's weakened state.

"I'm alright, just took a few licks last night—not as quick as I used to be," Pallas replied with a fading grin.

"Right, well, let's get that young buck closer to the fire. I had him over there for safekeeping. In case a bear wandered in for a snack while I was out," Thadius joked. Pallas chuckled briefly, but his bruised ribs ached. The men walked over to where the prisoner lay motionless.

"Grab a leg and we'll drag him over there," Thadius said.

The old dogs dragged the battered slave across the cave floor. The former soldiers were not fazed by the young man's dire condition. Thadius was comically brash, letting Citius's head bump into several rocks as they pulled his lifeless body across the cave floor. To Pallas's amazement, the boy never stirred.

"Helps to knock them around a little. The more comfortable you get, the faster you die," Thadius preached, dropping the body to the cave floor with a thud.

"Isn't that the truth. This boy is lighter than he looks," Pallas noted.

"The miners don't eat much. Most of them don't last long either," Thadius replied; he was now busy skewering the rabbits. The Roman looked at the slave lying by the fire, desperately clinging to life. He spoke into the flames, "Nero had that boy at his disposal for a few short years. In that time, the monster harvested enough salt to enlist the whole of the Northern Legion. It wouldn't have been long before he mustered an army of his own."

Thadius took a long swig from his jug. Then he passed it off to his guest. Pallas drank deeply. "This is damn good."

"It's my prized jug. Always told myself I'd drink it after I killed the man who walked out of the Northern Shaft," Thadius rattled off.

"Ah, but you spared this one. It seems the gods are with this young man," Pallas said, warming his bruised bones by the smoldering logs.

Thadius took a long, deep swig. "It was not a man that

killed my crew last night."

Pallas did not respond. Thadius passed him the jug; the tired wolf took a long draw.

The guard looked his guest dead in the eyes to finish his thought. "You were looking for Citius. Well, let me tell you, that man is dead. It was a war hound that emerged from the mountain."

"Look, Thadius, I—"

"Like a war hound, this boy has been beaten, starved, and forgotten. His humanity is dead. He was like a cursed beast. No hesitation, no nothing. Empty black eyes like a wild animal—all instinct." Pallas's watery eyes met Thadius's; the jug's fiery contents were taking their toll. Suddenly, the hunter's hand moved to his sword. Nicodemus's archers had entered the cave, fully armed. The motive was clear.

"You men are making a grave mistake," Pallas warned.

"Alexander was very clear on how he wanted this handled," Nicodemus declared.

"Was he?" Pallas snapped.

"Step aside, old man," an archer said to Thadius.

"Men, is this really worth dying over? You can have all the salt you can carry. I will tell Alexander you died in the struggle. Or you can die right here. The choice is yours."

"Pallas, you will not win over my men with the promise of salt. Besides, if you were to return to Alexander, we will have failed. You see, we have strict orders to dispose of you as well. After ensuring the boy is dead, of course," Nicodemus informed the wounded foreigner.

"Drop your weapons and go, Thadius," Pallas instructed. The elder grunt could see that the Greek's strength was failing.

"And leave my honor with these half-wits—no sir, that's out of the question. I have lived long enough to know that cowards die many times before their deaths." The unruly old dog's fear of death had long since faded; he would stand his ground.

"I wish I had known that I wouldn't need that filthy northern tongue of yours to converse with this fool," Nicodemus said, glaring at Thadius. "If I had only known, I would have had my men fill your back with arrows as you limped down the mountain. I do admit—it was advantageous to have that filthy rubbish you cough out. Especially when the starving rats were spilling out of the mine. No matter, my army should arrive by nightfall, the rest will be disposed of once we are finished here."

"Get on with it then," Thadius badgered. Pallas drew inspiration from this righteous man's willingness to fight at his side.

Nicodemus ignored the commoner and addressed the Greek. "That letter was an imperial death sentence. To think, you unwittingly carried it from Estor, all the way to Alexander's doorstep."

"To hell with you cowards," Thadius boomed, drawing his bow. He grabbed the last three arrows from his quiver. One shot was drawn at the ready; two more were clenched between the knuckles of his firing hand. Reloading would be done in rapid fire succession.

"You should know that Alexander was going to let you live. He petitioned to spare your life. To my amazement, Emperor Severus took heed." Pallas remained silent; he wanted to hear the truth. "Of course, those peasants had to run their mouths and ruin everything. Don't worry, I removed Amond's head from his shoulders myself. Darius is still in hiding, but he too will be found."

"Shut up and fight, boy," Thadius barked.

"My cousin had hoped you would die fighting before it ever came to this. You see, he knew all about Nero's theft—long before you brought him the evidence of corruption on Saltz Mountain."

"You seemed more than surprised by those great mounds of salt," Pallas snarled.

"Alexander was stealing the salt from himself to avoid including the Emperor. Did that thought ever cross your mind? Nero would never dare to cross Alexander—although I do admit there was much more salt at the camp than I had expected."

"And the weaponry—let's not forget about that, boy." The wolf's temper was rising steadily.

"No matter, what's done is done. Now we must ensure that no word of this ever reaches Rome." Nicodemus adjusted his shield to account for Thadius.

Pallas looked out at the soldiers. "Men, weigh your decision carefully. If you do this, not one of you will leave this cave alive. All the salt you can carry or death. The choice is yours."

"Look at you. You are in no place to be offering ultimatums. You're a good man, Pallas. I wish you had kept your nose out of this. Kneel and we will make this quick." The men locked eyes; the Greek unsheathed his sword.

"Lucinda is dead. So are your servants, and all of your hounds. That fishing village was burned to the ground. It will be said that you were killed by rebels while journeying back to Rome. If nothing else, you have earned the right to know."

"She knew nothing."

"That doesn't matter now. Kneel—I will not ask again."

The warrior's gray eyes went blank; all his adversaries witnessed the sudden transformation. All could feel his wrath reverberating off the cave walls. Pallas stood defiant; like a cornered wolf, he would fight to his last breath. A deafening silence permeated through the dim smoke-filled light cast by the crackling fire.

"Kill them," Nicodemus commanded.

The last of the arrows filled the air. Thadius fired away with impressive speed and accuracy. His last shot plunged into the largest archer's neck. The mortally wounded man grabbed for his throat as Thadius hurled his spear into the dying man's chest. Pallas dropped his arrow-riddled shield in exchange for a second blade. The first archer to charge at the wolf was cut down with ease. Nicodemus had an arrow lodged deep into his left shoulder. The fiery noble snapped it off and bolted headlong into the Greek's kill zone. Thadius kept one of the archers busy while Pallas waged war on the others. The remaining mercenaries were exhausted; the booze was getting to them and one had an arrow protruding from his chest. These novice swordsmen paid dearly for every misstep.

The noble's confidence began to dwindle as every failed lunge resulted in swift retribution. The wolf avoided a blow, then smashed the butt of his sword into his attacker's well-groomed face. Nicodemus stumbled back into the cave wall. The other archer heaved his sword at the dead-eyed warrior. The Greek moved quickly, but the man's blade slashed his shoulder. Without hesitation, Pallas countered, delivering a fatal blow to the mercenary's exposed neck.

Pulling himself to his feet, Nicodemus watched Pallas shove his victim aside. The assassin fell lifelessly to the stone floor. Thadius was locked in combat with the last remaining archer. His younger opponent was much faster. The elder had already sustained several dismantling blows. Pallas stormed forward, but it was too late. Nicodemus leapt at the opportunity, driving his blade into Thadius's defenseless back. Pallas charged at the last archer, mercilessly clothes-lining him before inflicting a fatal blow. Thadius had collapsed; Nicodemus kicked him hard in the face and the commoner went limp. Pallas stood fuming, with blood dripping down his wounded arm. His empty eyes were locked on the conniving noble.

"Your men were given the *honor* of a clean death. *You* will die screaming." Pallas let his second blade fall out of his bloody hand to the cave floor. Then he knelt down to take hold of a red-hot burning log from the fire.

The Roman charged at the fading warrior. His focus was mainly on the log smoldering in Pallas's right hand. The Greek hurled the fireball at the charging swordsman. His wounded arm showed no weakness. The flaming timber smashed into Nicodemus's shield, erupting into a barrage of glowing coals. Hot embers seared the young man's neck; he stumbled, dodging them awkwardly. The attacker heaved his sword haphazardly at the old man.

As Nicodemus rumbled past, the wolf snatched his wrist and sliced the tendons across the back of his right knee. Pallas's victim lost the ability to support his weight, but his momentum carried him forward. The noble tumbled through the fire's smoldering coals, knocking over the burnt rabbit skewers. The wounded man screamed out in pain, rolling back and forth to extinguish his smoking garments. Pallas yanked Thadius's spear out of a fallen mercenary and hurled it into the Roman's side. Nicodemus lay helplessly quivering on the cold stone slab.

Alexander's cousin watched in horror as Pallas reached down to pick up a rounded stone. The warrior stood over his enemy; he was transitioning back to reality. He could think only of Lucinda. He hoped she had been given a decent death. The wolf let the blunt weapon fall out of his hand. Relief instantly flashed across Nicodemus's defeated eyes.

"Your son lives," the dying noble garbled his last words.

A man of honor, Pallas dispatched the young man quickly.

Tears rolled down the lone warrior's face; he wept for his woman.

Barely able to lift his lungs to breathe, Thadius spoke, "Last night, a cowardly part of me wanted to kill him—kill Citius—before another ambitious man took his reigns. Be careful, you will not be the last powerful man who wishes to wield this weapon."

"Rest, Thadius—*rest*." There was great pain in his dying defender's tired eyes.

"Pallas, men are not meant for power."

God made us great

God made us strong

Great to defend the weak

Strong to strike down evil

If evil in the world should surround us

We will not shy away from the challenge

The opportunity to display our fearlessness

We fight to ensure mercy triumphs over judgment

We live for the greater glory of God

~ TOTUS TUUS

— John Carlyle O'Neill —

John Carlyle O'Neill is a storyteller from Washington, D.C. He draws inspiration from faith and family. *Salt & Sacrifice* is his debut novel.